THROUGH THE FIRE

First edition

This is fiction. Names, physical and personality descriptions, places, facts, theories, and events, even if existing in the real world, are the product of the author's imagination or are used in a fictional manner. Any resemblance to any person, living or dead, is coincidental. Where real locations are used, they are used fictitiously. The author warrants and represents complete ownership of this work and maintains the sole legal right to publish all material therein.

Cover art produced in Canva Pro.

Models shown in cover art do not necessarily endorse this work of fiction but are fictitious representations of the lead characters.

IN MEMORY

COURTNEY SASSER
10/20/1971-1/23/2022

To my foul-mouthed, squooshy-hearted sister and best friend…

I will miss you for the rest of my f*cking life.

Big love, sis.

CHAPTER ONE

"Seriously?" Thatcher muttered, slamming on the brakes as an older green Honda cut him off in traffic, only to brake hard in front of him. "Yeah, dummy. I slowed for a reason." He stifled the urge to honk and offer the driver the bird as he eased around the Honda and the stalled car blocking the lane.

He'd have stopped to help the stranded driver if he wasn't running late.

Maybe you could skip today and start Wednesday.

The temptation to skip the meeting was strong. He didn't want to go in the first place. Everyone else said he needed to go. His family gently inquired. Then pressed. He dodged. But last night…fighting with Kearny, that told him maybe they were right.

Kearny had recently moved out of their parents' pool house into a swank rental home in a gated community while their brother, Greer's, design and build firm worked on his future home. Thatcher, who'd been staying in the downstairs guestroom of his parents' house after being medically discharged from the army, eagerly moved into it. Last night, Kearny had knocked on the pool house door at seven, just as Thatcher was finishing a round of exercises for his mangled shoulder.

Grumpy over his snail-like progress, he'd snapped, "If you're here to invite me to a barbecue or something, don't. I'm not in the mood."

Kearny snorted, stepping inside without need for an invitation, tossing his still-folded cane on the little entry table he knew was to the left of the door. "Nah, man, I've pretty much given up trying to convince you. At least for now."

"Good," Thatcher said, pulling two beers from the mini fridge in the pool house's kitchenette. You couldn't really call a mini fridge, microwave, and two-burner hot plate a kitchen. He crossed the room in four limping strides and tapped Kearny's hand with the cold bottle. "Beer?"

Kearny nodded, took it, then held it out so Thatcher could pop the cap along with his own.

"How're you? How's Janine? Did she drive you?" Thatcher asked, stepping aside as Kearny edged three steps to the right for the closest of the pair of recliners he knew would be there.

Sinking down, his grin lit up the dim room. "We're great. Better every day. And, yeah, she's in the kitchen with Mom." Kearny responded so enthusiastically a cleaver of guilt sunk into his guts. He'd never seen his kid brother so happy. A chaser of wistfulness followed the guilt. He tried to make his voice smile.

"That's great. She's adorable, man, with that vintage retro thing she's got going on. And she's sweet. When she comes over to cook with Mom, she always brings me a sample."

Kearny's fiancée, Janine, was a real spit-fire. Not deterred in the least by Kearny's blindness, she'd called bullshit on his every excuse for why they couldn't be together. She didn't let his failed relationships or his trust issues determine their future, nor did she let Kearny bow out over fears that his blindness would drive a wedge between them. When he'd avoided her out of guilt after they'd been mugged, feeling helpless, she'd called him on it. When he worried he'd fail her or a future child they might have because of dangers he couldn't see, she'd called him on that, too. She was good *to* him and *for* him, the way any partner should be.

"Me, too," Kearny grinned. "She's a good cook. I'm going to get fat if she keeps it up," he joked, patting his flat stomach. He sipped his beer, then sighed heavily. "Seriously, Thatch, what are you doing?"

Here it comes, Thatcher thought. *The lecture. The actual reason you stopped by.*

He didn't answer.

"Dude," Kearny frowned, his nose wrinkling. "Is it you that smells so rank?" He stood, leaning toward Thatcher in the other recliner. Stepping closer, Kearny stumbled over the 5-gallon water jug he hadn't gotten around to hauling to the dispenser in the kitchenette, falling onto and bouncing off the coffee table before landing on his ass on the floor. "Oh, my God, what *is* this?" he cried, sniffing his forearm and dry heaving.

"Sorry, man," Thatcher said, leaping up and grabbing the roll of paper towels he'd been using for napkins from the floor beside his chair. He almost laughed at the squeamish disgust on his brother's face as he wiped at his arm, only to dirty his hand. Thatcher tapped his unsoiled bicep with the paper towel roll. "Sorry," he repeated, "It's just leftover hot wings and ranch."

"From how long ago?" Kearny gagged as he swiped furiously at his forearm and the side of his hand.

"I'm sorry," he repeated. "You okay?" He put a hand on Kearny's shoulder. "Need help up?"

"No," Kearny grumbled, tossing the wadded, dirtied towels in the general direction of the coffee table. "Just tell me what else is out of place before I kill myself."

"Everything," he admitted. "You're safest just sitting back down."

Kearny sat wiping his face with both hands, up through his hair the way he did whenever he was frustrated. "Thatch, c'mon. Everybody's tried to give you space, but, bro, I'm thinking it's time you got some help. You want to shut us out, fine. Okay. But let *someone* in there with you. Quit hibernating in here with this rotting food and whatever else is creating this funk. Get back to life, dude." He paused. The irritation and disgust left his voice. "Come back to us, man. We miss you. *I* miss you."

Thatcher let Kearny's words settle like dust motes into the room. It was the same refrain his brother had been on since about two months after he arrived home from Walter Reed National Military Medical Center last October. And he understood it. Theirs was not a mollycoddling family. At age seven, Kearny arrived in their family newly blinded by the car accident that killed his folks, prone to screaming, kicking, and biting when he got scared or frustrated in his new, dark world. Their parents, however, followed advice offered by local organizations for the blind, assigning him chores and involving him in family activities, and punishing him if he failed to follow the same rules as his brothers and sisters. This was how Thatcher knew their patience had limits and was wearing thin. Their pushing was not unwarranted, just unwanted.

Kearny, unruffled by the silence, settled back into the recliner and took another pull on his beer bottle, grimacing as he set it on the table between the chairs. "God, bro, it smells so bad in here, it's making the beer taste like ass. You gotta clean this place up. You're going to get roaches. Mom will kill you." When Thatcher didn't answer, he shook his head. "Thatcher, man, I get it. You're angry. I know all about anger and unfairness. Been there, done that."

"Kearny," he barked sharply, "you've got no fucking idea how I feel! If there's one thing I can't stand, it's people trying to tell me they know. You will *never* have to see the shit I've seen, *bro.* You've never been halfway around the world in the middle of the next place to Hell and had your friends, your fucking brothers—" he sucked in a dagger of air, "—blown up in front of you! So, do not fucking tell me you know anything about anything, because you don't know shit. You don't." As soon as the words left him, he wanted to reel them back in, to throw himself on the floor at Kearny's feet and gather them up before he heard them. Because the little twitch of his jaw, that almost imperceptible flinch, shamed Thatcher to his core.

"I know I'm not military, Thatcher," he said quietly, rising, "and I don't know a thing about what you've been through. I haven't seen the shit you've seen—fuck you very much for that, by the way—but just because I haven't lived your particular brand of pissed off doesn't mean I don't recognize the flavor. I know crippling rage, Thatch. I know wanting to go back in time, and I know feeling helpless. And until you work that shit out, you're useless to yourself and everyone else."

Kearny sidled to the little entry table, his hand finding his cane, and slammed out of the pool house.

Thatcher hurried to the door to go after him but froze with his hand on the knob.

He'd cut deep. Kearny needed time to cool off.

Back in the present, with a glance at the dashboard clock, Thatcher sighed. He'd be lucky to make it on time to his first PTSD/Anger meeting.

He swore again as he noticed how perilously close the needle on the gas gauge was to 'E' and without braking, swung wildly into the lot of a gas station, ignoring the indignant honk behind him.

Easing next to a pump, he jumped, startled when another honk blared next to his Jeep. He whipped his head to the side just in time to see the green Honda whip past him. Up close, he could see the driver was female. She flipped him the bird he'd stifled earlier and whipped her car into the next set of pumps.

Maybe I should invite her to the group, he thought with

a smirk.

One thing he'd learned from his ten-year stint with the Army was to pick his battles. There was a time and a place to bring out the whoop ass. This wasn't it.

He filled the Jeep with gas, then debated going inside the convenience store for a soda. Why not? He'd probably be late either way.

After filling a large cup with Coke, his phone pinged. He meandered toward the counter, hoping for some minor family disaster. Something to give him a valid excuse to turn back toward the Rise—his folks' home—where he was staying as he got his bearings and determined how to move forward without the army, a career he thought he'd have until retirement.

"Jesus" a voice exclaimed, pulling him up short. "It's not that hard to look where you're going!"

Holding up his hands in surrender, Thatcher gestured to the counter. "Fine. Go ahead. Go in front of me."

She tilted her blonde, pixie head to the side. "Oh, well, thanks," she retorted, turning toward the counter. "Considering I was already in front of you."

Watching her plunk the largest coffee cup they sold on the counter, he said, "Maybe caffeine isn't such a great idea."

The clerk's eyes grew wide as if to say, *Why the Hell did you poke the bear?!* He winked at the clerk as he tried to hide a smile. Oops. The blonde saw it and whipped around as he tried to rearrange his face into a somber, non-amused expression.

"Oh, fuck you! Are you my doctor? No? Good. Shut up. Keep your opinions to yourself." Slapping cash on the counter, she waited impatiently for her change, then stalked toward the door.

Out of the corner of his eye, he watched her fumbling with the cup in one hand and her change in the other. As he accepted his own change, she gave up on the change, tossing the handful of coins in her purse.

He stayed a step or two behind, not wanting to rile her further.

Her head was down as she searched her bag for something. He wasn't fast enough with his warning. A bicyclist whipped through the lot, looking at something behind himself, clipping the coffee cup right out of her left hand and the purse out of her right.

Coffee splashing around her shoes, she hollered, "Motherfucker! You're lucky you're on a damn bike!!"

Thatcher debated whether to help with the picking up of her scattered items. As he bent at the waist and scooped up her empty coffee cup, he saw the cyclist wheel around with a glare, ready for a fight. The blonde, crouched and gathering the few items that escaped her purse when it fell, didn't notice the guy coming her way. He stepped in front of her as the bicyclist buzzed past, yelling, "Bitch, you want to start something?!"

His jaw clenched and unclenched as he met the guy's angry stare. He could all but see the dude take him in and was glad he'd chosen to wear a long-sleeved shirt and jeans. If he hadn't, he might have gotten his ass beaten. Instead, the cyclist flipped them off and kept going.

He turned, catching the blonde's eyes and the way her jaw jutted out as he did. She'd probably never admit to him she was afraid, but he could see it well enough in her tight expression.

"Hope your day improves," he said softly, channeling his oldest brother, Parker. The guy was unfailingly nice. Instead of sniping back at her, Parker would try to cajole her into a better mood, or he'd flat out ask if she was having a hard day. "Whatever it is, it'll get better."

Her eyes narrowed at the gentle words he'd chosen over several others, and she stalked away without reply. Maybe he'd gone too far with that last bit. Because he, more than anyone, knew that sometimes, a bad day did not get better.

He ducked into his Jeep, fighting a chuckle as she ducked into her car…the old green Honda. Glancing ruefully at the clock on his dashboard, he stayed where he was until she squealed out of the lot, temper clearly not abated.

CHAPTER TWO

Neither the room nor its medley of occupants were what Thatcher imagined. The circle of chairs was close enough. They were meeting in an old community theater building, the chairs set up in the middle of the stage because the floor in front of it was a riotous mess of old props and partial sets. Sitting up on the stage made him feel on display. He already felt that way amidst a group that had already been meeting without him for three weeks.

Up until he enlisted, he'd lived in the same neighborhood and grew up with the same group of kids. He'd never liked the idea of being the new kid, having to find a place in a crowd. Being the new adult in an already cohesive group wasn't much better, he decided, ducking his head, avoiding looking at anyone as he took one of only two empty chairs left. Being late was even worse.

The last chair, directly across the circle from his, suddenly filled, cutting the chatter almost instantly.

"Hey, gang, sorry I'm late," the man said, sounding like a voice double for the guy who did the Allstate insurance commercials. Dropping his backpack at his feet, he reached into it blindly, his eyes finding Thatcher's. "Hello. Welcome. I'm George Tellis, group facilitator."

Thatcher kept to his tunnel vision, nodding at George, and said nothing. To avoid questions or being put on the spot, he now looked around the circle. They were a group of nine, if you counted George: a fidgety guy who looked ready to leap up — and do what, he wasn't sure; a girl, arms wrapped around herself as if she were trying to hold her guts inside, hair curtaining her downward-pointed face; a steely-eyed, scruffy-faced older man with the kind of body which spoke of past athleticism, gone to pot over too much of the wrong things; a guy about Thatcher's age, expressionless, eyes locked on his phone; Thatcher, himself; and…crap. The blonde from the QT station. She, too, stared at her phone, allowing him to take in her super short, whitish-blonde hair and lightly tanned skin, her camo capris and a tight little black sleeveless tee, a Celtic-looking arm band tattoo wrapped around her right bicep. Before he moved on to the person next to her, she lifted her head and met his gaze with silent recognition and a "don't mess with me" glare. Next to her sat a very large, balding man in basketball length shorts and a stained Denver Broncos shirt. On George's right, closing the circle, sat the bald man's polar opposite, a clean cut, late-thirties, slacks-and-dress-shirt-wearing guy who tipped his chin in silent greeting.

George, having drawn a clipboard out of his backpack, looked around as Thatcher had, slowly assessing each of them in turn. "Okay," he said, sitting back in his chair, "who wants to start? Rachel?"

The girl whose hair curtained her face looked up and shook her head, her mouth twitching as she fought tears. Her arms hugged her middle, as if to hold everything in. Thatcher knew that desire well and found himself silently rooting for her.

"Rachel, something's happening inside you," George said gently. "We've all been there. Tell us what's putting you there today."

She shrugged. "Nightmares. Same, same."

He'd been there, too. But she was young. So damn young. Had she seen action overseas? His chest tightened as she remained mute.

"The one about the robbery?" Twitchy guy asked, his face drawn in sympathy.

She gave a single nod. "I fell asleep at work too many times. I got fired. I try to sleep at night, but I either end up staring at the ceiling or I'm back in the stupid gas station with a gun in my face, slipping in a pool of Adam's blood." Her voice hitched. She covered her face with her hands and sobbed.

The scruffy man with the steely gaze shook his head, rolled his eyes, and looked at the ceiling. "Good God, Rach, do us all a favor and get on some meds. You cry more than my 4-year-old grandbaby, for Chrissakes!"

Thatcher felt stung, as though the words had been for him. A wave of icy hot anger bubbled upward into his throat.

"Hey!" the tattooed blonde from the QT called, eyes narrowing. "Don't be such an insensitive dick, Gil!"

Yeah, Gil, or I'll throat punch you, he thought. Or he would, if he could get up fast enough. Thatcher rubbed his left knee, which throbbed angrily. His heart throbbed angrily in communion. He'd have been up out of his chair and in the asshole's face in half a second.

Before.

Gil's eyes narrowed as he looked her way. "Shut up, Kit. No one's talking to you!" Turning back toward Rachel, he leaned forward and made exaggerated crying sounds. "Oh, boo hoo hoo. My convenience store was robbed two years ago. The suspect fired but missed me and my co-worker, but I can't stop having nightmares that he died! That's the actual reality—not the dream—for most of us, Rach, so put your big girl panties on and—"

Twitchy guy and George lunged after Kit as she launched herself across the circle at Gil. Thatcher's face burned as he made it to his feet too late to be of any help. The two of them were already pulling her back toward her seat before he managed to stand. He wished he'd brought his cane. He hated the thing, used it only on the worst of the bad days, but it would have made a passable substitute bat.

"Gil," George warned, "you know this group isn't just for military PTSD. This is a general PTSD and anger management group. You also know, because we've all been through this conversation before, that everyone's suffering is real and valid. Everyone experiences things differently. It isn't a sign of weakness to break down, any more than it makes you a monster if you lose your cool and lash out." George scanned the room as if to remind them Gil's perspective was also valid.

Thatcher wanted to roll his eyes at that. There was anger and there was pure douchebaggery. He couldn't bring himself to feel empathy for the guy.

"Yeah, whatever," Gil ground out. "Rach, I'm sorry, but c'mon, kiddo. I'm trying to get you to see things straight."

Rachel nodded but didn't look at him. Kit furiously shrugged out of Twitchy and George's grip and plopped back in her seat, pointing at Rachel.

"Don't you dare accept his half-assed apology, Rachel," she spat. In his mind, Thatcher gave her a standing ovation. "Gil doesn't give a shit about you or anyone else in this room. He's too busy being the only one here who actually suffered anything."

Silence draped itself awkwardly over the room. Thatcher looked at Kit, at her clenched jaw, at the way she leaned forward, hands gripping the edges of her chair so tightly her knuckles were white. He could feel the coiled energy, her desire to leap up and get in Gil's face. He guessed her problem ranged more toward the anger management side. Today, at least.

George cleared his throat. "Let's talk about this, clear the air. Rachel, how do you feel about what Gil said?"

Rachel shrugged. "He's not wrong."

"The hell he ain't!" The guy who'd earlier had eyes only for his phone, protested.

Thatcher silently agreed. He didn't want Gil to be right,

not since he talked to himself the way Gil had to Rachel. How many lectures had he given himself since he'd arrived back in Phoenix about manning up, growing a pair, getting "back out there"? And if Gil was right, if *he* was right, he was an asshole *and* a coward.

"Donnie," George held up a hand. "Let Rachel finish first."

"I mean," she said, looking at Donnie, "he's a jerk the way he put it, but he's right. No one died. Nobody got shot. I don't know why I keep dreaming about it like that's what happened. I don't know why I can't just let it go. I'm working office jobs now, or trying to, without getting fired all the time. I want to be past this. But it's not like I go to bed planning to have bad dreams. Every time I hear about a school shooting or about things like the concert in Las Vegas, it's like it's happening all over again. And I call off sick because I'm too scared to leave my house, or I turn down my friends when they ask me to go to movies or shopping."

"You were barely eighteen, Rach. They had no business sticking you on the graveyard shift, whether there was a co-worker there or not," Donnie argued. "Getting robbed, getting shot at, that's not nothing, even if Gil pretends it is."

George nodded. "Are you still doing the individual therapy sessions, Rachel?"

She shook her head. "I can't afford it. No insurance since I lost my last job."

"Remember, you can call me," George said. "Day or night. You've got my number in your phone?"

Rachel nodded.

"Anyone else? What are your thoughts, Jon?"

Twitchy, who'd moved his chair closer to Rachel's, gave her shoulders a final squeeze. "You got this, Rach. Don't think any different. You're going to look around one day and realize things have gotten so much better, you didn't even notice it happening."

Thatcher wanted to snort along with her. *Yeah? When? When is it going to get easier to get out of bed? To stop letting my family down, stop seeing their disappointment when I turn down their invitations?*

George waited. "Jon?"

Jon shrugged, tapping one foot on the floor. "Doing good, no complaints, no worries."

"What about your hearing? Isn't that coming up?"

Jon sighed heavily. "Yeah."

"How are you feeling about that?"

"I wish I didn't have to go." He swallowed. "What if they toss me in prison and throw away the key? I can't," his voice caught. Rachel put her arm around Jon now. He tried to smile at her, terror written all over the guy's face. Thatcher swallowed hard, pushing the image of Kyle away. Different terror, but the same. *Fear is fear*, he'd say. *Feel it, but act, anyway,* he'd tell his guys. Yet here he was, ignoring the advice that had once felt so easy to give.

"Your heart was in the right place. The judge will see that," the large bald man said.

Jon snorted. "Right, Terry. He's going to let me off because, hey, almost beating a guy to death is the appropriate thing to do for leaving his dog in a hot car."

Thatcher sat up in his chair.

"Okay, sure, you should have just broken the window and gotten the dog out and left it at that, but the idiot deserved it. Freaking hundred-degree day, and he leaves his dog in the car to go grocery shopping? And it's not like he popped in for a gallon of milk or loaf of bread. Dude came out with a full cart forty minutes later," Terry argued.

Jon shook his head. "I wish I had taken the dog and left him with a shattered window, not a fucking shattered jaw."

"Regret is tough to live with," George agreed. "But you said your attorney has camera footage to prove how long he was inside the store, and there was viral footage of your altercation. The man threatened you with a knife, Jon, when you wouldn't give him his dog back. Maybe you went a little farther than you needed to for self-defense, but there's definitely more than one side to this story."

Jon nodded. "I still wish I could rewind time. Take it back."

"But you can't take it back," the slacks-and-dress-shirt guy said. "When is it, again?"

"Two weeks from today," Jon told him. "9:30, the courthouse on Jefferson."

Slacks guy tapped it into his phone. "I'm going to try to come, Jon. If I don't have any interviews."

"Cool, man. Thanks." Jon nodded.

"Speaking of interviews, Mike, anything you need to go over today?" George turned his attention to slacks guy.

"I'm doing well, George. I've got an interview for an insurance job. I'm hoping it goes well."

"I hope so, Mike. What if it doesn't? What's your plan?"

Mike shrugged. "Not throwing a chair at the interviewer, that's for sure," he grinned sheepishly.

Thatcher fought a chuckle, then wondered why he wanted to laugh. It wasn't funny, not at all. He'd been on a few interviews, recently, himself. He wondered if Mike felt the same ennui. The same *what the hell does it matter? What's important anymore? What difference does any of it make if we just end up dead?* He was depressed, he knew. He recognized the stagnancy of it, the apathetic, heavy inertia. The pervasive thought that maybe death was better. At least then, his mind would be quiet. No relentless guilt. No constant replay, wondering *what if.* He hated the idea of psych medication so much that even his fear of group therapy paled in comparison, yet his logical mind said to get past the stigma and seek help. But his heart said to give the group therapy thing a try before resorting to meds. And like it usually did, it won out over logic. For now.

He fought the urge to rub his hands over his face, into

his hair. He didn't want Mike to think it was about him. The guy seemed in a better place; the place Thatcher wanted to be. Giving a shit about life again. Getting excited about something, feeling hopeful about something. Having a purpose.

George smiled. "That would be a good plan. Tell us again about the interview, for those of us who haven't heard it." He met Thatcher's eyes across the circle.

Mike shook his head. "Guy was nice. Buttoned up, professional, asking all the usual questions. Saw my military record on my application, thanked me for my service. It was going fine. I could tell he was impressed; I could feel him feeling good about me, and then we moved on to the bullshitting part of the interview."

"The bullshitting part?" George asked, his forehead wrinkling.

"Yeah. You know, the part where the real questions are done, and the interview takes it personal to get a final impression of you, not just as an employee, but a person. You know?"

"I do know," George agreed, nodding. "I've just never heard it put that way before. Bullshitting. Do you think talking about your personal life is bullshit?"

Mike gave George an exasperated look. "No," he said. "A little," he added. "What does what I like to watch on TV or do on the weekends have to do with whether I'm right for the job or not?"

"Is that when things started going south?"

Thatcher knew it had to have been. George was the "ask the question you—and everyone else—already know the answer to" type.

"I guess," Mike replied helplessly, shaking his head.

"How did we get from the bullshitting part to the throwing chairs part?"

Whoa.

Mike's jaw twitched. "Man, you know how. We've been

over this."

George glanced at Thatcher again. "Not everyone in the room has heard this story before. Maybe we can get a new perspective."

Mike looked at Thatcher. Up. Down. Dismissed him as having anything worthwhile to say, being the new face in the room and all. Thatcher looked away, looked down.

"The guy started talking hobbies, talking about sports. Football. Watching, not playing. Then he said his son played high school ball and things were looking really good for a scholarship. And then it's like he completely forgot about my service, because he says to me, 'He's been talking about joining the Marines, instead, and I told him only over my dead body.' And he laughs like I'm supposed to get the joke."

Thatcher's head lifted.

"How did that sit with you?"

"How do you think it sat, George? Jesus!" Mike shook his head. "It went over like a lead balloon. He didn't even realize it might offend me. He was that clueless."

"What did you say?"

Heavy silence. Mike looked down at his lap.

"Mike?" George prompted. "What did you say?"

Mike sighed wearily, grinning again. Thatcher clearly recognized the sarcasm.

"I told him his kid would be better off joining up and serving his country than becoming some NFL kneeling-during-the-Anthem pussy."

Donnie's mouth dropped open. "Whoa, dude! Really?" He sat back in his chair, shaking his head as he folded his arms.

Mike shrugged.

George held up a hand. "Remember, folks, we all have our buttons."

"Yeah, and disrespecting what all of us—well, most of us," Mike corrected, glancing at Rachel, "did over there by using the Anthem to push a racial protest is one of mine."

Breathe. Nothing wrong here but a little verbal disagreement, Thatcher told himself as his heart began to hammer and his palms began to sweat.

"But isn't freedom important to you?" Donnie asked, leaning forward now. "Equality for everyone, not just the chosen few?"

"Hey," Mike said, holding up his hands, "all I'm saying is if people are going to give Tebow shit for kneeling for God, saying a football field isn't the place for his display of religion, then the same should hold true for anyone kneeling, no matter what the reason."

Rachel stood. "Oh, my God. We have to get into all that bullshit here? I come here to get away from this stuff."

Gil waved a hand at her like he wanted to erase her. "That's a load of crap. You comè here to cry about something that didn't even happen! Sit down, crybaby, and let the vets hammer this one out."

George held up his hands. "Okay, guys, let's all have a moment of silence. Right now."

The warning in his usually placid voice brought compliance. Rachel sat and the circle went silent.

Thatcher took a deep breath, grateful to feel his heart slowing.

Crisis averted.

After a long pause, George sent a warning glance around the circle. "All feelings are valid in this room. But Mike, Donnie, instead of debating the politics of the NFL players' protests, let's get back to Mike and why he's here. Anger management. Expressing anger in healthy rather than self-destructive ways. Because causing yourself to miss out on a job, Mike, that's destructive, right?"

Mike nodded curtly, his arms folded across his chest.

Breaking the silence, Gil guffawed. "I don't see a problem with your reaction, Mike. Except maybe you don't want to pull that in an interview."

Thatcher didn't like that he agreed with Gil on that one, but he did. At least the interview part.

Mike nodded, his face coloring. "Roger that," he said, eyes glued to his lap. "It was stupid. Reactionary. I mean, I feel how I feel, but I'm better than that. Anyway, I didn't so much throw the chair. I stood up and pushed it in a little too hard. And not really at him. Just toward his desk."

"What could you have done differently?" George asked gently.

"I don't know another way to respond to that," Mike admitted. "I lost friends over there. For him to sit there and say over his dead body would his kid ever join the military, dude, he might has well have said I'm a useless, stupid loser for serving. Like what I did wasn't good enough for his kid."

Thatcher looked down at his lap, then closed his eyes as his slowing heartbeat did a rapid one-eighty…so rapid the room began to spin around him and he fought off flashes of unwanted memory. As if from a great distance, he heard the conversation continue.

"Okay," George's voice sounded muffled. "Now we're getting somewhere. When we lash out, it's because we're angry or afraid. So, Mike, what could you have said in response to the interviewer's flip remark?"

"I can't think of anything that wouldn't have had the same result," Mike shrugged.

"Why do you think he said it? Do you believe he genuinely thought less of you for your service and because of that, he doesn't want his son to enlist?"

"That's how it felt. Like it's good enough for this guy who wants his entry level job but not his golden football god of a son."

"Do you have kids, Mike?"

"Not yet. But I get it, George. You're thinking he's just afraid for his son. But I don't think that was it. You didn't see the derision on his face."

"Fine," George said flatly, nodding. "He's a snooty jackass who's okay with giving thanks as long as it's not his kid out there. There are a million other snooty jackasses out there just like him. What could you have said, instead?"

"I guess I could have said it's a dangerous job, but it looks awesome on a resume."

"There you go!" George smiled. "You acknowledged the snooty jackass' concern for his kid and reminded him it would be a good idea to hire you, all in one shot."

George let that sink in around the circle.

The spinning feeling slowed, then came to a lazy stop.

"What's your plan when the discussion turns personal?"

"Well, if it goes to football, I'm going to say I don't follow it and keep my mouth shut after that."

"Good plan," George smiled. "What is the only thing in the world we can control?" He asked the room.

"Our reactions," the group dutifully replied, even though some rolled their eyes.

Thatcher didn't have the energy or the desire to protest, to say he couldn't control when the panic rose in him, stole his breath, and shouted *GET OUT! GET OUT! RUN!*

George glanced at his wristwatch, something largely obsolete in the wake of cell phones. "We've got a few more minutes. Anyone else?"

"How 'bout Kit? She's been pretty quick to jump in on everyone else's stuff, but we don't know anything about *her* stuff," Gil goaded. "Been three weeks already, and we don't know why she's here."

Kit shot daggers at him but said nothing.

"Kit?" George asked.

Thatcher watched her. She shook her head. "Nope."

Something in the way she held herself piqued his interest. Like she wasn't going to let anyone push her around. The fact that she was sexy as hell didn't hurt, either. Her short, sort of choppy blond hair. Sturdy, but paradoxically fine boned, with a slender neck and delicate wrists. Musculature, like her tatted bicep, that suggested she was no stranger to hard work and lots of it, yet not too sharply cut. Still female, still soft looking where it mattered. Chest, hips. But fiery to the point of snarky, as evidenced by her narrowed eyes and her sharp tone as she caught him looking.

"Quit staring, Harpo!"

He lifted his hands disarmingly, fighting a quirk at the corner of his mouth at the Marx brothers' reference. And, truth be known, thinking of his brother, Greer, who nicknamed people to keep them at a distance. He wondered if Kit was doing the same.

George glanced her way, then Thatcher's. He let it drop. "Anyone?" He looked across the room, his eyes landing on Thatcher. "What about you? I haven't seen you in before. I'm sorry, I should have gone around the room before we started, let everyone say hello, exchange names."

No need, now. He'd "met" everyone. George, Jon, Rachel, Gil, Donnie, Kit, Terry, Mike.

The room looked to him, waited. He felt it creeping upward again, like chains winding around his chest. Tightening his throat, sending his heart into jackhammer mode, telling him to go, get out. Leave.

Danger!

Run!

He forced himself to remain seated, to suffer the weight of their collective gaze. To breathe.

"Thatcher. Myers," he choked out.

George considered him for a minute. In that minute, his mind continued to scream, though his body didn't move, didn't flinch. The breath didn't heave out of him in desperate, sucking gasps. But it urged, begged, *screamed* at him to flee. Something caught in George's eyes.

"Well, I think we did some good, honest work today," he said. "I hope you all have a restful day today and tomorrow, and I hope to see you again on Wednesday.

Grab some food from the table by the back door. Be careful making your way through this mess. They keep promising me they'll straighten up the floor so we can get back down from the stage, but I'm not going to hold my breath."

The group gave him a few token laughs but cleared out in a hurry. Even George didn't linger. Kit was last to leave, other than Thatcher, and she didn't give him so much as a backward glance. Thatcher sat in the empty circle until he felt his legs would hold him, fumbling to his feet. Easing down the stage steps, he glanced toward the table at the far door. A platter of mini subs and bags of chips littered the surface. Kit glanced around, pulling a plastic bag from her giant, floppy purse. She stuffed it full of mini subs, zipped it closed and tucked it in her bag, followed by a few single serve bags of chips. He ducked behind a large, sheet-covered item on the auditorium floor, watching her pass, head dipped low as though she'd remain invisible that way.

He waited until the door closed behind her with a heavy thunk to grab a mini sub of his own.

CHAPTER THREE

"You're late," her boss said as Kit flew in the front door of the grooming shop.

"Give me a break, Nanette. It's thirty minutes away if traffic is perfect, and it's never perfect."

"Take care of Mozart, will you? He never snaps at you like he does me," she replied.

Kit breathed again, grateful to have a boss that let her split up her four-hour shift on group therapy days, even though the shop generally got backed up in her absence. Stuffing her bag of mini subs in the dorm-style fridge in the wash area, Kit breezed back into the grooming and holding area.

"That's because we get each other," she replied, slipping into baby talk. "Right, Mozie?"

The grumpy old mixed breed with the snaggle-tooth wagged as she eased him out of the kennel. He'd snapped at Nanette more than once and had broken skin twice, so it was no wonder her boss preferred Kit handle him. For whatever reason, the dog loved her, wagging and gazing at her with adoring eyes whenever she was near.

"Crystal fed up with Lily yet?" Kit joked as she passed on the way to the wash room. "She was screaming and fussy when I left her."

"If she is, she hasn't said."

After she got the tap set to a nice temperature for the old dog's arthritic bones, Nanette's voice rose over the water.

"Any drama today?"

She chuckled. "There's drama there every day, you know that."

Nanette laughed, too. "What now?"

"Just Gil being Gil."

"Who'd he attack this time?"

"Rachel. She cries a lot. Gil gave her shit for always bawling."

"Everybody handles it differently," Nanette said, sounding much like George.

"New guy showed up," Kit called out, dropping the sprayer and pulling down the shampoo. She remembered the searing heat that coursed through her when she noticed him staring. And it wasn't merely embarrassment for the way she treated him at the QT.

"Yeah?"

She could feel Nanette waiting for more. "Quiet type. Jacked up leg. Walks with a hard limp on the left. Not sure about his insides."

"What about his outsides?" Nanette teased.

"Messed up leg," she repeated, shrugging though her boss couldn't see it from the grooming floor.

"*Looks*," Nanette goaded.

"Decent," she admitted, though she didn't want to.

The last thing you need is another handsome but useless man.

"Tell me," Nanette prompted in their shorthand. Talking over the shop noise nearly left them hoarse most days.

"Tall. Maybe six, six two. Good muscles, but rangier. Not overblown looking."

"Rangy?" Kit could all but see her nose wrinkle. "Like bean pole rangy, or—"

"Not skinny. Just, you know, not hulk big like movie military guys. Not like the Rock or John Cena. Normal guy plus a little extra."

"Ah. I think I'm getting an image. Go on."

"Uh…" Kit wondered what else to say. Then she

wondered if she'd said too much already. Too much, and Nanette might notice what Kit didn't want to…that she was attracted. "Light brown hair. Kind of shaggy. His eyes, though," she said without meaning to. The verbal diarrhea continued with, "They are a problem."

"How so?"

The flutter in her belly returned just thinking about them. Him. "The color," she said, focusing on Mozart's rinse.

"What about it?"

"Super unusual. True amber. Like, golden amber." *Jungle cat amber. Tiger eyes.*

"And how did you get close enough to see them?" Nanette teased again.

"He wasn't sitting that far away. And he was staring at me at one point, so—"

"Oh, yeah?" her boss' interest only increased.

Kit said nothing for a minute, running her hand through Mozart's fur, looking for any remaining sign of lather. Satisfied there was none, she tucked him in a towel and headed back to the grooming floor.

"Seriously? Golden amber?" Nanette asked, turning off the clippers and stroking her current client's fur.

"Seriously."

And the way *he looks at you,* she added silently. *Like he understands everything you've never even said.*

"C'mon, Mozie," Kit cooed, easing the dog onto grooming table next to Nanette's, clicking the restraint harness in place. She picked up the hair dryer and set it to cool. "Let's dry off."

"You like him," Nanette grinned.

Kit paused, finger ready to switch on the loud blower. "What?" she dismissed it with a wave of her hand.

"You like him. Golden eyes."

Kit rolled her own. "Stop. He said two words all day."

"Yeah? What were they?" Nanette stuck her tongue out

at Kit's death stare.

Kit stuck her own tongue out in reply. "His first and last name."

She wasn't quite quick enough with the blower to miss Nanette's final barb.

"You like him."

~~~

Determined to fly under the radar, Thatcher arrived at the next group session neither first nor last. Like Donnie and Gil, he kept to himself, offering them no greeting, nor they, him. He thought about Kit, about her sub hoarding. Forced himself to keep his eyes away from her as she thumped into the same seat as the last session. Laughed a little at himself as he realized they were all, in fact, in the same seats as before. No surprise. He'd been reading about PTSD for weeks, trying to find something to cure himself of it, hoping understanding it would make it go away.

No such luck, but he did understand their sitting in the same seat behavior as an attempt to control something, anything. Never mind that nothing he actually wanted control over was as tangible as a hard-plastic chair or the stage platform that echoed under twitchy Jon's bouncing heel.

George arrived last, which Thatcher thought might have been intentional. He could survey the room, get a bead on the overall mood, which today felt sullen but tense. No one but Thatcher met George's eyes. No one answered when George asked,

"How is everyone today? Who'd like to start?"

Thatcher, too, looked quickly away like an unprepared school kid hoping the teacher wouldn't call on him.

"I don't have anything to talk about, more something to
~~~

ask about," Terry said, looking around the circle. "You might remember about my brother, Lee?"

Mike nodded. "Autistic, right?"

Terry nodded. "I've got plans to visit him this weekend. A long weekend. I leave today and come back Sunday night. He's afraid of dogs, so I have to leave Boomer home. I don't have any friends here yet, and my family is in Colorado, same as Lee. And this morning, when I went to drop Boomer at the boarding place, they wouldn't take him because his rabies shot isn't current. I didn't realize it was past due. I got the shot for him last night, but they say it takes about two weeks to be fully effective and still wouldn't take him. Any chance one of you'd be willing to look after him until I get back?"

"Sure," Thatcher said, surprising himself. Kit, who he realized had been about to volunteer, glanced at him and shrugged. "I mean, if you don't mind the new guy stepping up."

Terry grinned. "Nah, I don't mind. Long as you give me your address and phone."

"Yeah, man, no problem." Thatcher said easily, glad the frantic beating of his heart wasn't visible.

What the hell? Why'd you say yes?

George smiled at them. "Now that it's settled, who's next?"

He wasn't looking at George, but he felt the man's gaze as it swept the circle a second time, then a third.

"People, I don't usually push, but this room is stagnant. And life, whether we like it or not, is about forward motion. So…Kit. Tell us something about what brought you here."

Thatcher glanced her way as her head snapped up.

"Why me?"

"Why you what?" George asked.

"Why did you pick me?"

"Why not you? Are you feeling picked on?"

Silence.

"Maybe all that anger needs a little release, Kit," George said, mimicking her crossed arms and slouchy glower. "So, I'm gonna hit the valve today. Let off some pressure."

Silence.

He let her wade around in it for a bit longer, then lowered the boom.

"Don't know where to start?"

Silence.

"Alright, I'll help you out, Kit. Why'd you go into the service?"

She gave George a look that, had she given it to Thatcher, would have left him torn between wanting to hide under his bed and, inexplicably, wanting to kiss her. Hell, he wanted to kiss her, anyway.

The attraction is strong with this one, he thought, glancing at her *Star Wars* shirt. Particularly at how tightly it molded to her chest.

"Because," she said, lifting her chin, "my deadbeat husband didn't want to get a job, and someone had to support our daughter. Everything he was offered was 'beneath' him," she air-quoted sarcastically. "I didn't do so great in high school, and I barely finished my associate's degree before I gave birth. I didn't know what else to do. I'd been on about a billion interviews without a single offer. I couldn't support us flipping burgers. I figured if he wouldn't get off his ass and try to get a job, he could at least take care of Lily while I worked. Just after she turned six months, I weaned her off of breast milk onto formula and signed up."

Thatcher felt gut punched. Husband? Daughter? Wow.

"Why the Army?" George asked.

"Too prude for pole dancing," she shrugged, voice dripping with hostility and sarcasm.

Gil's bark of laughter had her slouching further in her seat, tucking her chin toward her chest. George held up a hand in his direction. The thought of Kit slinking around a pole, scantily clad, made Thatcher shift uncomfortably in his seat.

"Why the Army?" George repeated softly.

"Army National Guard," she corrected. "Thought it was safer, less likely to activate and deploy."

Several in the room bit back knowing laughter.

"Yeah," she nodded, giving them all the finger. "Thanks. About three months after AIT, Hurricane Harvey hit, and the entire Texas Guard mobilized."

Whoa. Fresh out of advanced individual training? Rough, he thought.

"You're from Texas?" Donnie asked, brow furrowing.

"My husband's family was there, so we moved when I got pregnant. More support," she shrugged.

"What was your MOS?" Gil asked, leaning forward with a frown.

She coughed, looking down at her lap.

Thatcher tried not to be amused at the reddening of her cheeks, at the obvious backfiring of her choice. He knew a lot of guys who had chosen their military occupational specialty, or MOS, similarly, based on rumors about "least likely to" and "seldom-if-ever", like choosing classes for the easy 'A', only to get hit with a passionate taskmaster of a teacher. And it certainly wasn't funny, getting orders to deploy when you thought your choice of career made it less likely. But her sheepishness was endearing.

"C'mon," Gil goaded. "What was it?"

"I've talked enough," she said into her chest, head down. "Next!"

"Kit," George prompted, giving her a pointed look.

"92A," she mumbled, obviously hoping they wouldn't know what the number meant.

Jesus.

Silence fell heavily over the room. With the possible exception of Rachel, everyone knew logistics—92A—was one of the most frequently called infantry support groups.

Thatcher was grateful when even Gil kept quiet. He wondered what kind of psycho recruiter let a new mother choose logistics, ASVAB test results be damned. After a moment, George said,

"Thank you for your service, Kit."

When she offered nothing else, George prompted, "Who else wants to share today?"

"Nah, George," Jon said, shaking his head. "Can't leave it like that."

"Stuff it, Jon!" Kit groused.

"C'mon, Kit," Gil called across the circle, "rip it off. Like a bandage."

She shook her head, eyes shooting daggers at him. "I was part of a relief supply convoy. Our unit was only supposed to set up the supply chain, but the need was so great, we went from arranging everything behind the scenes to actively delivering. The LMTV I was on brought up the rear. Even though the floodwater was receding, it was still almost to the tops of our tires. I guess the weight of the five trucks ahead of ours undermined the saturated road. We began to slip off onto the shoulder, and then the shoulder disintegrated and we started to pitch sideways. There were eight of us in back with the supplies. As we scrambled to get off the truck, this guy, Chris, somehow got pinned at the ankle between the rear tire and the guardrail, and he went under the floodwater. A couple of the others went after him and tried to get him free, while I cut up a compressor hose to get him some air. The guardrail began to give under the weight, and the truck shifted again. I don't remember anything after that until I woke up in the hospital with a re-inflated left lung, fifteen stitches in my scalp, a lovely G.I. Jane haircut, and a monster headache."

When no one spoke, Kit tilted her head in Jon's direction. "You good, Peaches?"

"I'm sorry you went through that, Kit," George said.

Her iron façade slipped. "Yeah."

The soft agreement hit Thatcher in the center of his chest.

"You get a medical discharge?" he asked.

She met his eyes. "No. Hardship. Same day I was injured, my husband got off a plane here in Phoenix, dropped Lily off at my disabled mother's house with a letter that basically said, 'Hey, I didn't agree to this. Please sign these divorce papers.' Three days later, when I regained consciousness, my CO broke the news about my pending divorce and that my mother passed away and my daughter was with social services. Not because they couldn't reach my piece-of-shit, soon-to-be ex, but because he couldn't be bothered to take care of his daughter for the two weeks it would ultimately take for my hardship discharge to process."

"Two weeks?! Who'd you have to blow to get approved that fast?"

Terry sat up straighter in his chair next to Kit. "Seriously, Gil? That's what you're taking away from everything she just said?" He shook his head. "I'm sorry, Kit. God."

Thatcher couldn't have said it better, himself. Jackass.

Kit clearly didn't appreciate it, either, but it appeared she lacked the energy to snark at him. "Between the pending medical evaluation and the hardship request, it was fast-tracked."

Gil shook his head. "Fucking lucky is what it is," he groused. "Always the broads that get the breaks."

"Watch it, Gil," Thatcher threatened, wanting to take the asshole's throat in his hands and squeeze until the smart remarks stopped.

"Whoa!" Gil held up his hands. "The new guy *can* talk. Whaddaya know?"

It was way too early, but George suddenly stood. "I think that's a good place to stop for today."

I think so, too. Before I kill that son-of-a-bitch.

Thatcher watched the others make their way down the stage steps, amazed at the way George remained unruffled.

"Gil, I need you to come down the hall to the lobby area so I can update your paperwork. Everyone else, help yourselves to the refreshments in the back, and I'll see you Friday."

This time it was a platter of chicken sandwiches from some unknown location. Thatcher guessed the deli department of a grocery store, though there was no sticker or other marking on the loud plastic lid Kit pulled off. He wondered if she was waiting until he left to bring out the Ziploc. She took one sandwich and stood against the wall with it as Donnie and Terry grabbed two each, already wolfing them down as they headed for the exit.

Terry stopped as they were leaving, and they each plugged the other's information into their phones, agreeing to meet at a dog park near Terry's house so Thatcher could get acquainted with Boomer and Terry could provide all the supplies the dog would need for the five days his owner would be gone.

Thatcher limped to the buffet table as they left, facing no other competition for the platter. George overbought, for there were still several sandwiches in the first container and another unopened one. He considered trying to make conversation with Kit, moving to stand beside her along the opposite wall. As he opened his mouth, however, she reached over and pushed the hand holding the sandwich toward his face.

"Don't bother," she said, "I'm done talking for the day, Harpo."

Unable to stop the side of his mouth from lifting, Thatcher winked and took a large bite of his sandwich, fighting the urge to look back as he left. The urge he didn't fight was stopping in the hall to watch her finish eating. She unwittingly lunched with him, then pulled out another plastic bag and stuffed it with chicken sandwiches.

Thatcher wondered if George wasn't cluelessly overbuying, after all, but very deliberately doing so.

As Kit slipped out the far door with her big, slouchy purse full of food, he thought George was a very smart man, indeed.

CHAPTER FOUR

An hour later, still thinking of Kit, Thatcher steeled himself as he stood outside the swank house Kearny shared with Janine, relieved he'd gotten past the guards in the little shack at the gates to the community. Idling in his Jeep as they looked in the computer for his approved guests, he feared he might no longer be on the list. When the door swung open, Kearny asked, "What do you want, Thatch?"

"How—?" he began.

Kearny lifted his head and flashed a humorless grin. "Spidey sense. You know, all us blind people who haven't seen the shit you've seen have it."

He deserved that, and he knew it, but he couldn't quite stop the hitch in his breath. "I'm sorry, man," he choked miserably, hating the sting of tears…hating the emotional wreck he'd been since coming home. No, not since coming home. Since waking up at Walter Reed.

Kearny's forgiving embrace almost did him in completely. "Okay," he said softly as Thatcher held on tightly, trying desperately to regain control of himself. But he shook from the effort, and he knew Kearny felt it. "Okay, man," he said, tightening his own grip, no longer holding back. "We're good."

Thatcher sighed as some of the tension drained away from him. "Thanks."

A whine at their feet had Kearny jerking back quickly, head ducking in direction of the sound. "Dude, you got a dog?"

Thatcher shook his head. He'd gotten past rolling his eyes over all the things he did that Kearny couldn't see. "Dog sitting," he explained. "This is Boomer."

"Friendly?" Kearny grinned, eager to meet the dog.

"Yeah, man."

"Hey, Boomer," Kearny reached out, fingers curled into his palm, petting the dog when it happily ducked under his hand.

"Thought you might want to come with me to a dog park, hang out for a bit."

"Sure. Let me get some shoes."

He followed Kearny into the depths of the modestly sized but well-appointed home. Spying his discarded guitar on the sofa, Thatcher said, "If you're working, I—"

"Nope. I need a break, anyway. Fresh air and all that."

"You sure?"

"Positive. My muse could use some air," he joked.

"Everything going okay with Ashes Onward?"

Kearny's new rock band suffered a lot of scrutiny from critics and fans alike. The early buzz garnered when his fiancée, Janine's, boss broke the story open before the planned announcement was mostly positive, but Kearny's jokes sometimes were a deflection…a silent signal that he was actually suffering.

"All is well," his brother agreed, grabbing his cane. "Lead on."

An hour later, Thatcher and Kearny sat on a bench in a dog park nearby while Boomer loped around, playing with the other dogs.

"So…I've been going to a group thing," Thatcher said lightly, tossing the slobbery tennis ball Boomer had abandoned from hand to hand.

"Yeah?" Kearny smiled. "How's it going?"

Thatcher thought about it. "It's only been two sessions."

"So far, then?"

"So far," he paused. "Kind of a circus." Boomer returned, crashing against their knees. Kearny laughed and petted the retriever's broad head.

"Give it a chance. Too early to give up."

Boomer barked, and Thatcher held up the ball to see if the dog's interest had renewed. It had, and now the two dogs he'd been romping with also quivered, eagerly awaiting his throw. "Go get it!" he encouraged, sending the ball sailing with his right arm. "I didn't say I was quitting," he answered mildly.

"You been talking any?"

Thatcher shrugged, realizing Kearny couldn't see it. Habit. His silence was enough of an answer.

"Thatch..."

"Kearny, drop it, man," Thatcher warned as Boomer came galloping back with the ball, his doggie friends at his furry heels.

"Thatcher," Kearny rubbed a hand through his hair in a way that said he was getting frustrated.

"Stop trying to—"

"I'm not trying—"

"Yes, you are," Thatcher's voice rose. Boomer's tail drooped. He dropped the ball, sidling closer, flattening his furry body against Thatcher's knees. "Okay, okay," he told Boomer, stroking the back of his broad head. "Kearny, I know this whole situation is fucked up. I know *I'm* fucked up, and I know everybody just wants me not to be. Trust me, bro, if I could rewind all this shit..." his throat grew thick. Boomer put both front paws on his right thigh, looking for all the world like he was trying to become a lap dog. "I know, Boomer," he soothed, stroking the dog's neck. "I would go back in a second," he finished.

Kearny's hand found his shoulder. Squeezed.

Thatcher's stomach dropped at the voice in his head that reminded, *Yeah, but you're not going to wake up from this nightmare. They aren't coming back.*

"I'm sorry, Thatch. I'm not trying to push you or put on the pressure. I just…I hate—*we* hate—that there's nothing we can do."

"Believe me, I wish there was." Thatcher put his own hand on Kearny's shoulder. Squeezed back.

Boomer reared forward to lick his cheek.

"Alright, Boomer," Thatcher chuckled. To Kearny, he said, "Anyway, if you think I'm grumpy, you should see this girl in my group, Kit. It's like talking to a cactus."

Kearny grinned. "Prickly, huh?"

"Oh, yeah."

"She hot?" The mischief in his brother's smile was something, Thatcher realized suddenly, he hadn't seen in a long time.

Thatcher laughed, surprised at the fullness of the sound, the genuine feeling behind it. "Oh, yeah," he said again.

"Interested?"

"Sure. She's not hard to look at. Just hard to talk to. Pissed off at men," he added, then found himself telling Kearny about her douchebag ex, the way the guy dumped their baby daughter and a packet of divorce papers on Kit's dying mother without a backward glance.

"Shit, that's cold."

"Yeah."

"Well, no wonder she's prickly. You don't mess with a mama bear's cub like that," Kearny shook his head.

"No, you don't," he agreed. "Tried to help her out a little the other day. George, the guy who leads group, always brings food for the end of the session. Both times now, I've seen her stuffing all sorts of extras into her purse for later. I think she's having trouble making ends meet, not that she's said anything in group about it. But I dropped some groceries off at her place the other night. Tried to do it without her catching me, but—" he slapped his thigh just above his knee. Boomer came rocketing back, mistaking it for a command.

Kearny nodded at the sound.

"She bit my damn head off. Gave back the stuff that wouldn't spoil, along with ten bucks."

Kearny made a face.

"God!" Thatcher shook his head. "Turned me on so damn much, I almost tried to kiss her."

"Better watch out," Kearny shook his head. "Chick like that might punch you in the throat if you try."

"Probably would."

After a brief silence, the two of them basking in the late winter breeze that would soon give way to Phoenix's usual ridiculous temperatures, Kearny folded his hands over his stomach and sighed.

"Mom wanted me to try to talk you into family dinner."

He gave a sarcastic chuckle. "I should've known."

Kearny sighed heavily. "Thatch, you haven't been to family dinner in two months."

"I wasn't at family dinner for the better part of ten years."

"That's different and you know it."

He did know it.

"I can't, Kearny," he said flatly, too weary to warn. "Not yet."

One on one, or two on one, really, with just his parents, he could do. He could go to Parker and Melody's or Greer and Shelby's for a meal, no issues. But everyone together...he felt suffocated. Panicky. He'd had to lock himself in the bathroom four times at the last family dinner Kearny mentioned. Breathing. Holding the sink. Trying not to pass out. Finding things he could see, touch, hear, smell, taste. Over and over until his mother asked if he was feeling ill. All but running to the pool house the second it was socially acceptable to do so, which was when Parker and Melody begged off early to put their baby to bed.

After a few more minutes of silence and warm breezes, Kearny nodded. "Alright, man. My conscience is clear. I told them I'd ask, and I have."

~~~

"P.D.D., man." Kyle's last words, since you couldn't count the helpless gurgling sounds he made before going limp in Thatcher's grasp, faded along with the nightmare into the whir of the floor fan.

P.D.D.

Pay attention.

Don't get stupid.

Don't get dead.

His squad's mantra. Important words, packed into a quick little acronym. Meaningless now.

Thatcher swung his legs over the edge of the bed, wiping sleep-tears off his face, wishing Boomer was still around. He considered, not for the first time, looking into a PTSD dog of his own. The dog had been in his life for a short four and a half days, but Thatcher felt his absence acutely. Handing him back to Terry the night before had been harder than he'd imagined.

Without the dog forcing him out for walks and playtime, he wondered why he bothered to get up at all. It's not like he'd been doing the world any good lately, hiding in the little apartment over his parents' pool house after graduating from their downstairs guest room—a banner day, that one!

He limped to the dresser, his morning ritual, clenching his jaw against the vicious, gnawing ache in his left leg. It was always worse in the morning. He forced himself to look in the mirror before sliding his gaze to the four guys in fatigues, tapping the dog tags hanging from the corner of the frame—his—four times, acknowledgment of each life ended.

Why the hell am I the one still standing?

He touched Kyle's tags, trying not to think of his toddler
~~~

son, Matty. Those huge blue eyes, so innocent.

"It should be you, man. You should be with Wendy and Matty," he croaked, his head dropping forward.

He thought of Gabriela, his high school girlfriend and how maybe her picture should be on the opposite corner of the dresser. Another life ended. The first, actually. Where would she be now, if not for him? Married? Kids? Would she be a famous anything, the way she'd wanted to be?

How can you want to be famous without knowing what you want to be famous for? he'd teased.

I just want people to remember who I am. Like for a long time after I die, you know? Like Elvis. Or Lucille Ball.

An entertainer, then?

Not necessarily. Just lasting like that.

"Well, honey," he sighed at her smiling face in the photo, "you got your wish, didn't you? I'll never forget you."

He braced himself against the dresser, leaning as hard as he could on both arms, until the stupid thing clunked backward into the wall and he jerked back, white-hot pain shooting out from his shoulder in two directions, from arm to elbow and down his back to his waist.

His throat hurt, a ball of pain he refused to release, his chest tight as he fumbled with the drawer pull and clumsily pulled out a fresh pair of boxer briefs. The dexterity was returning to his left hand more slowly than he'd like, despite following his physical therapist's advice to use his injured side as often as possible.

He stared lifelessly into his closet, dreading the day. Most were pointless, spent at physical therapy appointments or going on interviews for jobs he didn't want and couldn't get excited about, or wanted but probably couldn't physically perform—the latter just to watch the interviewers squirm.

He wished it were one o'clock already, time for another group session. Not because he wanted to talk. He didn't. He hadn't…not in the way that mattered. He offered support to the others, for their issues. He offered none of his own. He couldn't. Even thinking about his reasons for attending group caused the words to swell up in his throat. But it was a place to go…something to do instead of drift uselessly through the days.

Thatcher returned to the dresser to stare at himself in the mirror with contempt, wishing he could fix things with his family without having to sit in a circle of chairs on the stage of a community theater with a bunch of other broken people. But they were right. He was 28-years-old, a disabled veteran of the U.S. Army. Directionless. Adrift. He had no job, no purpose. He had trouble sleeping, a new fear of crowds and unexpected loud noises, and dwindling self-respect. Despite his family's assurances that they loved him and were there for him, he had trouble being around them. When a crowd consisting of your own family—granted, they were a large group—was too much to bear, something was wrong. Something that wouldn't fix itself with time or concentration.

Thatcher forced his eyes to remain fixed on his mirror image.

"It ends today," he told his reflection. "No more pity party. No more denial. You go to PT, you keep going to this group thing, and you start making shit right. You talk this time. You don't have to tell them everything. But say *something*."

The lecture backfired. His heart hammered in his chest. His hands shook. He swallowed hard as the world began to spin, and his breath came in ragged pants.

No.

No, no.

Breathe.

Don't let it take over. Don't let it do this to you.

Turning away from the dresser, he stumbled into the bathroom. Leaning on his good arm on the bathroom counter, his head spinning, his physical therapist's words came back to him.

Do your box breathing. Exhale slowly to the count of four. Hold your breath for four more counts. Inhale slowly for four. Then exhale again for four more.

When that didn't work, he tried another panic remedy, eyes roving around the little bathroom.

Name five things you can see...

"Mirror, sink, toilet, shower, lights," he gasped, the room still swirling.

Four things you can touch....

"Towel, medicine cabinet, light switch, shower door," he said, naming them as he touched each one.

Three things you can hear...

"Ceiling fan, bathroom fan." He wondered if that was cheating, naming two fans. "Water running," he said, turning on the shower tap as the spinning slowed.

Two things you can smell...

"Water," he said, sticking his hand under the spray to test the heat. He rushed out of his clothes and into the strangely comforting confines of the tiny stall. "Soap," he added, squirting some onto his palm.

One thing you can taste...

"Water," he repeated, opening his mouth to the spray. He'd already cheated with two fans, and he sure wasn't going to taste the soap.

He sighed, relieved. It worked. Most of the time, it worked. It backed the panic down to a manageable level.

Thatcher tipped his head back, focusing on the heat, the steam, the light scent of the soap. The clean feeling that would only last until a few hours' worth of horrible, ugly thoughts wound around his brain.

He felt like a damn sissy, falling apart in his bathroom, hyperventilating over the mere thought of speaking in the group therapy session. This time, however, he didn't bargain with himself. He didn't decide to skip group, reasoning with himself that he'd be ready to try again "if I can just have today and tomorrow to mentally prepare for it." That bargaining bullshit was what kept him hamstering on a wheel.

He scrubbed his hair clumsily with his left hand, wincing at the pulling sensation caused by the thick scars all over his bicep and shoulder.

"It ends now," he repeated in the echoey shower chamber.

CHAPTER FIVE

Kit sank onto the sofa with a weary groan. Barely nine o'clock, and she could fall asleep right now. After four hours of dog washing and four hours of community service at the food pantry, her feet were killing her and her back ached. She bit into the last of George's latest offering, a breakfast burrito, casting a reproachful glance at the stack of mail and her checkbook on the coffee table.

Thatcher flitted into her thoughts, a distraction from figuring out her finances. Without wanting to, she felt a pang of empathy for him. George had called on him to speak, and like with every session so far, his eyes lit with panic. Panic he clearly thought he hid…but didn't. Then again, maybe she and George were the only ones who noticed. George, because he was a professional therapist. Her? She liked looking at Thatcher far too much. She'd seen his throat working, his Adam's apple bobbing as he swallowed several times. She'd seen his jaw clench and unclench. And then his palms, resting flat on his thighs, curled up.

George moved on to Donnie, and she'd watched Thatcher slowly relax. By session's end, he was still a mystery.

Quick movement at the corner of her eye drew her attention to the screened security door. A shadowy figure there had her grabbing the baseball bat she kept in the corner of the living room. She thought briefly of the Glock in her bedroom closet, in the safe, but decided against it.

She'd never had to use the bat— or the gun — before, not in this neighborhood. She hoped she didn't have to use it now. As she reached the door, however, she saw the shadow figure again, further up the street. Limping.

Lowering the bat, she shoved open the security door and rushed onto the patio, her cry cut short as she stumbled over something solid and nearly fell down the three wide concrete steps.

Grocery bags.

A familiar Jeep rolled by slowly. She could just make out the shape of a hand lifting in greeting.

She stared after it, hands on her hips, tears and fury battling in equal measure.

"I knew it," she muttered, picking up the first two sacks, staggering under their unexpected weight. "Fucking Harpo."

She knew he'd seen her stuffing chicken sandwiches into her purse after group last Wednesday. Then the burritos on Friday. Too embarrassed, she'd skipped bagging any of today's offering, KFC. She'd swallowed down the shame and the rude comment she'd been prepared to make in answer to the prying questions or, worse, derisive comments she feared might come next. But by the time she reached the parking lot, his shiny red Jeep was backing out of its space.

George. Fucking George and his "everyone help yourselves" thing. Transparent. She wasn't stupid. He'd never brought food in before, but the one time he'd brought donuts, he'd caught her with three of them, grinning when she'd sheepishly claimed to have missed breakfast. After that, he'd brought food in every time. She knew what he was doing, just like she knew what Thatcher was doing.

She hefted the leaden bags onto the counter, tears sliding down her face, then made another trip outside for the other two. With each item she pulled out, her shame grew. Since she couldn't bear the feeling, she forced it to swing toward pissed off.

Gallon of whole milk, brick of Kerrygold.

Jesus, you can't just do cheap store butter? You've got to buy this wonderful grass-fed, natural stuff?

Carton of eggs, a rotisserie chicken, pound of ground beef—more of the organic, grass-fed stuff—and bag after bag of fresh fruit and vegetables. Rice, pasta, crackers, and cans of tuna followed. She put the refrigerated items away, trying not to notice his groceries were nearly the only items in the thing, save a few half-empty bottles of condiments, a block of cheese she kept scraping mold off of, and Lily's milk and juice.

Storming back into the living room, swiping at her face, she grabbed her purse.

Ten dollars. Two measly fives. All she had left until Nanette paid her on Friday. With her gas gauge hovering near 'E', did she dare risk stuffing the non-perishables back into one or two of the sacks with the two bills inside so she could sneak them into Thatcher's Jeep at tomorrow's group session?

Fury warred with gratitude. It wasn't as though she couldn't use the lovely groceries or that she was an insufferable bitch. It was that she hated that she couldn't do it on her own, couldn't feed both herself and Lily. It killed her to rely on the kindness of strangers, or near strangers. George. And now Thatcher. She'd die before she'd let Lily go without. She'd choose Lily every time. Until she found a better job, something full-time, she'd make it work. Somehow. That's what she told herself. And told herself again each session as she smuggled as many of George's offerings as would fit in a gallon-size freezer bag in her big ass purse. But the truth was, without George, she'd be starving even if Lily remained fed. With George, she was still hungry sometimes, especially in the weekend stretch, when she had to get from Friday's session to Monday's.

And now, having skipped today's offering, she'd have had trouble getting to Wednesday. Or would have.

Thatcher.

Her breath caught. She could picture him, his amber eyes staring solemnly at her. Judging her. Maybe not harshly. But pityingly. That would be worse. So, so much worse.

Kit tossed one of the two fives into each bag with the non-perishables.

Though she thought she'd fully decided the matter, she paused at the archway from kitchen to living room. She thought of Lily, sleeping in her crib, and nearly marched back into the kitchen to stock her pantry. But then she thought of David, of where relying on someone got you.

She clicked off the light and headed back to the living room to face the stack of mail.

~~~

"Kit, what the hell?" Thatcher called at her back as she strode quickly to her car after Wednesday's session.

He'd waited for her to smuggle bagels and cream cheese into her purse, then slipped out the door after her, hoping to strike up a conversation, only to catch sight of two grocery bags nestled in the front passenger seat of his Jeep, sans the perishables.

Okay. He'd known she'd seen him. He'd driven by slowly enough to ensure it. Not because he wanted her to know it was him. He didn't. But then he saw her with the bat and put two and two together and decided he would rather she see him than be afraid of some creeper lurking outside.

She turned, walking backward, and called out, "I don't need your help or your charity, Prince Valiant!"
~~~

Prince Valiant. That's a new one.

He ducked to see her as she closed herself into her car, placing his left hand on the frame in hopes she wouldn't just drive out from under him.

"Everybody needs help sometimes, Kit," he said.

"Keep your eyes on your own paper, Harpo," she sighed, turning the ignition.

Nothing. She frowned and tried again. The engine sputtered to life, and her relieved smile hit him low in the belly. She'd grimaced many a time in group. But he'd never seen a real smile, and it hit him hard, her face lit up and open instead of always shuttered.

"I'm not exactly silent in class anymore. Better think up a new nickname."

She put the Civic in reverse, forcing him to step back. "The rest aren't fit for polite company."

Her words were acidic, but…was that a smile she was fighting?

"Since when are you polite?" he teased, just to see what she'd say.

"The fact that you're not under my tires is proof enough, Groceries!"

Now it's Groceries. She could give Greer a run for his money with the nicknames.

His mouth twitched as he swallowed a laugh.

Kit propped her elbow on the door of the car, a fist tucked in front of her mouth to hide her grin. But he saw it.

He ducked into the Jeep feeling good, thinking of Kit's smile…the first genuine one he'd seen. It did things to him. He shifted in the seat, wincing, and realized that for the first time, he didn't dread his next stop: physical therapy.

Or maybe he did, he decided, when his therapist, Cesar, a burly Mexican with a smile as big as his heart, put him to work on a new regimen.

"Getting too good at your exercises, Sergeant. Time to scale up." He groaned as Cesar eased his left leg up perpendicular to his body and gently leaned into it. "You're tight. You doing your stretches, Mano?"

He winced as Cesar eased his leg further back toward his chest. "Yeah. I'm just not as flexible as you want me to be."

Cesar laughed. "You're more flexible than you think. You gotta push a little. Not a lot. It's a fine line, but I think you're too scared of setbacks to push yourself enough. Give it one percent more than you're comfortable with."

He thought, not for the first time, that Cesar was talking about more than PT. He'd admitted to the guy that he'd started going to the group he'd suggested, and now the guy wouldn't quit asking about it.

"You tell them anything yet?" Cesar asked, as if he'd heard Thatcher's thoughts.

"Who?" he played dumb.

Cesar hissed in disapproval. "Group."

"Not yet."

"Mano," Cesar began, "you —"

"I will," he said.

Cesar hissed again. "My boy, Socrates, said 'The secret of change is to focus all of your energy not on fighting the old, but building the new.' You need to build some new, Mano. Can't regrow the muscles the surgeons had to cut away, but you can strengthen what you have left. But your heart, Mano, that's a muscle, too. And it can heal. But you gotta take the first step."

He snorted. "Are you my physical therapist or my psychotherapist?"

Cesar's mouth hitched up at the corner as he shifted to work Thatcher's arm and shoulder. "I like to think I'm a little bit of both. With me, you get two for one on your therapy."

Thatcher snorted again. "Careful. Some idiot will sue you for practicing without a license."

Cesar gave him a look, pausing a stretch that left his arm

angled awkwardly.

"Not me," he added. "But someone."

Cesar resumed the stretch. "You just focus on you, Sergeant," he said. "Therapy ain't going to help if you only sit and listen to other people doing their work. You gotta do your own."

Eyes on your own paper, Harpo.

That wasn't what Kit meant when she'd said it, but her words came to mind. He'd caught her watching him nearly as often as she'd caught him looking at her. Standoffish as she might be, her eyes flickered with interest. It made him want to speak. Keep her interested. Inevitably, her eyes flitted away each time he met them, like a butterfly evading capture. She was as elusive as the "healing" Cesar dangled like a carrot. He knew better. The carrot was something you chased but never caught.

CHAPTER SIX

On Monday, after a grueling session where Rachel cried over her latest attempts to find a job despite insomnia and suicidal thoughts, Mike worried over whether the latest interviewer—the insurance job—was going to hire him or not, Jon fretted again over tomorrow's 9:30 hearing for the assault charge, and Terry and Gil played "who's a bigger badass" with their war stories, Kit waited impatiently for the room to clear. She still had food at home thanks to Thatcher. But old habits died hard, and Nanette needed her help at the shop. Every minute spent waiting for the others to partake of the pizza before she could stuff her purse with whatever would fit in the usual plastic bag was a minute Nanette had to play the role of receptionist, dog washer, groomer and housekeeper.

Weekends were hard. Nanette insisted that Kit needed the prime dating nights off to "sow her wild oats", so she had Fridays and Saturdays off. Sunday mornings, when the shop was closed, her tax free $40 was earned giving the place an extra deep cleaning. Under normal circumstances, that meant George's Friday session offering had to last through the rest of the day on Friday, all of Saturday, and all of Sunday. By Sunday, when Nanette did her grocery shopping, there was seldom any stash of food left in the shop.

Her stomach tied itself in hungry knots. She'd had one egg for breakfast. One slice of toast with a tiny pat of that lovely Kerrygold. A juice glass of whole milk.

Habits.

If it wasn't for George, and now Thatcher, she'd probably have knocked over a QuikTrip by now.

Talk about embarrassing. She'd become *that* girl. The one that smuggles Tupperware to a buffet. She'd be damned if Lily would ever go hungry or dirty. She could skip a few meals if she had to or cut back on volume. But her little girl would *never* go without. Not while she still drew a breath. After the lights and water, car and home insurance, and diapers—God, diapers were expensive! —there was barely enough for gas for the car and airtime for her crappy burner phone. So, generally, she looked for free food where she could find it. Before George and the donut event, her favorite thing was to duck into Sam's Club on Saturdays with Lily in tow, claiming she was there for the pharmacy, which didn't require a membership card. Then she'd load up a cart with a few things she would ultimately put back on the shelves, all so she could avoid looking obvious as she went from sample station to sample station. When the samples were bad or fewer in number than usual, she'd scrape together enough change from the bottom of her purse for a hot dog or slice of pizza.

Now here she was, waiting to hoard slices she could enjoy with Thatcher's salad fixings before they went bad. She absolutely would *not* allow them to go to waste.

Kit pretended to check messages on her phone as the others slid slices onto napkins and left. All except Thatcher, who was actually texting back and forth with someone. Kit wished he'd finish up, grab a piece of pizza and leave. She couldn't exactly smuggle pizza after all but throwing his groceries back in his face last Friday, could she?

Fuck.

Twenty-five years old, making under-the-table minimum wage, with a toddler, living in her dead mother's paid off house, trying to figure out what to do next. And hogging more than her share of whatever George brought for them to enjoy. Yeah, she was a winner, all right.

Thatcher's gaze found her as he tucked his phone into his back pocket. He looked at the pizza box. She could all but hear him counting off the slices before he wandered off with another of his cheeky winks, empty handed. Still, she hurried through the pizza gathering and the walk of shame, furtively glancing around to make sure none of the rest of the group was anywhere in sight before she hurried across the obstacle course that was the theater floor.

So far so good. Parking lot mostly empty, except for…fuck. Thatcher's stupid Jeep. He was behind the wheel, head bent over his phone again. He didn't look up as she hurried past. Maybe he wouldn't see her.

Kit wondered if he was texting a girlfriend, surprised at the little sizzle of disappointment and the follow up punch of jealousy. She had no claim to him. Didn't want one. But her mind conjured an image of those silly, gorgeous eyes of his and her stomach went hollow from more than mere hunger.

The door to her mom's Honda squeaked so loudly she wondered if it would fall off. She felt rather than saw Thatcher's head lift, turn her way. So much for an invisible getaway with her six slices of pepperoni.

"No!" she moaned as the engine failed to start. "No, no, no!" she added as she turned the key once more. The Civic sputtered a laugh at her and died again. "C'mon, baby, please," she coaxed, "please, please, please. Not now. Not today. Not here."

The engine caught, then died. She dropped her head to the wheel, fighting off an ugly cry.

"Need a lift?"

Her head jerked up so fast she got dizzy.

"Valiant," she sighed, resigned to forever embarrassing herself in his presence. She climbed out of her car, glancing toward his Jeep.

"Got time for lunch?" he asked.

"No," she said, though she knew when she called Nanette to tell her she'd be late, her boss would say she'd be fine until Kit could make it in. Even if she wouldn't.

"It's on me," Thatcher added, flipping his keys in his hand.

"No. I have to get to work."

"C'mon. You have to eat."

"I just had a slice of pizza."

"No, you didn't. I was there, remember?"

He didn't suggest she start with what was in her purse, which surprised her. And stabbed her with shame. He was trying to help her save it for later, knowing him.

"Completely free," he added. "No strings."

She rolled her eyes at that. "Nothing's free, Groceries."

"No," he agreed. "But I know the owner, and he'll let me work off our meal if I ask him. No strings for you. Strings for me."

"Get real," she snorted. "Like I'm going to let you do that."

Kit stood beside the Jeep and wondered how much the bus would cost, if she could figure out what route to take to get her to Waggy Waggy for her shift.

Thatcher started around the side of the Jeep. Kit realized what he meant to do and hurried to grab the handle.

"Stop trying to rescue me," she snapped, ducking into the passenger seat before he could open the door for her. When he didn't answer, she looked out the window, watched the world slide into reverse as he backed out.

"It's just lunch, Kit. It's not the big deal you're making it out to be."

Maybe not to you.

She kept her eyes on the world outside the passenger window.

"Don't lie to me to force your charity on me, and it won't have to be a big deal, Valiant."

He'd barely turned out of the lot before he was swinging

into the lot of the paint store next door and switching off the engine.

"I can't pretend to know you, Kit," he ground out, staring at her with those amber eyes of his, "especially since you're locked up tighter than Fort Knox. But if you've got a daughter and you're stockpiling free food like it's the only meal you'll get and now you've got a broken car, you need help. So, suck up your pride and have a free meal with me. Maybe, I don't know, talk to me for a few minutes. Do the kitchen work if it'll make you feel better about the food."

She hated with every fiber of her being that he knew her situation and that she needed to accept his offer. Six slices wouldn't feed her through the rest of today and tomorrow and Wednesday until group. Or they wouldn't have, without his groceries. Lily was covered. Lily would always be covered. But she couldn't be at her best on the food she was pilfering. She had to keep the lights on, the air conditioning running, water flowing, the car running. And she couldn't do it, couldn't be her best for Lily, if she kept burning the candle at both ends. She had to keep accepting the free babysitting Nanette's wife, Crystal, offered. She had to keep looking for another job, though she hated to stab Nanette in the back that way…take the free sitting and use it to find something that would have her quitting the grooming shop at her earliest opportunity. Or at least it felt that way, despite Nanette's assurances they would be fine if she had to take a full-time job elsewhere, that they would work out a reasonable cost for Lily's daycare at that point.

She didn't have to like it that Thatcher was so observant or so insistent.

"Fine," she slouched in the seat.

He shot her a look she didn't want to think too much about and started the Jeep, slid it back into traffic.

After fifteen minutes of driving with only his phone's playlist to stave off the silence, Thatcher swung the Jeep into a restaurant parking lot. The sign, emblazoned with the silhouette of a Phoenix bird rising from a nest of flame, read "Phoenix Rise Grill".

Whoa. Wait a second.

Phoenix Rise Grill. Thatcher.

No.

Kit glanced over at him, wondering but saying nothing. Her mind conjured news articles, her memory sifting through articles and interviews. Before she could ask the question she wanted to ask, he switched off the Jeep. He made no move to exit. From the corner of her eye, Kit saw him draw a deep breath, turning her head only slightly to see his knuckles going white on the wheel. She considered asking, but her stomach won out, growling so loudly she couldn't fathom he hadn't heard it. Her questions forgotten, she watched him with concern, her mind sifting through a whole new set of questions.

He took another, deeper breath.

Kit leaped out of the Jeep. "Fine. You win. It smells amazing, even all the way out here. Let's do this. Chop, chop, Valiant!" She clapped her hands and headed for the entrance.

It resembled an overgrown Mediterranean villa, boasting an outdoor patio with an air curtain and a dark green mesh canopy strung with white Christmas lights over a pergola style roof. A perimeter of super fine misters offered delightfully temperate seating even, she guessed, in the middle of summer, though they felt chilly now.

A ramp up the side of the patio was the main entry into the restaurant, and as Kit neared it, the scent of barbecue quadrupled. Her mouth began to water as she reached for the handle, then hesitated to look back at him. Thatcher reached past her and put his own hand on the handle. He, too, came to a halt. Kit guessed his reason for hesitation had something to do with the white-knuckle moment in the car. She wanted to ask him about it, but she didn't know how. Before she could, he swung the door wide and stepped inside.

"Thatcher!"

Kit looked up at the man rushing forward. He had the same freaky amber eyes, except his were behind spectacles. Although his face was a bit fuller and more time worn, it was a clear representation of Thatcher's future.

Oh, God. He did, she thought, her mind returning to the articles, to his name…Thatcher.

He brought me to his father's restaurant.

Her earlier suspicions confirmed— that he was *that* Thatcher Myers, the wounded brother of rock star Kearny Myers, shocked her into shy silence. Kit swallowed hard as Thatcher drew another deep breath.

"Hey, Pop."

The two men embraced, and Kit could see some of the tension drop away as the man's bear hug lingered just long enough but not too long.

"Pop," he said again, gesturing toward her, "this is Kit. Kit, my father, Arthur Myers."

"Artie," Arthur said, offering his hand. "Kit, is that short for Kathleen? Katherine?"

"Just Kit, actually. I was named after a character in a movie," she told him, feeling the usual heat creep up into her cheeks.

"Yeah? What movie?" Thatcher glanced at her with interest.

"*A League of Their Own.*"

Artie's eyes narrowed. "Right! The movie about women's baseball, when the ladies kept baseball going as the men went to fight WWII!"

Kit nodded. "That's the one."

Artie's eyes lit with delight. "That's interesting! I named my first four kids after cities in Arizona. And then, when my wife, Della, and I adopted four more, they either started with or decided to change to Arizona names, too."

Kit tilted her head as she considered Thatcher. She almost blurted that she knew, but she held her tongue. Now was not the time. "Really. Wow. I didn't realize there were so many city names that would work as kids' names."

Artie shrugged sheepishly. "I suppose some people would think it's strange. But we've enjoyed showing our kids the places they're named after. It made for some fun family vacations. Anyway, welcome to Phoenix Rise Grill. Make yourself at home. Any friends of my kids are always welcome."

Thatcher tipped his chin at Artie, back to looking tense. "We're, uh, going to sit in the back, Pop."

Without warning, he grabbed her hand. A pleasant warmth crept upward from his curled fingers. One look at his face kept her from tugging her hand back and halted the request she'd almost made to sit on the patio. He was strung tight. Kit knew better than to challenge him on it.

More utilitarian than the booths at the front of the house, the two booths tucked between the kitchen and the back office, one on either side of a short aisle, were decorated similarly but more simply. The walls bore the same light paint but the tables were plainer, lacking the carved trim of the front booths. Each wall had a beautifully matted and framed family photo, however.

Thatcher handed her a menu.

"I'm going to wash up," he said, hurrying away.

Kit watched him go, wondering what had him so jumpy.

She turned to the menu in her hands. Artie and Della, younger, graced the cover along with a few paragraphs. They told of a devastating fire at Della Luna's Italian Kitchen in Philly, a restaurant that had been in Della's family for several generations when young Della Ricci fell in love with a bus boy. A quick study and hard worker, the bus boy rose rapidly through the ranks…waiter, head waiter, then filling in for the prep cook when he was in a car accident. From there, he worked the grill until, with

Della's father, Chuck's, blessing, he proposed to Della and stepped into the role of manager when Chuck fell gravely ill with cancer. Artie took over the day-to-day operations and kept the place running for six years until a faulty gas valve started the fire that burned the beloved local fixture down to nothing but ashes.

Heartbroken, Artie and Della decided to start fresh in a new place. Della picked Phoenix because her best friend, Marilu, lived there, and she liked the rebirth symbolism of the city's name. For the same reason, they opted against an Italian menu. They were determined to rise from the ashes of an old dream. What started as a single location anchoring a strip mall had now, thirty years later, become a state-wide chain of eight restaurants, one in honor of each of their biological and adopted children, whose photos were scattered throughout each property.

The short final paragraph encouraged patrons to come in, sit down, enjoy a meal, and get to know the family.

Welcome to Phoenix Rise! the final line read.

Kit's eyebrows rose. She held the menu, still closed, and stared at the cover. What would it be like to have a family so large? She had no siblings. Her mother was dead, and her father, though more of a sperm donor, could be alive or dead and she wouldn't know or care. Her mother's only brother had died as a teen in a diving accident. Kit and Lily were the only family each of them had.

"They made those menus to celebrate the thirtieth anniversary of Phoenix Rise."

Thatcher's voice behind her made her jump. He slid into the single width seat across from her, the booths in the back meant for quick employee breaks. They probably seldom held two people at once.

"Wow," Kit said, wondering whether to admit she knew the story. "That's pretty amazing, what they went through and recovered from."

He nodded, looking around as if he were trying to see it

from her fresh perspective. Or what he believed was a fresh perspective. She'd never been to the restaurant, but she knew the story thanks to Kearny's past interviews. Still, Kit looked, too. Something about the place felt like home, like being with a family she never really had. She said none of it to Thatcher. Instead, she studied the framed photo on the wall of their booth. A little plate under the photo read, "1992".

"That's Mom holding my sister, Sedona. Pop's holding me, and Parker and Eden are standing."

"Cute, Groceries. I see where you get your eyes from." It slipped out before she could stop it.

His mouth quirked. "You noticed, huh?"

She said nothing.

"Do you have any brothers or sisters?"

"No." She didn't look at him, didn't want to see if there was pity waiting there. Felt the awkward pause, or maybe imagined it. She didn't have to pretend when she asked, "What are the rest of their names?"

"In order of age," Thatcher said, "Parker, Greer, Eden, me, then the twins, Payson and Page, Sedona, and Kearny."

He seemed to wait. Right. She narrowed her eyes.

"Kearny Myers? From Smoke/Fire/Ash?"

His mouth quirked again. "My baby bro," he agreed, a note of pride in his voice. "But that's Ashes Onward now."

Her eyebrows lifted again. Glad to be able to admit she recognized him from more than just group, she nodded. "Right! And you're Thatcher. You're the reason he freaked out in front of the audience in Houston. You were injured and the promoters didn't want him to cancel. I was supposed to go to that show to celebrate the end of AIT but got sick. Shit, Valiant!" Kit clapped a hand over her mouth, horrified. She'd said too much. Way too much.

Thatcher's face was pale.

Kit's stomach dropped. She lifted a hand, reaching for him, but he slid his arms off the table, into his lap and sat back. She drew back her own, sorry to have ruined the moment.

A fresh-faced young waitress appeared out of nowhere and greeted him shyly. "Hey, Thatcher, good to see you," she said simply. "Your dad wanted me to take your order, if you're ready."

"Can you give us a sec, Andie? I don't think my—Kit—has had a chance to look over the menu."

"Sure," she nodded, vanishing.

Kit occupied herself with the menu. By the time she looked up again, the waitress was on her way back and Thatcher was closing his menu, though she suspected he knew the whole thing by heart.

"I'm going to try the burnt ends with a side of slaw and fully loaded mashed potatoes," she said, smiling her best friendly smile, trying to ignore how it felt forced and rusty.

As soon as Thatcher ordered the same thing, Kit stood. "I'm going to wash my hands," she said, and ducked through the archway she'd seen him disappear through earlier.

Returning from the restroom, Kit heard Artie's voice and glimpsed him from behind in the little hallway, near the dining room, stage-whispering to the waitstaff.

"It's okay to say hello, but do it one at a time. He's having a little trouble with big groups, even family. Don't take it personally or make it more than it is. Our boy is improving every day, and we want that to continue. Okay?"

After a chorus of quiet agreements, he added, "Also, Thatcher tells me his guest is a proud woman, but she's a single mom who's having a hard time right now. Andie, have Bruce give her super big portions so she'll have a nice doggy bag to take home for seconds. And Nee, Thatcher says she's insisting on working it off, so save the easy chores, okay?"

Kit ducked back into the bathroom as Artie clapped his hands twice and ended the impromptu meeting. She leaned against the wall across from the sinks and tried not to cry. Artie's speech proved how much love surrounded Thatcher, how easy it was to understand why he kept offering help. He came by it honestly, from a hard-working man who'd raised four biological kids and adopted four more. A man who clearly loved his kids down to the marrow of his bones.

She took a steadying breath, washed her hands again as the door opened so she wouldn't look like she was hiding in a bathroom. It was going to be harder, now, to keep her distance, but she wasn't up for another heartbreak or for Lily to form an attachment to another man who might not stick around.

When she slid into the booth, Thatcher's head was tipped down toward his phone. His thumbs tapped out a message to someone even as his eyes lifted to meet hers. He set the device aside and gave her a smile.

"Everything okay?" he asked.

She felt heat creep into her face. "I wasn't gone that long, Valiant." *Yes, you were. Because you were eavesdropping on Artie.*

He tipped his head. "It wasn't an accusation."

"Tell me more about your brothers and sisters," she said. "Do you have a favorite?"

"Absolutely not," he grinned.

"Yes, you do. You look so guilty right now!" she laughed, suspecting she already knew what he'd say.

Thatcher coughed into his hand. "Kearny."

"Why?"

Thatcher shrugged. "We shared a room growing up. Closest brothers in age. Plus, he's got this happy-go-lucky thing going most of the time. Maybe not when he first came into our family, right after losing his folks and his eyesight in the car accident, but once he started to regain his footing, he was this silly, funny kid who was usually smiling."

She didn't bother to pretend she didn't know Kearny's

history. Any serious fan who followed Smoke/Fire/Ash knew about the car accident that killed his folks, and also that he'd started the concert her friends had been to in Houston with a furious rant about corporations and businesses choosing greed over people. And of course, she knew his rage was directed at Silver-Mars Productions, the company bankrolling the better part of their tour, for making veiled threats about his future in music if he left the venue to fly to Thatcher's side after he was injured overseas. Had she been there, she'd have joined the rest of the audience in chanting, "Fuck Silver-Mars! Go home!"

Returning to the conversation, Kit said, "It must have been really hard to go through all of that at the same time."

Thatcher nodded. "He was seven years old and pissed. His grief started out as anger. Red-hot, scratching, biting, kicking anger. If he didn't know how to do something, or if one of us startled him, he'd lash out. But just when you decided to hate him or leave him alone or whatever, he'd have one of his easy-going moments, and it was like you could see who he was before it happened. A happy, goofy little doofus. Pretty soon my folks realized he just wanted to feel normal again, like everyone else and not like the 'weird blind kid.'" His fingers curled into air quotes. "Mom found this program that paired Kearny up with a visually impaired adult, and they spent every Saturday together for a few years, hanging out and having fun. He took special classes during the week, but his Saturdays with Ray brought him back to being that happy kid. Pretty soon there wasn't much he wouldn't try."

Their food arrived, the plates so heavy Andie had to bring them one at a time. Kit grabbed her fork and pretended to be shocked at the volume.

"Oh, my God, did you bring us each a whole cow?" she asked, secretly jumping up and down inside even though a part of her wanted to roll her eyes and snark about it, too.

"Trust me," Andie smiled, "you'll be glad for the

portions when you're enjoying more later."

Artie came by at the moment Kit decided it was the best food she'd ever tasted, but if she had another bite she'd explode.

"Need any help with dishes or bussing?" Thatcher asked casually, wiping his mouth.

Artie tried to wave it off, but Kit stood up with a smirk.

"With a house that full, someone's gotta be in the weeds. Point them out, and I'll take care of it."

Thatcher's grin widened. "You never mentioned you had restaurant experience."

"You never asked, Groceries," she said sweetly, her eyes never leaving Artie's. She winked at him. "I don't have my food handler's card anymore, but I can bus with the best of them. Just grab me a dishpan."

Kit felt Thatcher's eyes on her as she followed Artie into the kitchen.

CHAPTER SEVEN

Thatcher had hoped to spend more time with Kit, but she wasn't having it. She thanked him for lunch, but when he asked what her plans were for the rest of the afternoon, she smirked.

"I'm best in small doses, Valiant, really," she said, buckling her seat belt.

"Shouldn't I be the judge of that?" he asked, grinning at her.

"I've got mommying to do."

Thatcher nodded. "That's true 24/7."

"It is. But my babysitters have a shelf life, and I have to get to work. Can you drop me?"

"Fair enough. Do you want to go back to your car to wait for a tow or straight to work?"

"Work." She rattled off the address.

She shut down his attempts at making other plans. Lunch or dinner the next day. A movie. Hell, even a trip to the park with Lily earned him a cross look and a clipped reminder.

"Small doses, Valiant. You have to trust me, here."

Hours after he dropped her at the cheery little grooming shop, his phone began blowing up. Assuming Pop had lit up the family wire with gossip about his lunch date, he ignored the buzzing of his phone and kept up with his PT exercises. But when it signaled a fifth time and vibrated itself right off the coffee table, he glanced at it on the floor and saw the screen lit with "9-1-1" and a number he didn't recognize.

He'd barely swiped to answer when he heard, "Thatcher?"

"Who's this?" he asked, rubbing a hand towel over his face, under one arm.

"George. From group." His voice held a steady, grim note that dropped Thatcher's heart to his knees.

"Yeah?" he finally answered, sitting down as his knees began to shake. It'd only been about two weeks, but he didn't want anything bad to happen to any of the members of the PTSD group. Not even Gil. And why else would George be calling?

Images he didn't want began flashing through his mind. Chaos. Blood. He sucked in a breath and waited for George to tell him someone from group had died or, more likely, taken their own life. The room began to spin lazily, though he forced himself to breathe in "fours".

"I just got back for evening group, and Kit's car is here. Have you seen her? I tried calling her cell, but I can't get her."

Relief hit him so hard he would have fallen if he wasn't already sitting. "Her car broke down. I gave her a lift to work. It's still there?"

"Yeah. And at seven, this becomes an event parking lot for the downtown sports complex. Anybody still here gets impounded. If she doesn't have the money to tow her car to a mechanic, she's *really* not going to have the impound fee."

"I'll take care of it. I've got a friend who owes me a favor."

"I'll try calling her again so she doesn't panic if she finds out it's missing from the lot."

Thatcher wanted to ask George for her number, but he knew it was private information that the man would never share without permission. "You can give her my number if you reach her."

As soon as George disconnected, he called Parker's friend, Tony, to call the debt from their poker game three months ago…one of his failed attempts at socializing. He'd won three hands before he'd had to excuse himself to the bathroom to settle an anxiety attack, and he hadn't given the guys a shot at canceling their debts in another game.

Tony's apologetic tone had him pinching the bridge of his nose between two fingers. "Sorry, man, but that's Regent Towing's lot. They collect the fees, and they tow anyone who stays past seven. I know the owner, so I can probably work something out to pick up the car, but I can't grab it before seven without the owner's permission."

"Shit. Does she have to be with the car, or can she give the okay over the phone?"

"As long as the information she gives us matches what's on the registration, it's fine. Start by making sure the registration is in the car, because if it isn't, a verbal permission over the phone is invalid, at least at my company. Keep trying your friend and let me know. I can post a driver in the area, but if something else comes up…"

"Understood. Thanks, man."

Thatcher held his phone for a moment, considering the options. Since he didn't have her number, he'd have to physically find her. The question was where to try first: Kit's house, or the grooming shop? The grooming shop was closer. Better to try there first. It was only just going on five o'clock. Plenty of time to find her. After a quick shower, he hopped in the Jeep and drove back to the grooming place, only to find that on Tuesdays and Wednesdays, the place closed at four. Figured. Any other day besides Sunday, it was open until seven.

Hearing laughter, Thatcher followed the sound to a side gate.

A handmade sign read *Salespersons will be fed to the dogs. Friends may enter freely.*

He turned the knob and poked his head past the gate.

"Hello?"

A group of about a half dozen women lounged around on a shady patio while another stood at a grill, just starting to drop burgers.

One woman stood and stepped toward him, still laughing at something one of the others said. "Were you looking for information on Waggy Waggy?"

"No," he answered, taking in the bright colors and jungle of potted and hanging plants. Misters along the patio eaves kept the area cool and the plants watered. "I was looking for Kit."

The woman's eyes shuttered warily for a moment, then widened. "You're amber eyes!"

He felt a rush of heat go through him as he realized she must have talked about him. Which meant she was thinking about him, at least a little. Enough to discuss his eyes with someone, apparently.

"I'm her boss, Nanette. You know," she hitched a thumb toward the front building. "Waggy Waggy."

"Right. Cute name." He waited a beat, then glanced at the circle of other women. "Is she here?"

"Nope. Dropped her off, myself, about an hour ago."

"Damn. Do you know how I can reach her?"

Nanette regarded him warily again. "Why?"

"Well, her car broke down this morning, and if she doesn't move it by seven, it's going to be impounded."

Nanette's eyes widened. "Oh, no! That would be just what the poor thing needs, wouldn't it?"

He didn't know how to answer that, so he didn't.

"Let me call her. I'll tell her what's happening."

"Tell her I can pick her up and take her to her car and a friend of mine can tow it. On the house. Guy owes me a favor."

He watched her wander a short distance away, poke the screen of her phone. She glanced at him several times as she spoke. Frowned. He wasn't sure whether to feel relieved that she'd reached Kit or annoyed that Nanette's news was met with what appeared to be a lot of resistance, to the extent the woman's voice rose.

"Hey, what choice do you really have? Do you have the money to get it out of impound? Because I think that would be even more than a tow. I can—" Even at a distance, he could see the woman roll her eyes. "I swear to God, Kit, you're like a mule sometimes! The guy's offering a free tow. Why the hell won't you take it?" She glanced his way several more times, cocking her head at him as she regarded him with the beginnings of a small smile. "Fine, have it your way, Kit, you stubborn idiot!"

His heart fell as Nanette poked her phone again, this time in short, angry movements.

"You're Thatcher," Nanette said almost accusingly.

"Yep."

"Tell you what. I'm going to trust you. I'm going to give you Kit's address in hopes you can convince her to let your friend tow the car. If you use it to stalk her or show up without her permission other than just this once, I'll—"

"I won't," he promised, not telling her he already knew the address, that he'd only come to Waggy Waggy because he'd figured Kit would still be there. "I only want to help her get her car."

She disappeared into the building for a few minutes, then reappeared with paper and a pen. Jotting the address on the back of a grooming flyer, she gave him another once over.

"I see what she means," Nanette said cryptically.

"About?" he asked.

"You," she replied. "Go on. Get her car before it's impounded."

He nodded. "Thank you."

She stayed him with a cool hand on his arm. "Keep trying."

"I'm sorry?" he asked, searching the woman's face for answers. But like her Boho clothing, the woman was a filmy, dizzying mystery.

"Keep trying. She'll let you in eventually." Turning, Nanette made it clear the conversation was over.

Kit's house was large with a tidy yard. If she was keeping up with the bills for the place on a grooming shop wage, or trying to, Thatcher reasoned, it was no wonder she was in trouble. In daylight, he could see the stucco finish was worn in places and the eaves and fascia needed new paint. He eased up the three wide concrete steps into the cool shade of the front porch with its large columns and cracked Saltillo tile floor.

"What now, Valiant?" she sighed as soon as she saw him, even though he knew she knew why he was there.

"Let's go get your car."

"I can't do that. I have Lily and no car seat." She leaned against the front door jamb.

"Give me the keys. I'll go meet the tow truck." He held out his hand.

She didn't move. "Groceries…" Kit looked over his shoulder, out at the street. "I can't afford a repair right now, so there's no point in towing it."

"Nanette told you it'll be impounded, which'll be about $250, right? And then every day you don't pick it up, they'll charge a daily fee until you do."

Kit's head tipped back toward the ceiling. "Fraaaaack," she moaned.

Thatcher's mouth twitched. He forced the grin away as she dropped her head again and glared at him. "Frack?" he asked. "Since when are you worried about your language?"

Kit tossed her head toward the inner depths of the house. "Since I don't want Lily speaking like her mommy, Valiant. It's too late for me, but she's still got a chance." Her smirk had him fighting his own.

"If we call my friend and you give him some

information about yourself and the car and permission for the tow, I'll go down there, I'll get Lily's car seat out, and he'll tow the car to another buddy of mine for a look. Depending on what's wrong, either he'll fix it or my brother, Greer, and I will."

She folded her arms across her chest. "I just told you I can't afford to have it repaired right now." She sighed. "But he could just tow it here, right? And when I get the money together, I can—"

"Kit…" Thatcher raked a hand through his hair, glancing downward as he sensed motion at her feet. "Hey, there. You must be Lily," he grinned as Kit scooped up the toddler.

"Lily Bug," Kit drew the squirming girl close and sniffed deeply. "You need to be changed." Stabbing the latch of the security door, she disappeared into the house calling over her shoulder, "Come in for a second. Excuse the mess."

What mess? Thatcher wondered as he passed a neat-as-a-pin kitchen and stood under an archway looking at the living room. Other than a blanket on the floor with a few scattered toys, it, too, was spotless. Not a speck of dust and nothing appeared out of place.

Minutes later, Kit reappeared with Lily on her hip. Blonde haired and huge eyed, the little girl reached a hand out, opening and closing it, a universal "baby wave" that made him grin. She broke into a wide smile and ducked against Kit's shoulder shyly. His heart turned to goo, the same as it had when he'd met his brother, Parker's, daughter, Hayden, for the first time.

"Hi," he lifted his left hand, mimicking her rudimentary hello gesture. She peeked from Kit's side and did it again, opening and closing her chubby little hand and giggling. "Hi, Lily. I see you." With a soft squeal, she ducked against Kit again. "Adorable," he said without intending to say it out loud.

Kit, however, rewarded him tenfold with a bright, genuine smile. "Yes, she is. Aren't you, Lily Bug?" Kit ducked and kissed Lily's neck noisily several times. She put Lily down on the blanket and shook a stuffed toy at her, the kind with buttons and zippers and buckles and various tactile patches. Lily grabbed it at once, studying it with wide-eyed wonder.

Thatcher watched her with what he feared might be a similar expression. He loved kids. Their innocence, their easy laughter. You didn't have to guess how they felt, didn't have to guard yourself against them. Except watching her, he flashed to another toddler's face, to a happy little boy's burst of bouncing, giggling joy at seeing his father on the stuttering internet feed from miles and miles away. He remembered telling Kyle what a cute little guy he was as he passed by on the way to his own computer. Firing back a hello in response to Kyle's wife, Wendy's, greeting. The room suddenly felt too close, lacking available oxygen. He strode back toward the kitchen.

"Valiant?" Kit's voice behind him, and the jingle of keys reminded him why he was there.

"Yeah," he shook his head, reaching for her keys. "Is the registration in the car?"

She nodded. "Glove box. Are you alright?" Her eyes roved over his face.

He knew his smile looked as forced as it felt. But he offered it up, anyway, and poked the code into his phone and scrolled to Tony's number. Pretended the reason that he didn't answer her was that he was too busy with the call. "Hey, man, I've got the owner with me. What information do you need from her in order to tow?"

"Put her on the phone," Tony said.

Wordlessly, he handed Kit the phone. Stood silently running through the 5-4-3-2-1 anxiety trick, which worked almost as well as performing the actions. He tried not to notice Lily rounding the side of the sofa, toddling toward them with her toy clutched in one chubby fist. Kit rattled off her driver's license and some other information and gave Tony permission to tow the car at Thatcher's direction.

"No, I need him to get my car seat out of it first," she was saying. "Yes. It's in the glove box. Yes, he'll have the spare key. No, no other keys. I'll have my main set with the house key. No. There's nothing valuable inside unless you count baby drool and lost Cheerios," she laughed.

Thatcher felt a zing of jealousy at the easy, teasing manner of her conversation with Tony. *Sure. For him, she's charming and funny and...nice.*

"Valiant!"

He looked up from his thoughts and realized she was holding his phone out toward him in one hand and a single car key in the other. Good. He didn't have to lecture her on leaving house keys with mechanics. Not that he had to worry about Tony's friend, Billy, and his crew.

"Great. I'll bring the car seat back to you after Tony picks up the car," he nodded.

"Just have Tony drop it here," she said over her shoulder as she corralled Lily in the living room. "C'mon, sweets, let's go play with your dolly."

Thatcher hurried out, calling over his shoulder, "Lock the door! I'll be back soon."

~~~

Kit sat on the blanket with Lily and tried not to think about Thatcher's face when he saw her. Charmed, like most people were. Because Lily was damn cute, and she wasn't just saying that because she was her mother. Her little girl had a way of wrapping total strangers around her little finger, though she was a bit fickle about it. Lily's sweet charm made it all the more infuriating that David couldn't
~~~

give a single fuck about her.

You really need to clean up your language, she told herself. *She's learning more words every day, and you don't want her to be a two-year-old potty mouth.*

She hadn't exactly had the best role models. Her mother was bitter and angry most of the time. Not that she didn't have valid reasons to be. She'd won the bad luck lottery when it came to husbands, losing her first in a drunk driving accident and her second unexpectedly to an aneurysm. The third, Kit's father, was the worst luck of all. He was the husband who walked out on his wife the second she was diagnosed with multiple sclerosis, for better or for worse be damned. Kit was twelve.

Her mother's prior marriages left her positioned well financially, in a paid-off house with a brand new, paid-off Honda Civic. Kit's father was a loser in search of a sugar mama. He got that in Kit's mom…a cougar to his thirty years of age. Kit knew she was a surprise for her middle-aged mom, a geriatric pregnancy that boosted him from boyfriend to husband. By way of thanks, he slept around, which Kit knew her mother suspected. Yet her mother seemed genuinely surprised when Keith Reilly left her almost before the doctor left the room after the diagnosis.

MS was not a cheap illness, and her mother hadn't worked a day in her life. Fifteen years of illness, hospital visits, quack remedies that didn't remedy anything at all, and eventually wheelchair and home health care costs had drained most of her savings and investments. What remained was a huge, lovely house too big and too expensive for just Kit and Lily. But she couldn't put it up for sale. Not yet. She broke down every time she picked up the phone to call a real estate agent. It was where she'd lived her entire childhood. It was her mother, full of her mother's dashed hopes and dreams, the things that she loved. Her style, her taste, her spirit.

She couldn't. Not yet.

But she couldn't go on this way, either, smuggling free food from group and grazing samples at Sam's Club on the weekends. Summer was coming, which meant the electric bill she already struggled with would skyrocket as the air conditioner bled dollar bills. Her Netflix membership, paid ahead for the rest of the year because of gift card loads, would run out. Not that the ability to stream television was a big priority, but as it was virtually the only entertainment option she had, it was worth worrying over.

She put on *Ask the Storybots*, which fascinated Lily to no end. Parent guilt be damned. If she needed a few minutes to herself, this was the way to get them. And she needed a minute.

To cry.

Kit put up the baby gate as quietly as possible, peering over the sofa. Satisfied that Lily was glued to the screen, she sank to the floor on the other side of the gate, tucked her fist against her mouth and let the silent sobs have her. About five months. That's all it had been.

Five months.

A lifetime, paradoxically.

Five months since she was injured in Texas, waking to find her baby abandoned and her mother dead. How she'd even cared for Lily for the few days before her death was a mystery. Most likely, the home health aides had done the lion's share of the work. And even though she had no way to know, no proof of what had happened, Kit could easily imagine how things must have gone. Her mother would plead with them to help her out, just until her daughter got better and came home. Just a few days, a week. Please don't let my grandbaby end up in foster care, she'd beg, too weak to get up and change her. I'll do anything. I'll pay you extra, under the table.

It would explain the last few drafts from her dwindling checking account. Checks made out to three women Kit didn't know, had never met. Large checks.

She didn't know whether to be grateful or horrified. Furious. She was all of those things and also angry that the money had been in vain. Because her mother passed away three days in, and whether the caregivers had been willing to keep up the ruse or not, they couldn't hide the facts from the coroner when he arrived to declare her mother dead.

Kit wept trying to imagine what her mother must have felt. Worry for her child, injured miles away where she couldn't ever hope to travel. Helplessness at her inability to rush to her daughter's bedside. Anger, grief, and who knows what else when Lily was dropped off without warning or a backward glance by a man who was, in the end, little more than a sperm donor. God. Those two things combined probably killed her mother. She might have lived a little—or a lot—longer, had the stress and uncertainty caused by those two horrible things not happened.

Kit wept for the woman she remembered, with the vibrant smile, infectious enthusiasm, and the ability to get up and keep going after one husband, then a second died. Struggling to rise that third time, with her legs weakened and her heart broken by a man who promised to love her until death and instead ran as fast as his healthy legs could carry him when the diagnosis came down and with it, the lifetime sentence of flares and remissions, gradually worsening symptoms and deterioration.

Kit wept for the jail sentence MS was for a woman accustomed to coming and going freely, traveling widely on a whim. Time with friends became time spent in her own living room, especially when the daunting task of loading up a wheelchair-bound woman for an outing became too much to ask.

Kit wept for her own guilt at letting David talk her into moving to Texas just when her mother's health went into a fast decline. Pregnant and feeling alone in a marriage that had barely begun and already felt mostly over for reasons she couldn't fathom, she'd done as he'd asked because she'd hoped it might draw them closer. And it had seemed to, at first. The closer her due date came the more distant David became. She saw more of his friends than she saw of him.

She wept because she couldn't understand how David's family didn't step in to help with Lily when he wouldn't. His mother, while not the warmest woman in the world, had seemed at least a little excited about her first grandchild. Social services assured her as tactfully as possible when she'd asked that none of the family members they'd contacted had been willing to look after Lily for even a few days. She couldn't understand that. Wouldn't. Ever.

And finally, she wept because her shattered heart, so full of a dark, sludgy hate, led her to the irrational decision to take a road trip back to Texas with her infant daughter in tow. She'd dropped Lily at the daycare center of a church she'd attended once or twice. And then she showed up at David's door with the baseball bat she now kept in the corner of the living room. She'd smashed every window in his shiny new silver SUV, and she would have smashed the hell out of him, too, if the sound of his approach hadn't been masked by tinkling glass. He'd seized her around the waist and wrestled her down to the front lawn while one of his neighbors called the police. She'd taken advantage of his distraction with the neighbor's call and managed to deck him in the nose, all the while screaming obscenities at him, calling him every horrible name she'd ever heard or could dream up.

By the time the police arrived, she'd been reduced to a sobbing lump on his weedy front lawn. She should be grateful he told her in front of the police and several witnesses that he wouldn't press charges, with the condition she would pay the glass deductible for his SUV repairs, stay away from him, and attend some sort of anger management classes or therapy. She was lucky for that, or

Lily would be back in foster care. Even though it made him look like some kind of soft-hearted hero, she was grateful he hadn't had her hauled off to jail.

Her thoughts of David did what they always did…replaced sorrow with anger. Kit wiped her eyes and stood on shaking legs, peering over the back of the sofa again. Lily was still mesmerized. She splashed a little water on her face, blew her nose, and moved through the house restlessly, looking for something to straighten or clean. Too efficient for her own good, there was nothing.

A knock on the security door startled her.

Thatcher stood on the other side. Kit glanced at her phone, surprised to see it had been over an hour since he'd left. Shocked at the duration of her little pity party, she peeked around him at the street but saw only his Jeep. No car seat.

"I had them tow you to my friend, Billy's shop. He'll call you tomorrow with a diagnosis and an estimate of when you can pick it up."

"Valiant!" She shoved open the door so fast she nearly slammed it right into his body. "Did I not tell you to just bring it here? I can't—"

"Relax, Kit. Bill owes me a favor. Same poker game. If it's something reasonable, he'll fix it for free. If it isn't, he's willing to work out payment arrangements. Or Greer and I might be able to handle it."

The man was suffering some kind of hearing loss from his time overseas. Maybe even short-term memory issues. Had to be. Otherwise, why would he consistently ignore her requests, steam-rolling right over anything she asked and doing whatever the hell he wanted, anyway? With a calm she didn't feel, she asked, "Where's the car seat?"

"In the Jeep. I'll give you and Lily a ride to work tomorrow, and I'll take you to get your car when it's done."

She shook her head, torn between taking his face in her hands and kissing the holy hell out of him and aiming slightly lower with a kick to his man parts out of sheer frustration. "Do you ever listen to anything anyone else says? Ever?"

"Not when what they're saying makes no sense. Without a car, you're either stranding yourself here or taking Lily on what would require about six bus transfers. Neither of those are good options."

He'd checked the bus routes? He'd actually sat down and mapped out her life for just one day, determining what she'd have to do to get to work via city bus? Who did that?

"Do you need to run any errands tonight?"

She shook her head again, turning to the side so he wouldn't see the stupid tears building up, picturing him puzzling over the solution he assumed she'd come up with…the freaking bus route. And he wasn't wrong. She'd already started poking around with it on her phone, trying to figure out which buses and what times and how long it would take to get to Waggy Waggy, grateful beyond words that tomorrow was not a group session day.

She didn't have the luxury of opting out for a day. Her attendance was a requirement, part of her agreement to get help when David refused to press charges against her. She didn't know whether anyone was following up on her promises. She'd paid the glass deductible and had just received a subrogation notice from David's insurance company demanding the rest of the monies paid for the glass repairs. She'd be working on that one for a while. David was in Texas, so she was easily staying away from *him*. But could he somehow monitor whether she was going to group? She didn't know, so she monitored herself. Attendance was *not* optional.

"Kit?" Thatcher was looking at her with concern. "Everything okay?"

She didn't know which of them was more shocked when she grabbed his waist, lifted up on her tip toes, and crushed her mouth to his. The purely animal sound that escaped him said he was not displeased with the turn of events. The hands that slid to her back, one traveling upward, the other down toward her rear, kept her from backing away, encouraged her to continue.

He tasted like coffee and sunshine. He felt surprisingly soft. His mouth, anyway. His waist, his shoulders were firm and hot, the muscles twitching under her wandering fingers. He voiced his approval of this, too, a low grumble that was half purr, half growl. His tongue greeted hers, welcomed it into his mouth, then danced hers back in a tit-for-tat, sweeping lightly along the inside of her lips.

She pulled away because she had to, because she was growing dizzy and delirious under the gentle sweeping of his hands along her back, at her waist, at her hips, tugging her closer to him, against his formidable erection. With a heavily drugged expression, he tried to tug her back again, but she stepped back and pulled the security door between them, gasping.

"One step at a time, Valiant," she breathed, almost ready to fling the door back open as his tongue flitted out to pull any lingering taste of her from his lips. The fact that he looked as unsteady on his feet as she felt on hers didn't help matters.

He backed slowly to the top of the stairs, glancing over his shoulder to ensure he wouldn't trip down them. "What time do I need to get you for work tomorrow?"

"Nine. Please," she added, wiping her own mouth with her hand. She couldn't keep tasting him there. She'd never survive the night.

He nodded, still looking dazed, and trotted down the steps, turning back and meeting her eyes. The heat she saw in them, even from that distance, had her firmly closing the security door and, despite the mild temperature, the front door.

Fucking Valiant.

CHAPTER EIGHT

Thatcher thought about Kit all the way home, through horrendous traffic and an overly insistent erection that, despite the distractions of music and stupid maneuvers by other drivers, refused to fade. He was grateful neither of his parents happened to be outside when he limped even more than usual from the half-circle driveway, through the backyard gate toward the pool house.

He really needed to get his own place.

Jesus, he'd wanted her so bad. Still did. Was rock hard with pent-up need, in fact.

Jerking off in the shower to a firm memory of her kiss-clouded face, the rise and fall of her pert breasts, nipples showing through her shirt as if it were soaking wet…well, it took care of the erection but didn't cure the lust behind it. Nor did it rid him of the desire to bury himself any which way he could in her…balls deep between her legs, nose deep in her cleavage, or with his tongue inside her core. It was all he could do to keep another erection at bay. He exercised as hard as his knee and shoulder would allow, ruining the effects of the shower. He texted with every last one of his siblings, which took a while, because they were all so glad to hear from him. None insisted on a call, for which he was grateful. A few sentences of back-and-forth typing took enough concentration that he was spared from torturous, heady images of Kit.

He read part of a spy thriller he'd been working through.

Cooked an ambitious late-night dinner in his tiny

kitchenette. It sucked, but it met the objective. Kept him distracted for a while. And renewed his interest in finding a new place to live. Even an apartment-sized kitchen would be better.

He dozed off in front of Netflix.

He woke, frantic, in front of the "Are you still watching?" screen, launching himself out of the easy chair toward his phone on the coffee table.

8:13 a.m.

Shit. Shit, shit, shit.

"Last thing she needs is another guy letting her down, jackass," he berated himself, moving as quickly as his first-thing-in-the-morning stiffness would allow.

He showered in under two minutes, just enough to get the stink of last night's sexually frustrated workout off him. He was on the road speeding toward Kit's place by 8:17 a.m.

She was waiting on the steps, Lily on her hip, when he roared to a stop at her curb at 8:38. He started to climb out, engine running, but she shook her head, rushing toward his Jeep.

"You're making me late, Valiant! Which," she snarled, ducking into the back to buckle Lily into the car seat, "isn't very valiant at all."

"You'll be there on time," he told her, climbing back behind the wheel as he realized he wouldn't do anything but slow her down.

"Really?" she asked, putting her belt on even as he sped away from the curb. "When did you discover time travel?"

He grinned. "We've got twenty-two minutes, Kit. You'll be there by nine on the dot. Or before."

He drove quickly but safely, weaving in and out of morning traffic, trying not to remember how he'd learned the subtle art of defensive driving and evasive maneuvers. Kit ticked off the minutes in a running commentary.

"8:49, Valiant," her clipped tone made him step up his

already tight driving game.

"Plenty of time," he assured her, though the slightest niggle of worry had him mentally mapping six different routes.

"8:54," she said, tapping out a message on her phone. Her voice was sickly sweet. "I'm just telling Nanette I'm going to be late."

"No need," he replied easily.

Watching him turn into a neighborhood, she lunged forward against her seatbelt.

"No, not—"

"Relax, Kit," he flashed her his best disarming smile. "You need to learn to trust people. This can be lesson one."

Three turns later, with the dashboard reading 8:58, he stopped in front of Waggy Waggy. "Right on time," he grinned.

She shook her head and leapt out of the car. "Lily's supposed to be with Crystal, and I'm supposed to be in the shop ready to work at nine. But nice try."

He tipped his chin toward a woman standing at the rear passenger door.

Kit startled. "Crystal," she said feebly, "I didn't see you come out."

Crystal, meanwhile, was already in the backseat unbuckling Lily from the car seat.

"Like I said. Right on time." He wished he could pat her on the ass. "Scoot, or you'll be late." Her eyes narrowed, but the corners of her mouth twitched. "What time should I be back to get you?" he asked.

"One-thirty."

He watched Crystal head for the back yard and Kit jog to the shop door at the front. He made sure to wink as she glanced back at him, hoping she lost control of her smile as he pulled out of the small lot.

When his phone rang three hours later, he didn't expect it to be her. He didn't recognize the number on his caller

ID. If he hadn't been applying for various jobs, he might not even have answered.

"I want the truth, Valiant," she demanded before he even said hello. "Did these guys really owe you favors, or did you pay your own money to tow my car?"

"Kit? How did you get my number?"

"You first."

"Yes, they really owe me. We play poker once a month at my brother, Parker's, house. Instead of cash, we offer freebies or junk we don't want anymore, favors, whatever. I had a couple of good hands. No big deal."

"No money changed hands?" her voice, full of suspicion, assured him they had a great many more lessons in trust.

"None."

"So, I owe you two pretty good favors," she surmised warily.

He opened his mouth to object, but grinned against the phone instead. "Guess so. How'd you get my number?"

"I threatened the mechanic friend of yours with a free kick in the junk if he didn't give it to me. He'll have my car ready at four."

Thatcher laughed picturing Billy's reaction to her threat. "I'm glad now that he got nailed by a pissed off ex once in high school. Made him properly reluctant to refuse."

"You've got my number now, Valiant. Don't abuse it, or I'll nail *you* in the junk." With that, she was gone.

"Goodbye," he huffed at the phone before saving her number in his contacts.

~~~

"Don't use me like that," Nanette groused, brushing the tail of a young golden retriever.
~~~

"Like what?" Kit called from the wash room where she was soaping a chocolate Labrador.

"I don't care if you're five minutes late here or there."

"You care when I get back late from group," Kit pointed out.

"Don't use me as a reason to push Amber Eyes away!" she hollered back over the rush of water.

Kit shook her head. Ever since that first day, Nanette had been bugging her to act like a normal grown up and go out on a date with Thatcher. She'd pointedly reminded Kit that she gave her Fridays and Saturdays off for a reason, and that reason was so she could dive back into the dating pool.

"Open those legs, Kit," she'd joked. "They might get stuck in the closed position."

She'd fired back a joke of her own about battery operated boyfriends. Truth be told, that sort of date was getting a little old. Especially when she had those damn amber eyes on her at group, reminding her what it felt like to have his lips and hands on her. Short lived though it had been.

"Nanette, I'm not pushing anyone away," she answered calmly, the water turned off as she soaped up the Lab's sturdy body.

"Like hell you aren't! You just told me the other day you don't want Lily getting attached to anyone. But how can you find someone if you don't spend time getting to know them?"

She didn't answer.

Thatcher would be back in just under an hour, and she'd been coaching herself all morning on how to get her car from his mechanic friend and get the hell away without kissing him again—or letting him kiss her. Kissing him was a dangerous proposition, because last time, she'd wanted to press against him up on her tip toes until all their best parts were lined up perfectly. She wasn't a saint. She wouldn't go so far as to say she'd never have sex with someone she wasn't in love with, because she loved sex as much as the next healthy human. She didn't tie a lot of meaning to it like some women. She'd read enough romance novels—a guilty pleasure, especially *because* they didn't mirror real life—to know that a good many people still equated sex with weddings and babies and happily ever after, even if they pretended not to. But by the end of the book, the girl and the guy were always headed toward happily ever after even if he hadn't proposed yet. She wasn't worried she'd get her rocks off with Thatcher and start shopping for wedding dresses.

She was thinking of Lily. Lily didn't know yet about the impermanence of love. She didn't want Lily to learn that particular lesson if it could be avoided. The less time she spent with Thatcher, the less chance she would have to fit all of those good parts together. And the less chance Lily would have to learn how fleeting love could be.

Kit thought that for once, Nanette had let a subject drop. But when she walked Humphrey back to the grooming area and clipped his collar back on, Nanette glanced at the clock.

"Twenty-five minutes to go until Amber Eyes picks you up. I've already told Crystal we've got Lily until eight tonight." Nanette winked at her. "Have a little fun for once. On us."

Kit sighed. "You're incorrigible."

"I never suggested otherwise."

"I barely know the guy. I'm not going to go off and have sex with him between now and eight o'clock tonight."

"I didn't say you had to go that far. Maybe make out a little. Have some dinner," she shrugged. "Talk to another adult for a few hours."

When Thatcher pulled up with five minutes to spare, Nanette reached out and tucked $40 straight into Kit's bra with a cheeky grin.

"Stop trying to cop a feel," Kit joked, digging it back out again.

"I only have eyes for my Crystal, kiddo," Nanette fired back.

"Payday isn't until Friday."

"That's not payday. That's a quarterly bonus. If you're so opposed to him helping you out, buy him a late lunch or some dinner to thank him."

"Well, since this is your money, you'll be buying that lunch, so—"

"Have fun!" she sing-songed. "Bye!"

Kit grabbed Humphrey's collar. "C'mon, boy, back to the kennel until Nanette's ready for you."

"Bye!" Nanette said again, pointedly, as Kit closed the kennel door.

Kit threw a hand over her shoulder as she grabbed her bag from the wash room. She made a point of not answering.

~~~

Thatcher lifted his head as Kit eased into the Jeep beside him.

"Where's Lily?" he asked, glancing in the back as if he'd somehow missed Kit buckling her into her car seat.

"Nanette said I should come back for her after I pick up my car, in case there's a delay."

"There won't be. He'll have it ready at four if he told you four."

Kit shrugged. "Thank you for the ride," she said, buckling in, the $40 all but burning a hole in her pocket. "Let me take you to lunch."

"I have a better idea," he said. "You game?"

She wondered what might be in store. Tried to fortify herself against those damn eyes and all the other sexy parts that went with them. "Sure," she said carefully. "Just make
~~~

sure we're at the mechanic's place by four."

"You have my word," he grinned.

His idea was a picnic at Sahuaro Ranch Park, one of the oldest ranches in the greater Phoenix area. The seventeen-acre property featured original buildings, orchards, a picturesque rose garden, and free-roaming peacocks. Midday on a weekday, there wasn't a huge crowd. Kit had heard of it but had never been. She would much rather have had lunch on the lawn outside the old main house building, but Thatcher set up their picnic in the designated area. After a delicious spread of crusty French bread with cheese cubes, grapes, and a variety of cold cuts, they wandered the grounds.

"They only do tours on the weekends," he said apologetically as they scattered a few sunflower seeds for the peacocks.

"Oh, my gosh, aren't you handsome?" Kit gasped as one of the males, on the prowl for a mate, fanned out his tail feathers. She fumbled for her phone. The camera was crappy, but it would have to do.

Thatcher teasingly struck a pose. "That's the nicest thing I've ever heard you say."

She stuck her tongue out at him. "Move it. You're blocking my shot."

She took a ridiculous number of pictures of the peacock before a park volunteer wandered by and warned them not to get too close.

"Otherwise, you might have him trying to mate with your legs!"

Kit laughed as Thatcher made a face and limped backward a few feet. "Aw, are you scared, Valiant? I won't let the big, bad birdie get you."

He made another face, sidling closer to her.

After watching the strutting male make a play for one of the peahens, Kit let Thatcher take her hand and hustle her away from the area, laughing when he suggested they might need some privacy.

"I love your laugh," he said, grinning, squeezing her hand.

Just that quickly, reality crashed in. She took her hand back. He shot her a questioning look, but she kept walking, back toward the rose bushes they'd passed earlier. The sun-dappled grounds were postcard pretty. Kit took a few more pictures as they circled around to the picnic area.

"You've seriously never been here before?" he asked as she sipped from the water bottle.

"Never. My mom got sick when I was twelve. She didn't usually feel good enough to do much," she told him, surprising herself. The less she shared with him, the better.

"I'm sorry," he said, grabbing the large soft-sided cooler, now empty.

"Me, too," she answered.

He glanced at her, those damn eyes of his filled with genuine concern. "Was it something chronic? Was that how she died?"

Kit swallowed and nodded, surprised at how fresh the grief still was. Five months wasn't a long time, but remembering that first awful conversation with her CO caused her throat to swell up, her eyes to water. "MS," she rasped, blinking fast, shaking her head.

Don't ask me anything else.

He seemed to catch on to her mood, which only made the threat of tears increase.

She walked quickly back to the Jeep, feeling like a jerk, knowing he was probably limping faster, trying to keep up. But she needed the distance. She couldn't talk about her mother. Anything more than the quick exchange she'd just had with Thatcher would tear her apart for hours.

Avoiding the breakdown, she mused, was probably why she did nothing to stop him from pressing his body against hers as he tossed the cooler bag in the back of the Jeep, nor did she protest when he lowered his mouth to hers. She ignored the warning shivers that raced down her spine, the heat that flushed through her belly, the way her traitorous hands fisted the back of his t-shirt as he rocked gently against her, catching her lower lip between his teeth and giving it a little tug. She let his tongue trace her lips and dip into her mouth to slide against hers.

It was his groan that brought her back to reality. It brought her back to awareness and to the realization that her hands had somehow wandered, found his ass, and were tugging him closer—God, closer—to her where she ached. Kit awoke to the parking lot, to the possibility of families with little children happening by. She looked up into those heated amber eyes, so hazy with lust she almost didn't care about those possible families or their impressionable little children.

She reluctantly moved her hands from his ass to his chest and felt the thundering of his heart under them, the heaving of his lungs as they filled with air he'd lacked while devouring her. What she didn't do, didn't want to do, was force him far enough back to lose contact with his erection. It nestled against her belly, made hot little pulses of need beat in her, down low, mere inches yet also miles from where his hardness met her body.

I want that. I want that so bad.

The admission gave her the strength to force him away from her.

He swallowed, and she wanted to put her mouth against his throat where it bobbed.

"We'd better go," she croaked.

How easy it would be to pick up her car and lead him back to her place where she could, in the privacy of her own home, fit him against her again. Let him inside her body if not inside her heart. Her life.

Nanette's giving you this chance, stupid! Take it!

She could. She could bring him home, into her bed, for a few hours of what was sure to be wild sex if how she felt just kissing him, just letting him press against her, was any indication.

She buckled herself in beside him, faintly aware he was watching her. His little cough, the way he tried to be discreet as he found a more comfortable position in the driver's seat, spoke volumes. The handsome bulge she glimpsed before turning to look out the window called to her, promising naughty things.

Do it, the devil on her shoulder urged.

Not a chance, she and the angel on the other shoulder answered, though her resolve wasn't quite as strong as the angel-Kit would want it to be.

Music filled their silence, as usual. The world blurred by as he drove quickly, easily through thickening afternoon traffic.

She didn't even know where the mechanic's shop was located, but she dreaded arriving all the same. Because she'd have to decide what she would do. Invite him over? Invite him out somewhere else? Out would be easier. Safer.

It wasn't like he wasn't on board. He was as hard as one, even now, she discovered as she sneaked a peek at his lap. And he seemed as intent on avoiding her eyes as she tried to avoid his. His fingers tapped the wheel with the beat of the music. Despite his seeming nonchalance, the cabin of the Jeep felt charged with need, with anticipation, with a…waiting. Like a dirty movie on pause.

Kit nearly groaned, stopping herself at the last second. She had to be the one to stop it. Thatcher was stuck on go, if his body was any indication. She had to be smart about it. Lily. A few hours of free babysitting didn't change the fact that Thatcher might not be so ready for casual sex. No strings sex. Service with a smile, nothing more. She could do that. But all she had to do to put a damper on that plan was think of Phoenix Rise Grill. This was not a man, she suspected, who took sex as lightly as she wanted to. He was all about family. About ties. Entanglements.

Maybe she was assuming something she shouldn't. Maybe he was just as eager to scratch an itch and leave it at that.

Her belly pulsed down low again as her mind raced with images of them tumbling across her bed, of finally getting to feel that healthy erection against her naked skin, the tip of him against her and then inside her.

Yes, please, she thought, tucking her fist against her mouth. With her face turned fully toward the passenger window, he couldn't see her greedy smile.

New subject, she commanded, forcing herself to catalog the shops and businesses they passed. She counted houses on the street corners, watched a woman jog with a dog almost as tall as her waist.

When Thatcher turned into the parking lot of the automotive shop, she'd decided to thank him for the picnic and part ways. He didn't, after all, know that Nanette forced freedom on her until eight. She could use picking up Lily as an excuse to end their time together.

She didn't want to.

It was torture, walking beside him into the auto shop. Why she didn't tell him to stay in the Jeep to remove Lily's car seat, she didn't know.

Billy Gresher, Thatcher's friend and the shop owner, shook her hand and discussed the repairs he'd done. It sounded like a lot more work than Thatcher had led her to believe, but he winked at Thatcher and said, "We're even, buddy. I'll get you back at the next game."

Kit folded her arms across her chest. "Are you sure I don't owe you anything?"

Billy shook his head and winked at her. "A bet's a bet. I'll be more careful not to lose next time."

A technician held her key out, and Kit noticed her Civic was now parked next to the Jeep.

Thatcher nodded at Billy. They clasped hands in that man-shake, half-hug thing guys did. "Thanks, man."

Kit hurried to her Civic, ducking away from Thatcher's hand when it wanted to rest at the small of her back. *Don't touch me, Valiant, or I'll cave.*

He seemed reluctant to let her into the Jeep to get the car seat, moving slowly. She ducked into the back seat, similarly hesitant. Losing her resolve would *not* be a good idea. All too soon, though, the car seat was out of the Jeep and installed back into the Civic.

"Thanks again, Valiant," she said, offering him a smile. A poor consolation prize, she knew, in lieu of what they both wanted.

Four-thirty. Four-fucking-thirty. She could have a few hours before reality returned.

No.

Please?

No.

Kit felt a sinking inside. Disappointment, like an anchor, made her body feel heavy as she opened the car door and plopped into the driver's seat.

He rounded the Jeep toward her side, and her heart picked up speed.

"Want to grab a coffee or something?"

She wanted to grab *him.*

"Sure," she said instead, following him to a Starbucks three miles from her house.

The elephant, however, sat stubbornly in the coffee house. On the table between them, if she had to guess. They made painful small talk about the weather, which would be rainy and cooler next week if the weathermen were right. She sifted through the pictures from their picnic, deleting the ones that were blurry or the lighting too dim. She rehashed the wonder of seeing peacocks just wandering around. He told her a funny story about his sister, Payson, being terrorized by a hungry peahen on one of the earliest visits he could remember.

Kit thought for a few moments she might be imagining

the tension, but Thatcher shifted on his chair like he had ants in his pants. In turn, she wanted to settle his restlessness by sitting on his lap.

Stop it, she lectured herself. *You have to face this man in group three times a week. You can't start something with him. If it ends up going nowhere or ends badly, you'll still have to show up at group.* Kit had agreed to six months. Whether David was watching or not, she would fulfill the agreement. This new argument was a good one. Her body seemed to be listening to her, seemed to be settling into its normal place again.

"When do you have to get Lily?"

One casual question, and she swung right back to dirty thoughts, lustful desires.

"Not until eight," she blurted without thought.

Fuck.

"Want to catch a movie or something?"

Or something.

She shrugged. "What's playing?"

He read off some titles to her. None of it meant anything. She didn't go to the movies. At best, she found something on Netflix. No twelve-dollar ticket or twelve-dollar concessions to worry about.

"Pretty crappy choices," he frowned. "I guess summer blockbuster season is still a way off."

"Want to come over for a swim?" Kit nearly clapped a hand over her mouth. Funny, but her mind wasn't screaming at her like it should be. Her inner critic should be demanding to know what she was doing, but…crickets.

"A swim?" His brow furrowed. "Kind of cold yet, isn't it?"

She shrugged. "Probably."

"I don't have any trunks," he said, sipping his drink. Unless it was her imagination, he was sipping faster.

"You have underwear, right?"

He nodded. "No fair wearing a real suit if I have to go in

my boxers."

She rolled her eyes. "Swim or don't swim, Valiant."

Kit gulped the rest of her drink and stood up.

"Swim," he said, rushing clumsily to his feet.

He clearly understood that "swim" was code for something else, because he was right on her bumper all the way back to her house, and she constantly checked the rear view to make sure he was still there.

Thatcher's patience was impressive. He waited for her to gather towels. He waited for her to remove the dowel from the sliding door's track and the pins from the top and the middle of the frame. He seemed so much more patient than she felt, wanting to rip the door open, burst through the screen, run for the water…find an excuse to wrap herself around him.

Where the hell were all those smart alarm bells when she needed them? Where was the voice of her conscience now? It was Nanette's voice, telling her to have a good time until the clock struck eight, that's where.

In the back yard, he kicked off his shoes, then lifted his shirt. He bared about half of his chest before he went still for a long second. Catching her eye, he swallowed, his jaw clenching, and something sparked in his eyes. She wasn't sure if it was anger or challenge, so she pulled off her shirt, revealing her bra to him.

He swallowed hard again, looking away as he pulled the shirt off the rest of the way with a wince. It was then that she noticed his shoulder. Gnarled, puckered skin covered his left shoulder, zig-zagged with angry red lines. She reached, he ducked away.

"Still tender," he said tightly. She nodded.

He gave her that pissed off yet defiant look again and opened his fly, shoving the denim down in short, jerky movements.

His left thigh, knee, and calf were the same. The skin just above and just below his knee was deeply lined, his thigh and calf dipping inward in places they shouldn't, portions of muscle irretrievably lost, skin likely grafted over the areas from other places on his body. He met her eyes only fleetingly now, but she saw both defiance and stark fear before he looked away and resolutely stepped down into the pool.

"Christ, that's cold!" Thatcher gasped, standing with her on the steps. This time when their eyes met, she saw only amusement.

They loudly protested the cold water with giddy, breathless laughter.

Kit felt her nipples turn to stone and saw his eyes go hazy as he noticed them. She had a few second thoughts about taking a dip. It probably had his good parts shriveling up in protest.

"Hot tub, instead?" he asked, tilting his head toward the patio.

"Broken and empty," she shook her head apologetically. "This was a bad idea. C'mon. Let's get dressed and go back inside."

He followed gratefully. Thatcher fumbled back into the jeans he'd shed onto a patio chair. Kit's heart sank. She hadn't thought about anything but getting closer to him. The fact that he seemed ashamed to let her see him, all of him, put a new crack in her already battered heart.

He eased down on a lounge chair to put his socks and shoes back on.

She didn't ask. Wanted to, but didn't.

He didn't offer.

But he didn't duck away when she lifted a hand to his face. He ducked toward her, reaching, seeking.

Warmth returned quickly as their mouths crashed and slid, tongues darting. Like a dirty movie taken off of pause, they went right back to the place they'd been in earlier, against his Jeep. Except she had no shirt to twist in her hands, and instead of clutching his ass to get him closer to where she wanted him, she was straddling his lap, still in just her bra and panties, mindlessly rubbing herself against his rapidly rising crotch.

With his lips on her throat and his hands on her hips, Kit bit her lip to stifle a moan. She was embarrassingly close to orgasm after going without since a few months before Lily was born. Thatcher didn't seem to mind a bit that she rocked eagerly against him. His appreciative growl as he slid his hands to the clasp on her bra suggested the pace was just fine with him. She'd just lifted up to work on his fly when her phone nearly vibrated itself off the patio table.

No! Not now!

She debated letting it roll to voicemail. It might be spam, after all.

He agreed, though he couldn't hear her thoughts. He clutched her tighter, his nose nuzzling her cleavage.

The phone stopped and she relaxed into him. She'd just unzipped his fly when it started up again. She sighed and pushed herself up off of him. "Hold that thought, Valiant," she ordered, tossing her towel over his lap so she wouldn't have to see the eager bulge there. "Hello?" she asked, rubbing her nose as it tickled with frustrated tears.

"Hey, Kit, I'm sorry to bug you," Crystal said apologetically, "but Lily has a fever. It's probably nothing but it's kind of high…103, and—"

"I'm on my way," she choked, glancing back at Thatcher as she rushed toward the sliding door.

See? This is life reminding you this—he—is not a good idea.

He rose slowly, questions in his eyes.

"I'm sorry, I just didn't feel right not telling you. I hope—"

"I'm on my way," she repeated, ending the call. Kit turned toward Thatcher. "I—"

"—have to go," he finished ruefully. He nodded. "I hope everything's okay."

“I’m sure it is,” she forced herself to say lightly. “Unfortunately, it means I’ll be spending the evening at urgent care with Lily instead of something more fun.” When his brow furrowed, she said, “Fever. Probably no big deal, but—”

“You should make sure,” he agreed.

“Yeah. Thanks for understanding.” She said this as she ducked into her tank top and slid back into her jeans, damp panties be damned.

“Do you want company?”

She shook her head. “You’ve never met me when I’m worried, Groceries. Not a good thing. I’ll see you at group tomorrow.”

He nodded but didn’t move.

She met his stupid gorgeous eyes. “Recess is over, Valiant. Go home.”

CHAPTER NINE

Thatcher held off as long as he could, but his fingers itched to dial Kit, to make sure Lily was okay. He paced and prowled the pool house apartment like a wild animal. He tried the usual distractions…PT, texting his brothers and sisters. Streaming a movie. He even went back downstairs and skimmed the net through his folks' pool until every stray leaf, two drowned bees, and a stray water-logged receipt were in the trash. His body remained miraculously under control despite the persistence of Kit-related flashbacks. A good thing, seeing how his mother wandered out, no doubt dressed in her typical late winter lounge pants and light sweatshirt, a pair of flip-flops announcing her presence before he actually saw her.

"Hey, Mom," he said, a glance confirming her evening uniform down to the flip-flops. Kept skimming even though there was nothing left to capture.

"Hi, baby," she said cheerfully. "You're not thinking of swimming. You'll freeze."

Yeah. Pretty close. He fought the corner of his mouth at the thought of him and Kit ankle deep in what might as well have been ice water. "Just…thinking," he finished. "Pop home yet?"

She strolled the perimeter of the pool, glancing up at the sky. "On his way," she said. "I remember when I could sit out here on a lounge chair and stare up at a blanket of stars. We had only two neighbors then, both so far away you'd have to drive out to see them."

"Times change," he said, remembering tucking up against her on that lounger as a kid, the in-and-out of her breath as she stroked his hair and told him stories. He missed that pure feeling of safety, like the whole world was gently breathing and nothing could go wrong. He was twenty-nine years old, but he'd have given anything to curl up next to her again if he could get that feeling back.

"That they do," she replied. Her wistful tone suggested she was sharing some version of the same memory with him.

Thatcher limped to the far wall and placed the pool net back on the hook. His mother came to stand beside him, and he tipped his head back to search the sky with her. Pointed out a star to her, one of the few bright enough to be seen these days.

"Make a wish," he said, feeling rather than seeing her soft smile.

"Have you eaten?" she asked. She was always asking him that these days. He'd gained back some of the weight he'd lost during his recovery, jeans no longer threatening to slide down to his ankles. Her instinct to feed him hadn't quite caught up yet.

"Not yet. Maybe in a little bit." He slid his arm around her waist, bumped her lightly with his right hip. Looping her arm around his waist in reply, she squeezed gently.

"Come inside, have dinner with Dad and me."

He started to decline, but she squeezed again.

"It'll just be the three of us and my pasta e fagioli."

She'd hit his weak spot. He loved her pasta e fagioli. Turning to meet her eyes, he grinned. "Dirty pool, Mom."

She grinned back at him. "It's sparkling clean, thanks to you." She squeezed once more and released him. "Dinner in twenty minutes."

He watched her go, then glanced at his phone. As was common in a restaurateur's family, they'd be eating at nine o'clock. Was it too late to call Kit? Would he disturb Lily if he did? Children could be cranky when they didn't feel well. He stood staring at the green and red icons under Kit's name, trying to decide between them. He heard the sound of an engine. Pop was home. Thought again about how he needed to find an apartment. As the engine cut off, he poked the dial button, reasoning that he would be distracted all through dinner if he didn't call her, and his parents would worry about him.

"Valiant, what did I tell you about using my phone number?" Kit's dry question contained no malice, no heat. What it did contain—curiosity? hope? —had his dick twitching just a little.

"How's Lily? She okay?"

"Yes. A little Tylenol, some rest, she'll be fine. See—"

"How are *you*?" he asked, wanting to extend the conversation. He wanted the sound of her voice, to feel the husky tones ripple through him. *Keep talking.*

"She's fine, I'm fine. Happy little family. Gotta go, Groceries. See you at group."

"Wait, I—" Thatcher stopped. A quick glance proved she'd hung up. He let out a rush of air, disappointed.

He glanced at the house, at the downstairs windows lit with soft light. He could all but feel his mother's pleasure at his acceptance of her invitation to dinner. Could imagine his Pop washing up with a whistle at the news. He couldn't duck out. Didn't want to, exactly. He wanted to keep the sound of Kit's voice in his ears all night, let it wash over him. Because he'd realized while talking with her, even for those precious few seconds, that he'd felt a trace of the easy comfort he'd recalled from his childhood. No similarity in his feelings for her compared to his mother, of course. But the comfort was similar. The feeling of home, of ease, was the same. It was hard to give up after not having it for so long. Longer than adulthood. Longer than the military.

With a deep breath, he let himself into his folks' house.

~~~

Lily had been asleep since they left urgent care. Kit stood in the doorway to her room and watched her sleep, one fist curled up near her cheek, her rounded little baby belly rising and falling. She fought the urge to feel her forehead. The baby monitor was on. With the tiny bit of congestion in her lungs, Kit could hear her breathe. A mild case of the sniffles, likely triggered by the unusual weather fluctuations of unseasonable warmth followed by the chill of a cold front on its way.

She wandered through the house, looking for something to straighten or clean, but things were still good. She settled in front of the television with leftover pizza a la George and tried to lose herself in a show.

It would have been so easy to scratch that itch. She'd been halfway there already. More than halfway, if she were honest. Another few seconds of dry humping Thatcher's crotch and she'd have had her first non-solo orgasm in over two years. Lily's conception was very likely the last time she'd gotten laid.

Focus, she told herself, fixing her eyes back on the screen. Maybe she should find a show she hadn't watched and re-watched several times. One that wasn't currently featuring the two main characters about to get busy.

Tossing her paper plate and half-eaten slice of pizza on the coffee table, she grabbed a throw pillow, pressed it to her face, and screamed into it. Lily was priority one, always would be. But she wished with everything she had that the timing had been better. Just long enough to get their rocks off. Getting the call about Lily any time after that would have been better. Ideal, even. No time to cuddle. No chance of Thatcher getting any long-term, family-type ideas.

Would he, though? Maybe she was reading too much into the fact that he had a large family. They seemed close,
~~~

especially if Kearny's devotion to his brother on stage that night in Houston was any indication. But did that automatically mean he would want the same? A family? Maybe he'd be thrilled to roll around with her and call it a day.

The more determined he was to pry his way into her life, the more she wanted to take that tumble with him…right into bed. What she didn't need was his grocery-buying, car-fixing, cape-wearing superhero shit. She wasn't his to rescue. In her experience, the rescuer always became attached. Look at stray dogs. You take in a stray, intending on finding them a home, but you fall in love, and suddenly you're buying leashes and bowls and kibble and you've got vet bills and another whole *being* to worry about. She wasn't a dog, but the concept was the same. Too much care and feeding could lead to an attachment she didn't want. Not for herself, and especially not for Lily.

It was good that David left when he did. Lily's memory of him, in the unlikely event there was any at all, would fade with time and distance. She was too young to hurt over it. Someday she would ask who her daddy was, why he wasn't around. It was hard enough knowing the truth would hurt her no matter how gently it was delivered. Kit didn't have the right or the desire to put Lily through that more than once. There was no way she'd let her daughter fall in love with a man who might up and walk away the way David had done. Because one daddy figure walking away, you might get over that. You might escape feeling like some broken, bad thing in you made it happen. Kit had no such delusion about her own father. He left because her mother got sick and he didn't have the balls to man up and deal with the misery of chronic illness. He didn't leave because of Kit. Not *only* Kit. She was part of the whole "inconvenience" package. Sick wife, young daughter who still needed looking after for a while. No, thank you. Mic drop. Exit, stage left.

You might understand that *one* piece-of-shit-jackass-waste-of-breath dad walking out was not your fault. But *two*. Two and you would start wondering if you were to blame. And no way was she ever going to risk Lily feeling that way. She was the grownup. Her choices mattered. They had consequences.

David was a mistake she wouldn't make twice. He was handsome...shorter, stockier than Thatcher. Rougher looks. But attractive. They'd fallen hard and fast for one another. David had tried to be gentlemanly, to keep it at chaste goodnight kisses, even five dates in. She'd been the one who couldn't wait, didn't want to. They'd spent the weekend in bed with only bathroom and meal breaks. She learned she was pregnant not long after.

She wouldn't take back Lily's birth, but for a long time she'd thought if she could go back and find a way to close the endlessly wide gap that formed between her and David seemingly overnight, she'd do it. Resentment crept in at the way he kept his distance from their daughter, having as little interaction as possible before and after she was born. No touching her belly to feel the baby move, no talking to her swelling tummy. No doting daddy stuff from David at all. Further resentment grew in Kit at her own inability to draw him closer after she was born. She'd thought maybe if he looked after Lily while she worked, he might discover the same bottomless love she felt for their precious girl.

What an idiot.

Kit sucked in a breath at the memory of her stupid excitement when she'd received a letter from him during basic training. He missed her, he'd written. And the baby missed her mom. Wasn't there any way to back out of this and come back home?

Idiot.

It wasn't worth all that. All the crazy, girly, smiley, hearts-drawing silliness she'd given it. Given *him*. Turns out he'd only missed her because taking care of Lily was too much of a cramp in his lifestyle.

Kit sighed and tossed the throw pillow back into the corner of the sofa. She picked up her plate from the coffee table and went back to her slice of pizza, now cold. And the food wasn't the only thing gone cold. Thinking about David was the perfect extinguisher for her particular fire. She'd lost the itch for sure.

CHAPTER TEN

Kit's refusal to spend time with him was frustrating. On Wednesday, Thatcher suggested lunch. She turned him down. Lily was still not feeling well, and fussy sick kids and restaurants didn't mix. Thursday, same. On Friday, Kit's day off, she turned down breakfast. *I want to sleep for a week, Groceries. I won't even be conscious until noon unless Lily gets up earlier.* Another picnic lunch? *You and I can handle lusty peacocks, Valiant. Lily could get hurt. And anyway, I've got errands to run that I've been putting off all week.* Dinner? *I'll see you on Monday at group. Baby steps, Valiant.*

That easily, she shut him down not just for Friday but the entire weekend. He considered a million invitations but had a feeling she'd only snap at him for calling back.

"I don't know," he told Kearny as they sat down to dinner Saturday night at his house. "Maybe I should back off. I don't know if she's ever going to give me a real chance."

"Dude, she's a single mom. It's all on her, and—"

"Yeah, but it doesn't have to be. If she needs help, I can—"

"You can what, Thatcher?" Janine asked as she set a plate down in front of him, loaded with pot roast, red potatoes, and roasted asparagus. "Swoop in like Prince Charming and fix everything so she's got time for a date? It's not your job to play the hero." She winked to soften the blow.

"Well, maybe I should ask *you* to marry me," he joked, pulling her down so she sat on his right thigh. "This looks delicious. And it's not entirely untrue that a way to a man's heart is through his stomach." She giggled and kissed his cheek. "Not to mention this sexy Donna Reed thing you have going on," he added, eyeing her halter dress with its cheery lemon print.

"Already spoken for," she said, waving his words away as she stood and turned to plant a kiss on Kearny's lips. His brother growled and pulled her down on his own lap.

"Go home," he said in Thatcher's direction, kissing Janine deeply.

"Get a room," Thatcher fired back. "Don't invite me to dinner and then suck face all night."

Kearny chuckled as Janine freed herself and took her seat at the table. "Don't be jealous. You'll get there. If she's as guarded as you say she is, maybe you should follow her advice. Baby steps, man," Kearny said, cutting his roast.

"Why the hell do I tell you shit just so you can throw it back in my face as advice later?" Thatcher mumbled, taking a bite of his own roast. Damn. *This*. This was what he was missing. Home cooking. He was more than capable of a similar meal, but it was a pain in the ass in the pool house apartment's tiny kitchenette. "I've gotta get my own place," he said aloud, closing his eyes in appreciation of the flavorful, tender meat. "I have to get back to food like this. The junk I've been eating isn't doing me any good."

And it wasn't. He was convinced he'd have made more progress with his shoulder and leg by now if he was putting better quality fuel into his body.

"What's stopping you?" Kearny asked. "Isn't Mom feeding you?"

"She tries to. It's not about that."

"I know," he nodded. "Just kidding, man."

"Then what *is* stopping you?" Janine asked.

"Laziness," Thatcher admitted, making them laugh. "It's so much work, packing and moving and unpacking and buying stuff I've never had to buy."

"Is that why you stayed at home between deployments?" Janine's natural curiosity made her a great columnist, but Thatcher found himself wishing she weren't so interested in everyone all the time.

"On leave," he corrected. "You don't go home between deployments. You're stationed at a post—a base—and you work there unless you're deployed, get sent on TDY, which is temporary duty somewhere, or you get a PCS…a permanent change of station. After OSUT, my first duty station was Fort Carson." He watched her brow furrow and winced. "Sorry. One station unit training. It takes the place of doing basic at one base and shipping off to another for AIT." He winced again. "Advanced individual training. But, yeah. It's a hassle to break leases and pack up and toss stuff in storage all the time. Being single, I was stuck with barracks life until I made E-6, Staff Sergeant, unless they offered a non-availability waiver because housing was too full or some other reason, but the two times I was offered it, I didn't see the need. My roommates were always decent. I let guys I knew who hated their roommates take them. If they'd been a nightmare, I might've been more inclined to snatch up a waiver."

"Wow. How many moves did you go through?"

Thatcher didn't like talking anything military these days, but Janine's innocent curiosity somehow made it possible for him to answer past the lump forming in his throat.

"Three PCS moves in ten years. Like I said, after OSUT my first duty station was Fort Carson. I PCS'd in my third year of duty to Fort Stewart, Georgia, and while stationed there, I had TDY in Fort Hood, Texas, for six months, and at Fort Drum, NY, for eight months, but I was lucky enough to PCS back to Carson late in year seven. That was my last post before I was medically discharged. In between all of those, I had several overseas deployments. Combat and non-combat."

"Gosh. That has to be rough, moving around all the time." Janine said.

"That's the army," he shrugged.

"Are you looking for any particular area?"

Thinking of Kit, he replied, "West Valley. Maybe Peoria."

Kearny's nose wrinkled. "Why so far?" After a short pause, "Oh. Got it."

Thatcher shook his head and rolled his eyes. "She's only part of it. You can't stick anywhere around the 17 anymore, unless it's really far north, like the Rise. Too many tweakers. It's either east or west. Most of the jobs I've been looking at are out there, and yeah, Kit's out there, too. It just makes sense right now. If that changes, I can move when my lease is up, pain in the ass though it is."

"What sort of work are you looking for?" Janine asked. She had all sorts of connections, he knew. The girl was not one to burn a bridge or miss an opportunity. She was even on good terms with her former employer, *Phoenix Blink*, despite the nightmarish things that had gone on there.

"Not sure yet. Maybe something non-profit."

"Military focused?" she asked.

He froze, fork midway to his mouth. "Not necessarily. There's a lot of help needed, and I figure I might do a little volunteering around to see if something clicks."

"It's a great way to find a job," Janine agreed. "And one that so many people overlook."

"How long can you afford to do that, though, just volunteer?" Kearny asked.

"Let me worry about that, bro," Thatcher chided. He knew his brother didn't mean it the way it came across. "I'm not broke. Not much time to spend the small pittance I've earned for the last ten years."

Kearny's eyebrows rose. "You've got a point. *I* never

see you spend a dime," he flashed a cheesy grin.

Janine and Thatcher groaned together. She knew as well as anyone else in the family that Kearny could get annoyed by the cluelessness of the general public, but more often than not, he laughed at his own expense. His way of showing the world he was fine the way he was, that he didn't need or want anyone's pity. He'd been like that since he was a kid.

"Sorry," Thatcher joked, shaking his head. "But you chose to live with the guy."

"That's right," she said with a dreamy smile in Kearny's direction. "I did."

Sure, it would be nice to have what they had. His folks were still going strong, still slow danced in the kitchen to the 80's throwback, under-cabinet radio. They still grossed their adult kids out with their occasional PDA. But he'd rather they publicly displayed their affection than became polite strangers the way he knew some long-term couples did.

Thatcher could play the what-if game with the best of them…what if Gabriela hadn't been killed? Would he have gone into the military at all? Would they still be a couple? If not, how long would they have lasted? Who would he be today if life had unfolded differently? Unanswerable questions, all. He put his fork down on his empty plate with a sigh he hoped sounded like contentment. He was done talking about his love life, or lack of one.

He wasn't done *thinking* about it, though. He thought about Kit all day Sunday, looking forward to group whereas he usually felt at least a little dread.

He should have dreaded this one, actually, because it started out bad and went downhill fast.

Jon, whose hearing had gone well, was in fine spirits. He got some community service hours and his required time spent in the anger group extended but no jail time. Life was looking up. Mike, who did not throw any chairs or otherwise offend his interviewer, got a Dear John letter from the company and a promise to keep him in mind for the next six months.

"I really thought I had it," he sighed. "Meanwhile, my rent isn't getting any less past due."

Thatcher glanced his way. "Speaking of rent, anyone have any input on apartments on the west side? I'm looking to move."

Mike frowned. "Well, I have it on good authority that *my* apartment will be opening up soon," he groused. "Nice place. No carpet, just that fake wood-look vinyl and pretty quiet until the kids get out of school. First floor," he sighed, arms folded across his chest. "View of a little park with a barbecue and one of those round cement tables with the benches. The kids let off their steam there for several hours a day, but I drown it out with the TV or music." With another heavy sigh, he told Thatcher the name of the complex.

"What's your unit number?" Thatcher asked. As jaws began to drop, he put up his hands. "I'm kidding. Sorry. Bad joke. Mike, man, things will look up."

"Right!" he snorted. "Well, you can ask the office about unit number 1818, cause I'm sure it'll be vacant soon."

"That last job was in insurance? Do you have a license?" Thatcher asked, wondering if his sister, Sedona, who was a fraud investigator for a major insurance company, might know of any openings at her company or any competitors.

"No. They promised to help you get licensed if you got the job."

"What other sorts of work have you done?" he asked.

"Just about everything, which is why it's so damn frustrating that no one wants me now," Mike seethed.

"Restaurant work? Construction?"

"Some construction, yeah. Not much. But a couple of summer jobs in college and some Habitat. Never did any restaurants, though."

Thatcher made a mental note to ask his brother, Greer, if his company needed anyone. Looking around the circle, he said, "We'll all be on the lookout, right?"

Everyone agreed.

"I'm serious, though," Mike said, "if any of you can help me move, sign up now. Evictions don't give you a lot of time to get your shit together."

"Jesus, kid, stop whining," Gil moaned, shaking his head. "You're always focused on the doom and gloom and how everyone is out to get you. You didn't get this job because you threw a chair. You didn't get that job because it's just not your lucky day, you're losing your apartment, wah, wah, wah. Shut your whiny ass up and go sign up for every temp agency you can find. Go flip burgers if you have to. Sell your plasma. Pawn some stuff. When push comes to shove, you shove back or you fall on your fucking face. You wanna keep falling, Mike, be my guest."

He should have known it would set Kit off, given her similarities to Mike's circumstances. Short on cash. Underemployed, unemployed. Close enough if it didn't make both ends meet.

She stood up and let loose a tirade that started with Gil being the worst excuse for a human being she'd ever met and ended with her telling him that the reason he was so foul is that he knew there wasn't a person anywhere on earth that would call him a friend. Gil's face grew redder and redder until he launched himself toward her at her next words:

"You keep this shit up, Gil, you're going to die alone in a tiny little hovel and no one will know or care until you're just a disgusting odor stinking up the neighborhood!"

Unafraid, Kit met him toe to toe, face to face, and finished her words within spitting distance. Thatcher pulled her back out of Gil's reach as he moved to hit her, George palming Gil's chest to keep him from following.

Gil spat a stream of profanity at her that made a room

full of former soldiers and marines begin to blush and when George let down his guard, lunged toward her again.

"Enough!" George called. "Gil, you're done for today. Go home. Cool off. Come back on Wednesday."

"What about—"

"I'll be talking to her, too, Gil, but you're the one trying to throw punches. Go. Now. Before I have to call security."

He should have seen it coming. He should have known Gil wouldn't just pass Kit's chair at the edge of the stage. But he didn't. He didn't see it coming. Frankly, he wouldn't have thought Gil was in good enough shape to grab her by her shirt, pull her right out of her chair, and fling her off the stage in one fluid movement.

Thatcher flipped him to his back on the stage floor with his good arm and leg and pinned him there, right knee on his stomach. "I don't know who it is who raised you," he seethed, "but in case you missed the lesson, you don't put your hands on a woman. *Ever.*"

George didn't have to pull him off of Gil, because in the next instant, Thatcher was joining several of the others at the foot of the stage stairs where Kit was already busy pushing everyone away, struggling to her feet by herself. Thatcher caught her as she faltered forward.

The tears in her eyes that he knew she'd sooner die than shed told him she was in pain. Hurt. Donnie hurried down the steps with her chair, setting it down behind her. Thatcher helped her ease down into it, glancing up as George led Gil down the other, farther set of stage steps.

Kit insisted to each person who asked that she was fine, but when George returned from seeing Gil out moments later and asked whether she needed medical attention, Thatcher blurted a 'yes' over her 'no.'

"Two seconds ago, you couldn't stand up on your own. You're going to urgent care at the very least," he warned.

"Valiant, chill out," she replied wearily, rubbing her temple. "And no, George, I don't want to press charges against Gil. Just maybe mention to his P.O. that he's not making enough of an effort with his anger management studies."

"Kettle, pot, Miss Incendiary," George smirked, trying to bring them all down off the ledge. To the room, he said, "Let me just say right now that what went down in here today is *not* acceptable, and it is not going to happen again. It is never appropriate to react with violence, and Gil has been dismissed for today. Do any of you want to talk about what just happened?"

Silence.

"Okay, then. We're going to end things here today. Get some grub from the back, and we'll see you again Wednesday."

Everyone cleared out quickly, ignoring the platter of subs. Thatcher couldn't blame them. Group was supposed to help bring down their stress levels, not ratchet them up. His own heart was still beating somewhere in the vicinity of his throat. If Kit felt him watching her, she didn't show it. He noted the careful way she walked to the food table and the way she had to try twice to lean down to remove the plastic cover over the subs. He saw her regard the three chairs across from the table, choosing to stand, instead. But she let him stand close enough that his arm brushed hers as he lifted his own sub to his mouth.

"Are you sure you won't let me take you to urgent care?"

"I'm sure," she replied after swallowing. "I have to work."

"You're going to lift dogs like that?" he challenged, staring at a bulletin board full of notices and personal ads.

"No choice," she shrugged. He pretended not to see her wincing at the motion.

"Sick time?"

Now she met his eyes. "Valiant, I get paid in cash, under the table. No benefits. No work, no pay."

He knew she'd served less than twenty-four active months in the Guard. If he recalled correctly, that was the minimum threshold to receive any benefits after discharge.

Shit.

They finished their subs in silence. She didn't try to hide her food smuggling from him any longer. She just whipped out the Ziploc and filled it up matter-of-factly. But she didn't meet his eyes. And when she limped to the door, he followed her out.

He gently backed her up against the door of her car, and she let him. That she also let him lean in and kiss her senseless told him even more about her pain level. She didn't even *try* to pull away with an excuse about being late. As her tongue flitted out and traced his bottom lip, sending a shock of pleasure straight downward, he waited for her hands to hit his chest and shove him away.

They didn't.

Instead, she began making soft little happy noises that were half sigh, half moan. Those noises increased the shockwaves to his groin. He was unmistakably hard now, and she responded to that sensation by tugging his hips tighter against hers.

His greedy groan didn't stop her, either. What stopped her, to his fevered dismay, was that he thoughtlessly clutched her hips, and she yelped like a trod-upon dog.

"Sorry!" He immediately threw up his hands.

She sighed, licking her lips, and clutched his waist with trembling hands, settling her forehead against his neck for a moment before kissing him there.

"It's okay, Valiant," she said, lifting her head to look up at him. His cock twitched at the flushed appearance of her face and the dazed look in her eyes. "I'm glad you did that. I have to go, or I'll be late."

"Kit..."

She shook her head at his silent request and slid behind the wheel.

He watched her go, then realized her car had been the only thing hiding his massive wood from anyone passing by and hurried to his Jeep. He cranked the air down as far as it would go, still tasting her on his lips as he licked them.

Using the phone sheet from group — purely optional, but everyone other than Gil allowed the others in group to have their numbers — Thatcher sent a text to everyone.

I'm going to check on how much it will take to catch Mike up on his rent, if anyone wants to chip in.

A flurry of texts came in fairly quickly.

Donnie's was first. ***Yeah, man. Just let us know. I can probably put in a few bucks.***

Terry chimed in. ***How do you want us to contribute? Crowdfunding? Money transfer app?***

He hadn't thought about the logistics. Not like he could walk into group with a coffee can like people used to do. Shit. He replied with a text asking if the others had access to a money transfer app he used with his family.

Another few texts came in. Rachel, Jon, and even George. Everyone was eager to do what they could and would be standing by for word of the total.

Thanks, guys. I'll let you know, he typed.

CHAPTER ELEVEN

His mother called just as he wheeled the Jeep into a space for prospective residents at Mike's apartment complex.

"Mom, can I call you back in a few minutes? I'm right in the middle of something."

"It won't take but a minute. I just wanted to invite you to a family barbecue this Saturday."

He felt her waiting, likely holding her breath. And when he didn't answer quickly enough, her sigh carried the weight of months of disappointment.

"Okay, son. Enough is enough," her voice suddenly exploded over the line. Instead of the sad notes beneath a layer of understanding that he expected, her anger caught him by surprise. "I know you've been though something that none of us will ever understand, but you'll never heal from it if you don't get back into life. There's no answer that I will accept from you other than, 'What time, mother? What can I bring?' And the answer to that, kiddo, is just yourself. Your smiling face at noon this Saturday is all that I need."

"Mom, I—"

"Nope," she said sharply. So loudly, in fact, that he had to hold the phone away from his ear. "I said, 'What time, mother? What can I bring?' is the only thing I want to hear."

When he said nothing, wondering if she knew he was pinching the bridge of his nose, she prompted,

"I'm waiting."

"What time, mother? What can I bring?"

"Just yourself," she answered, irritation still plain in her voice. "And no last-minute calls to cancel. I'll see you on Saturday."

She was gone before he could tell her he might bring a friend, so he texted the words to her and received a prompt—and much sunnier—reply:

Of course! You don't need permission!

He put his phone away. Great. Just picturing the madhouse of bodies all over the patio made his palms begin to sweat. He glanced toward the glass door of the apartment office and considered coming back at another time, no longer certain about taking a tour. But the thought of returning to the pool house, where his parents could and probably had been monitoring his every movement, had him easing out of the Jeep.

The smiling receptionist, Jenny, was all too happy to show him several vacant apartments on the community map, gushing about the newly renovated fitness center, the three sparkling pools—the one behind the office being heated year-round—and the in-unit washer dryers.

"And, if you opt for a ground level unit, we've moved to an all wood-look vinyl flooring scheme that our newer residents are raving about. Some units even choose to pay a little extra for accent walls from our approved paint colors list," she said, pointing at a picture frame on the wall that contained several tastefully colored squares.

He nodded. "Can you show me something on the first floor?"

It would be better than huffing up the stairs, especially on the rare occasion that it rained. When it rained, his bones ached like an old man's, his limp more pronounced and his left shoulder twinging insufferably.

"I have several. Do you prefer something closer to the front office area or something more secluded?"

"Could I see all of the ground level options?"

Thirty minutes later, he'd seen the three currently available options. Jenny's small talk and disarming chatter had led him to acknowledge that yes, he'd been injured overseas. No sense lying when she'd guessed the tattoo on his forearm was military and asked sympathetically if the limp was from his service. He could have snapped at her to mind her own business, to not make assumptions, but he saw no reason to lash out at her over her observational skills. And it wasn't like she hadn't asked in the most tactful way possible.

But now she was throwing him looks that suggested an interest in him that went beyond that of a leasing agent trying to secure a tenant. He chose to ignore those looks.

"We've got another two ground level units that might become available in the next month, also, if these—"

"These are fine. I like 1909, the one almost in the back corner of the complex." He liked that all of the windows except the kitchen would face north. It would keep the heat level down.

"Great. Are you interested in moving in immediately?"

He shrugged, easing into the utility cart next to her. "Let's talk about the rent and other details first."

Being jobless wouldn't exactly endear him to the front office, so he figured he'd have to disclose his investment portfolio and include the small amount in profit share he received from the Phoenix Rise Grill. He figured he'd offer to prepay whatever lease term was most affordable and see if that swayed them further.

Although the offer to prepay the lease period and his request for either reduced rent or a replacement of the ancient fridge and stove in his chosen unit surprised Jenny, a quick conference with her boss and a call to the corporate headquarters determined that they would waive the income requirements—though not the background check—if he were to pay the entire lease period's rent in full up front, by cashier's check. Rather than reducing the rent, however, they would meet his request for new kitchen appliances, which was actually what he'd hoped for when he saw the stove and heard the jetliner-takeoff sounds the fridge was making.

"Great," he agreed. "I'll need the appliance replacement promise noted somewhere in the lease. I also need you to tell me the amount past due for unit 1818."

"I'm sorry?" Jenny asked, brow furrowing, fingers pausing over her keyboard.

"Unit 1818," he repeated. "The rent is past due, and I need to know by how much so I can bring it current and stay the eviction." When Jenny said nothing, just exchanged a glance with the office manager, he said, "I know the tenant. He's a friend. I know he's about to get evicted for non-payment of rents, so I want to help him out."

After another brief conference, she came back and advised, "The overdue rent totals $2,619, which is two month's rent and includes the late fees."

"Would you be willing to waive the late fees, help a guy out?" He gave her what he hoped was a charming smile.

Jenny clearly held no power in her position, but her smile suggested she'd like to give him anything he asked for. Another discussion behind the closed door of her boss' office yielded an affirmative response. "If you are able to provide a separate cashier's check or money order for that amount, we will waive the late fees as a courtesy."

Thatcher nodded. "Do I need to sign something to hold 1909?"

She assured him they'd be fine without it if he was coming straight back.

He accepted the sticky note she offered with the deposit and full lease period amounts for 1909 and the past due rent amount for 1818.

When he turned to leave, he said,

"Jenny, I hope you'll keep my identity a secret from Mike, the guy in 1818."

She lifted her eyes from the screen, her fingers pausing on the keyboard. "You don't want us to tell him who paid the rent?"

"No, I don't. Just tell him it was some concerned friends."

She gave him another gooey-eyed look, sagging slightly in her office chair. He could all but hear the "aww!" Being keenly observant, however, she quickly straightened, her face sliding back to all business. "Sure. No problem."

"I'll be back soon."

Just as he pulled into the parking lot of a grocery store where he planned to get the money orders, Thatcher's phone rang. He assumed it was one of his brothers or sisters and without looking, answered, "Yes, yes, I'm coming on Saturday. Go ahead and spread the word."

His hand froze where it rubbed the back of his head when a voice replied,

"I'm sorry? Is this Thatcher?"

"Yeah. Sorry, who's this?"

"Nanette. We met the—"

"Kit's boss," he answered grimly. "Is she okay?"

"Of course not. She's a stubborn idiot, but she's not fooling anyone. She's moving like a 90-year-old. I'm kicking her out of my shop until she brings me a doctor's note."

"Good call," he said. "I'm on my way. I'll take her to urgent care, myself."

"I knew I could count on you. See you in a few minutes!"

He called the apartment office and asked Jenny if she'd accept his credit card to pay for Mike's past due rent, explaining that he had a sudden emergency to deal with. A brief hold ensued while, he guessed, she conferred with her boss again. When she came back to the line, she took the information and warned that if the charge failed to clear, the stay of the eviction would be lifted.

"Understood, ma'am. Not a problem," he said.

"I can't hold 1909 for you without the deposit, and that one, I can't take by credit card."

"It's alright," he sighed. "I'll come back another time and see what you have available then. Thanks."

He could all but feel Jenny's disappointment as the lost rental opportunity. "I appreciate your willingness to help clear his obligations. Remember, don't tell him who it was."

"I won't. I hope to see you back soon," she said as he ended the call.

Kit was slumped sullenly in a waiting area chair when Thatcher pushed open the door to Waggy Waggy. Though he'd known better than to hope she'd be happy to see him, he wasn't prepared for the eye daggers she shot him. He should have been, but he'd thought maybe they'd progressed a little past her usual jaded, narrow-eyed looks.

"Hi, Thatcher!" Nanette greeted sunnily enough for both of them. "Thanks for doing this."

"Sure," he nodded, plucking a business card from the holder by the door.

"You just rest up, Kit," Nanette dismissed. "We'll keep Lily for you tonight."

"You don't ha—"

"Thanks, Nanette!" Thatcher called over the sound of the blow dryer, reaching down for Kit's arm.

She ducked away and stood without his help, her lips pursed, still shooting him her best death stare. "I'm not an invalid," she seethed.

He gave her a grin and held the door for her.

Silent treatment. Great.

He didn't bother glancing her way as he drove several blocks to the nearest urgent care with x-ray capabilities. She said nothing as she angrily poked information into the tablet the clerk handed her. They sat in a bubble of cold quiet as the rest of the pained, sick customers around them chatted and healthy kids waited with exhausted-looking parents, hopping in and out of chairs, darting around the waiting area, which seemed to grow smaller and smaller by the minute.

Kit made a face at a wide-eyed toddler until the little boy let out a deep belly laugh. His mind's eye instantly flashed to Kyle's son. Change this kid's eyes from brown to blue, darken the hair a couple shades. He imagined that other little boy growing up without a daddy to hold him patiently on his lap with a jiggling knee, and the walls of the already impossibly small waiting room sucked in around him like shrink wrap.

"Valiant?" Kit asked as he shot to his feet seconds before her name was called by a medical tech. Too bad they both knew he wasn't psychic.

"Kit Reilly?" the tech called again, waving at Thatcher, mistaking him for her patient.

He followed at Kit's heels, ignoring stares from the waiters, hearing only the echo of his ragged breath in his ears. The inner door closing did him the favor of closing of a little of the panic, the closeness.

"Are you alright, sir?" the fresh-faced technician asked.

"Crowds," Kit told her, grabbing his hand and tugging him behind her into the exam room. "I'm Kit."

The technician looked back and forth between them and her eyes lit with understanding. To Thatcher, she said, "Why don't you have a seat here in the exam room while I take your wife for x-rays?"

He nodded, too relieved at all the available oxygen to correct her. He sank down in the hard plastic chair and watched the door swing closed. The impersonal, sterile room with its dull beige walls and random medical posters calmed him. It could have been minutes or hours, but waiting for Kit to return to the room was eternal. He shot out of the chair like it was on fire when the door finally opened and the technician's voice floated in after Kit.

"Have a seat. The doctor will be right with you after we've reviewed your films."

Kit looked at the newly vacated chair for a minute, deciding to stand. "Feel better?" she asked him.

He nodded. No use denying what she'd seen.

"What was that about?" Her eyes searched his face.

"Nothing." He leaned against the exam table. "Crowds, like you said."

"We were in there for almost half an hour before you lost it," she pointed out in an uncharacteristically soft voice.

"I didn't lose it," he denied.

Kit snorted. "You were halfway to the parking lot when they called my name."

"I can only handle crowds for so long before I…can't anymore," he offered, hoping she'd bite.

"Might help to talk about it," she suggested casually. He pretended not to notice her curious looks as he re-examined all of the posters he'd already memorized. "I mean, you've never said a word about yourself in group."

"Like it helped you so much?" he challenged, meeting her eyes now.

"Yeah, it did, actually," she nodded.

He shook his head and folded his arms across his chest, ignoring the protest from his left shoulder.

She snorted back and added an eye roll, but before she could say anything else, the technician returned to gather additional details.

The reprieve, unfortunately, didn't last. A few seconds after the door closed behind the technician again, Kit's voice found him.

"Come on, Valiant. Give me something. One sentence about what really happened just now."

He didn't want to be pissed off at her, not right now

when she was busy playing tough ass and shoring up her own walls. He sure as hell didn't want to realize he was doing exactly the same thing…with her, with group, with his family.

But he was.

He was also frustrated enough about her impenetrable fortress to give her less than what she deserved.

"I can only handle so much crowd before I have to get away."

She rolled her eyes again, but this time he caught a flash of pain in them. It stabbed him in the gut. Before he could offer her more, the door swung open once more, the doctor already talking.

"Well, Mrs. Reilly, good news. No broken bones. Bad news, it'll be a few days before you should consider doing anything strenuous. We want to rest the hip and shoulder as much as possible to see if they improve by next Monday. If not, you may need an MRI to rule out a bone bruise."

She paled. "Well, if we're done here, I just need a note so that I can go back to work."

"I'll give you one for Monday," he nodded.

Kit's eyes narrowed in Thatcher's direction. "Who did you talk to, Valiant?"

He held up his hands. "When would I have spoken to anyone?"

"While I was—"

"There was no secret discussion," the doctor told her absently, keying information into the exam room's computer. "You advised Marci that you work at a dog grooming salon, correct?"

"Yeah," she agreed wearily.

"And you regularly lift large breed dogs?"

"Small ones, too. More small ones," Kit replied hopefully.

"You need a few days off from anything strenuous or weight bearing. Only a few," the doctor told her.

"Four days, though? Four working days? People who have surgery are cleared for work quicker than that!"

"Mrs. Reilly," he said patiently, rising from his place in front of the terminal. "Let me show you something." From one of the drawers, he pulled a large mirror. Thatcher moved away from the tiny cabinet and sink area as the doctor guided Kit to stand facing the door and held up the hand mirror. "Lift the back of your blouse and lower your pants a bit and look up here." He gave the hand mirror a little shake.

Thatcher's breath caught at how dark and ugly the bruise at her right hip was. He whistled low, drawing a frown from Kit.

"I'm concerned this might actually be a bone bruise, and if I don't like how you're moving on Monday, I want to send you for an MRI."

"So, what if it is a bone bruise? It just takes longer to heal, right? Is it a big deal?"

"It can be. Although rare, it can lead to a complication called avascular necrosis. That's when the bone or a portion of a bone dies, increasing your mobility issues and the chance that you'll need surgery."

She paled again. Or more. "Okay," she conceded, "so I take four days off and take it easy. Will that actually help, or am I just spinning my wheels?"

"I wouldn't suggest time away from work if I didn't think it was necessary and helpful. And it wouldn't hurt to increase your calcium, protein, and vitamin D for a while. Those are things that will help you heal, especially if it is a bone bruise."

After printing off her discharge instructions, he told her to return Monday morning or follow up with her GP. Then, looking at Thatcher, he said, "Now, if you wouldn't mind sir, please step out so I can speak privately with Mrs. Reilly for a moment."

"Miss," Kit finally said. "We're not married."

Thatcher nodded. "I'll be in the Jeep," he told her, wondering if his own face paled at the thought of going back to the crowded waiting room.

Kit stormed out ten minutes later, at least as much as she could storm anywhere. "Let's go, Valiant. I need to drop this paperwork off at Waggy Waggy."

"Just bring it with you on Monday," he shrugged.

"Waggy Waggy," she said, pulling the seatbelt across her body with a violent jerk that left her stifling a cry of pain. She responded to his pointed look with an eye roll and a deep sigh.

"Kit, it'll be okay," he said, "you don't—"

He'd faced IEDs, sniper fire and elementary-school-aged suicide bombers, sometimes all in one day, but her look scared him out of arguing.

"Waggy Waggy," he agreed.

She fumed the entire way. He felt the irritation radiating from her skin. She was almost vibrating with it. Before he could round to the passenger door to help her climb out, she'd winced her way out of the Jeep and stormed inside ahead of him.

She tossed the doctor's note down on the reception desk, giving Nanette a recap of the diagnosis. Her next words felt like a punch in the gut, though. "The jackass actually kicked Thatcher out of the exam room and asked if I wanted to call the police and press charges against him."

Nanette pointed her clippers, still humming, at Thatcher as he stood in the doorway. "On him?"

"He told me there had to be more to the story than a simple fall, and—"

"There *was* more," Thatcher stared at Kit. "You were thrown down from stage height by a guy with four inches and about eighty pounds on you!"

Nanette reared back. "Are you serious? You didn't tell me that, Kit!"

Kit's paleness finally broke with a bloom of color. She

gave Thatcher a long-suffering look. "Nanette, can't I just help you out with the office stuff? Phones, filing, desk work. Desk work, Nanette."

"Absolutely not. You're going to follow the doctor's orders and rest up until Monday, and then before you come in, you're going to go to urgent care for the follow up appointment and to your group thing. You're going to leave Lily with us tonight, and you're not picking her up until dinner time tomorrow. You're going to *rest*, Kit. No cleaning your house top to bottom, no volunteering at the food bank. Nothing." Nanette pointed the clippers at her, then turned toward him. "You watch her, Thatcher. If you don't, she'll probably go hiking or rock climbing or something equally stupid."

He fought a smile and nodded. "Yes, ma'am," he said.

Kit, on the other hand, was determined to find a loop hole. "You're my boss, Nanette, not my mother. I can take care of myself and my child, and I don't need a babysitter. Especially not Groceries, here!"

Nanette's face changed from that of friend to that of boss. "You're damn right I'm your boss, Kit, and I'm also your friend. And as your friend, let me just say that as your boss, I don't want to fire you. But you bet your pretty little camo pants that I'll do it if you don't get out of my shop and let Thatcher look after you, at least for tonight. If you want to be your usual pain in the ass self, at least wait until tomorrow night to do it. Lily will be fine with me and Crystal."

Kit sighed loudly. "Whatever."

"No. Not whatever." Nanette's voice rose. "Kit, take care of yourself! Eat a decent meal, get a good night's sleep, and for once, keep your damn mouth shut when Gil pisses you off."

"I didn't—"

"Oh, yes you did! I know you. I know exactly how you operate. You've been a little defender of the underdogs as long as I've known you, and you don't care a thing about yourself when you're standing up for somebody else. You got your ass handed to you this time. Learn the lesson, Kit!"

When no one moved or spoke for over a minute, Nanette flung an arm toward the door to the shop. "Go!"

Thatcher met the woman's eyes as Kit slumped out of the lobby and gave her a little nod before ducking out the door.

CHAPTER TWELVE

She was determined to piss him off so he'd leave her to lick her wounds in peace, but stupid Valiant was taking Nanette's orders as seriously as if she were his CO. He stopped at Walgreens to pick up her prescriptions, the first for three days' worth of hydrocodone-acetaminophen and the second for high dose ibuprofen.

She offered him a clipped 'thank you.'

He didn't answer. He was probably afraid she'd bite his head off as she'd done with Nanette. But he didn't seem angry. He tapped the steering wheel to the music, occasionally mutter-singing a chorus. He swung into a Safeway, gave her a warning look when she opened her mouth to protest. Who was she kidding? Four days without pay, with the electric bill already due…she'd be eating rice and ramen for a month. If that.

Kit tried to enjoy the breeze through the open window, tried to pretend she was an ordinary productive human. It was just after four now, plenty of full-time jobbers on the road, headed home. She was just one of that gang. Maybe even taking a little vacation. Quick grocery run before dinner with her—Okay not her husband, no matter what the doctor thought. She'd fucked up her actual marriage somehow. But maybe her boyfriend. Thatcher had to like her enough for that, even right now. He was shuttling her all around town and acting like her personal concierge. He had to like her enough for boyfriend status in her little "what if" musings, right?

So…dinner with her date, then maybe she'd pack a suitcase. Head to her beach rental. Yeah. She and Lily and Groceries would finish out the week at the coast or something. Golden bronze skin, sun bleached hair, rangy limbed…

No.

She shook herself. Her little beach fantasy faded. She was an under-employed single mother living in a mortgage-free house she still couldn't afford with a fifteen-year-old hand-me-down car and no real prospects for the future. She could blame the economy for the scarcity of jobs, but unemployment was at its lowest recent levels. It was her. She was too "rough around the edges". Too angry. Talked back too much.

Thatcher returned with two handfuls of reusable grocery bags.

"Anything else you need or want before we head back to your place?"

She bit her tongue, forcing back the smart remark that surfaced and shook her head, instead. She ignored the happy little home fantasies, the same romance novel happy endings she read books for but claimed not to believe in. She shut down the stupid filmstrip that wanted to run in her head, to continue the silly beach fantasy, the one that starred her and Lily and fucking Valiant, laughing and golden, frolicking in the sand and splashing in the water.

Reality crashed down as she saw her mother's house come into view. The ugliest, most run-down house on the block with its slightly weedy front yard and the eaves with the weathered paint and the deteriorating stucco finish. An eyesore amidst its well-kept neighbors. She was grateful not to have an HOA breathing down her neck, while her neighbors were probably hatching a plot to form one. She stared at it as the engine cut off, this place she daily considered selling but couldn't bear to. Not now. Not yet.

If Thatcher saw it the same way, he didn't let on. He

followed her to the door, shopping in hand. He turned off into the kitchen and ordered, "Pajamas. Couch. Now."

"Aye, aye, Captain," she flung back, no small measure of sarcasm in her voice. Why couldn't she stop doing that to him? Because if she wasn't snarky, she'd let him in too close. Damn Valiant.

"Staff Sergeant," he corrected.

There was no use arguing. He'd just railroad over her like always. Like with the groceries and with the car. She let him bustle around. And bustle he did. The fridge and freezer doors opened and closed, followed by cabinet doors. Pots and pans clattered, the sink ran, and silverware scritched against plates. Aromas rose that made her stomach twist in on itself and her mouth water.

He appeared in her increasingly dim living room first with two glasses of ice water, then with a pack of instant ice.

"Sit up," he ordered, tucking the paper-towel wrapped pack between her right hip and the sofa cushions before vanishing again.

He reappeared moments later with two plates, handing her one. She tried not to smile at the way he'd cut her food into manageable bites.

"We could've done this at the dining room table," she protested.

"Nope," he said, easing down next to her. "This is definitely a Netflix and chill sort of day."

"Suit yourself, Groceries." A moment later, she asked, "What is this?" and speared a crumbly, crusted piece.

"Panko crusted salmon, sweet potato home fries, and roasted asparagus. Enjoy."

"You cook?" she tucked a bite in her mouth and tried not to moan.

"Sure. All us kids know our way around a kitchen. Not my favorite thing by any means, but it has its benefits."

It was good. Son of a chef good. She moaned before she

could stop herself and he shifted beside her.

"You didn't have to go to all this trouble. A salad would've been fine."

"You need better than smuggled junk food and salad, Kit. You deserve better."

Kit looked away from him and at the TV screen before he could see the hot, stinging effect of his words. Instead of answering, she turned up the volume on an episode of *Friends*. No matter how loud the volume, it couldn't drown out her awareness of his thigh, his hip, his body so close to hers, not quite touching but closer than necessary on her long sofa. She could feel the warmth of him.

If he noticed, he didn't let on. He settled in amicably, chuckling at the sitcom hijinks, his fork scritching on his plate from time to time. She fought off another stupid daydream that this dinner in front of the TV after a long day, not needing to talk, was an ordinary thing. Just a ho-hum night, Lily playing quietly on the floor or perhaps already tucked in. When he finished his meal and sat back, flinging an arm across the back of the sofa, she pictured herself tucked against his chest, his hand toying with her hair, something she'd always loved.

Food, real food, was like a potent sedative, tugging at her eyelids even as she leaned forward to set her plate on the coffee table, promising herself she'd take the plates to the kitchen in a few more minutes.

Instead, her next awareness was of cotton under her cheek. Cotton that rose and fell under her, the comforting weight of a hand on her right shoulder and a cold sensation there. Kit lifted her head, fragments clicking into place. She was draped across Thatcher's chest, his palm anchoring another instant ice pack against her shoulder.

"What time is it?" she rasped. A different episode of *Friends* was just ending.

Thatcher yawned, lifting his left arm slowly. "Mm. Late. Just after midnight."

“Shit!” Kit sat up, looking for her plate.

“I did them,” he advised, reading her mind. “Didn’t want the dishes getting crusty.”

“When?”

“Right after you conked out. C’mon. I’ll tuck you in,” he said, rising carefully, his face an adorable mix of sleepy seriousness.

“Because I’m ten?” she joked, her hands muffling her voice as she slid them over her face.

“Because the doc gave you three days’ worth of heavy meds, and I don’t want you to fall on your face.”

He had a point. Standing, her body felt heavy and slow and her eyelids kept slamming shut of their own accord. She let him tuck an arm around the middle of her back, safely away from her bruised shoulder and hip, his hand burning where it met bare skin where it peeked out between her tank top and pajama pants. If she wasn’t so damn tired or so old-lady sore, she might try to get that hand to wander.

She insisted on removing her make up and brushing her teeth. He stood in the doorway, nonchalantly watching her movements in the mirror, ducking out when she met them in the glass and said,

“A little privacy, please.”

He stood just outside the door until she emerged, standing by as she slid into bed.

“I’ve been doing this myself for many moons now, Valiant,” she told him dryly.

“Yep,” he agreed, pulling the sheet up. “Blanket?”

“Nope.”

“’Night,” he said, kissing her forehead, one hand lightly cupping her cheek. She forced herself not to nuzzle against it.

Her heart hammered in her chest as she considered, in the space of a second, all his possible reactions to her sleepy offer. “Stay,” she mumbled.

He answered with the rustling of jeans falling to carpet and the bouncy jiggle of the mattress beside her. He didn't fit himself against her as she hoped, but it was enough.

~~~

"Dammit, Kyle…" Thatcher pressed the gaping wound in his chest hard, already feeling warmth oozing into his palm. "Don't."

He tried. Tried to talk, to form words around a pained moan. Thatcher closed his eyes and then met Kyle's.

Desperation.

He knew.

He knew what was happening, Thatcher saw it in his eyes. Knew he wasn't going to make it out of this stupid brown, weedy field littered with bits of concrete and rebar and old gray swatches of rags that might have once been clothes.

He saw the bewildered blue gaze of someone wondering how to stop what was coming, how to find a miracle in a place so void of them. Felt the shudder of death's hooves galloping through him. His buddy. His brother.

"Ssss," Kyle tried. Blue fucking eyes aging backward, his face morphing into the soft face of his son.

Matty's eyes, puzzling, looked back at him.

"Don't," Thatcher choked. "Kyle, no. No, dammit! Stay with me!"

He sobbed as the eyes stared back, forever questioning. Asking if this was really how it ended, here in this desolate, piece of shit country.

Why?

"Hey…"

Someone touched his shoulder where it burned and bled.

"Hey…"
~~~

"No," he sobbed, clutching Kyle's broken body tighter against him, until it yelped.

Thatcher leapt backward, scuttled on the desert floor until—

A strong hand gripped his wrist just before he fell backward off the bed.

The bed.

Thatcher blinked and scooted away from the edge of the mattress. Kit's sleepy eyes blinked back. He eased down on his back, heart still feeling like it might burst out of his chest. She reached up and stroked his stubbly jaw wordlessly. He turned toward it, toward the warmth of her hand. He met her eyes, tried to decide whether they were green or gray. Settled on both, a trick of the lighting. And still couldn't stop flashing back to those blue eyes.

"Tell me," Kit urged.

He forced the words down, down, and closed his eyes, pretending sleep was mere seconds away, though he knew she knew better.

"Tell me," she repeated softly, the sleep she'd beat him back to creeping into her voice.

"Can't," he told her and Kyle both at once. Pictured Kyle's scoffing face, the kind he'd made frequently as they'd exchanged barbs as often as encouragement. "Not yet," he croaked to Kyle's image. He rolled toward her though, onto his right side, away from the edge of the mattress. That would've set his PT back, for sure, falling off the bed.

"Hmmm," she said, and ran a drowsy hand down his left bicep until it fell, nestled against his lower belly. A tingle went through him. Interested, but too rattled to do much about it, he rolled onto his back to break that contact. Sleep would never find him with her hand there, though it made for a nice distraction. He desperately wanted to pull that hand a few inches south, guide it up and down.

He felt her grow heavier beside him as her

consciousness decreased, surprised as he felt himself pulled closer to sleep. Sometimes after one of his dreams, he was up all night. Kit’s slow breathing beside him, however, coaxed him closer, himself.

CHAPTER THIRTEEN

Kit woke to the sound of raindrops pattering on the window and the bed disheveled but empty beside her. Rubbing her head where it wanted to ache, she eased out of bed, glad Thatcher wasn't there to see it. She gratefully swallowed the single pill he'd left on the night stand with a bottle of water, lifting her head at what sounded like thunder.

A quick peek through the slats of the closed blinds confirmed it. A late March thunderstorm. The weatherman was correct for once.

She couldn't help but feel a giddy pleasure at the idea of a day at home, rain falling, with no place to rush off to. Worry and guilt galloped right after, however.

Thatcher, however, was mellow this morning, moving shirtless through her kitchen, jeans slung low so that when he glanced over his shoulder at her, she caught sight of his "V" and briefly considered brunching on something other than the omelet he was making.

She remembered waking in his arms, the feeling of uncomfortable tightness, his sleep-thickened voice. "Don't!" he'd sobbed. She remembered him backing away from her, horrified, until he almost fell off the bed. Would have, if she hadn't grabbed his wrist and given him a hearty tug.

Kit wanted to ask, but his relaxed manner and the rain kept her from doing so.

He proceeded to pamper her all day, between watching

the rare, steady rain and yet more episodes of *Friends*. He confessed to her he hadn't watched TV in so long, it was nice to experience a binge session like the ones his siblings sometimes posted about on social media. He gently rubbed arnica gel into her bruises, though she had to clamp her mouth closed to keep him from knowing how much it actually hurt. He helped her ice them off and on throughout the rainy afternoon and kept feeding her the most delicious meals she'd had in months.

He was half-asleep beside her on the sofa when she idly checked her phone and found a flurry of missed group messages between Thatcher and the people in their group. As she read through them, her eyes began to tear up. She nudged him gently with her elbow.

"Hmm?" He roused, sitting up instantly, alert and ready.

"You paid Mike's overdue rent?" She tried not to let her voice wobble but failed.

Thatcher shrugged. "I fronted it. Most of group paid his rent."

She shook her head. "That's…" She swiped at her eyes. "I'm sure he'll appreciate it." After a brief silence, her voice cracked. "I really wish I could help."

He slid the back of his hand against hers. Just that. She sensed he was waiting to see if she'd pull away. She left her hand against his and waited to see what he'd do next. After a long moment, he curled his fingers around hers and squeezed. "Someday you'll be in a better place and be able to," he replied huskily, his amber eyes meeting hers earnestly.

Damn you, Valiant. Making me like you more and more.

Kit ignored the voice and curled up against him. If he was surprised, he hid it well. Normally fidgety, getting up to do some chore or another, Thatcher sat next to her for a good several hours that afternoon.

She hated to see him leave. He hated to go, judging by the way he lingered in the doorway after carting Lily and her diaper bag inside and settling her to play in the living room. But she couldn't just bring some guy into her life to play house. Lily lost one father, an absence she was oblivious to. The older she got, the more she would remember. No way was Kit going to do that to Lily…allow her little heart to form an attachment to some guy her mother felt a physical attraction to.

And in spite of these thoughts, she offered no argument when he stepped back into the entryway and said, "Let me help you with dinner."

He put a pot of water on to boil and pulled macaroni from the pantry he'd just stocked again yesterday. When she made a face as she bent to scoop up Lily, who'd toddled back toward the kitchen, he swooped in and scooped her up, winking at her.

"C'mon, Lil' Miss, let's get some grub."

Lily, lacking proper socialization beyond Nanette, Crystal, and Kit, usually screamed bloody murder when strangers touched her. But she just blinked at Thatcher and reached a chubby hand out at his still-stubbly face.

"Let's wash our hands," he enthused, sitting her on the edge of the sink. "See, Lily, like this," he said, pumping soap into his right hand and rubbing it over both of hers. He didn't bat an eye when she let out an eardrum-rupturing squeal and clapped her hands, sending a burst of soapy water upward. He just grabbed a clean dish towel from the counter and sopped up the errant water. "All clean," he sing-songed moments later, chuckling at her attempt to parrot him.

"Awkween!"

Kit stood in the archway as he very competently plunked her into her highchair, buckled her in, clicked the tray in place, and poured a small handful of puffed apple snacks in front of her before sliding to the stove to grab the macaroni. In a strangely graceful ballet, he dumped the pasta into a colander, poured Lily a sippy cup of juice, spooned the macaroni into a casserole dish, whipped up a homemade cheese sauce, and had the dish in the oven before Lily finished her leisurely snacking on the apple puffs.

"I'll set the table," she said, shaking herself out of her daze, relieved when he didn't object.

Dinner was everything she'd hoped for with David but never got. Good food, random conversation punctuated with the occasional burst of toddler babble.

This isn't real, she reminded herself over and over again. *This is a temporary thing. This isn't your life or your luck. Even if he seems perfect. Even if you don't mind risking Lily getting attached. He'll get tired of playing house.*

But the next thing she knew, Lily was tucked in her crib, and Thatcher was telling her to take a shower if she wanted. She wanted.

"Need help undressing?" he grinned, lifting his eyebrows suggestively.

"I'm not an invalid," she reminded him, catching on when he offered to scrub her back. And her front.

She *did* let him kiss her, let his hands wander a bit, but catching sight of Lily's clothes in the laundry basket on the washer brought her to her senses.

"Valiant," she breathed, stepping back, "We're not there yet."

Tracing her lip with one finger, he looked at her under hooded lids and said, "We will be."

She kicked herself all through her short shower, one during which she couldn't help but picture him sliding in behind her, his hands soaping her up instead of her own, one that had her reaching down to stroke herself, picturing his fingers there. But the first forward tilt of her hips toward those imaginary fingers put a stop to that. She sighed heavily in disgust, resenting her bruises.

Maybe it was sexual frustration that had her rolling her eyes at the sight of him doing the dinner dishes, the leftover macaroni casserole missing from the stovetop.

"Valiant, seriously," she said, tugging the kitchen sponge out of his hand, "I can do my own dishes without straining anything."

He shrugged and tugged it back.

"Valiant!" She winced at the unintentionally sharp tone of her voice, slapping the handle of the faucet down.

He turned to look at her. "Do you know, Kit, that being here, helping you, it's done more for me than sitting through group?"

"Not that you've given group much of a chance," she argued. "You haven't shared a damn thing. Like your nightmares, for one."

He stiffened. "I've said plenty. I don't sleep well. I get anxiety attacks. I feel…unfocused. Everything seems trivial, like nothing means anything anymore. Like nothing I could do now is important enough."

Kit nodded. It was true, he'd said those things, almost verbatim, and then he'd shut down when George tried to draw him out. "But you haven't said a damn thing about why. All of that, that's what. Group is about why."

"What's your why?" he countered.

"You know why I'm in group. Because I went to David's crappy little house and smashed up all his shit and tried to smash *him.* By some miracle, he agreed not to press charges if I kept quiet about him abandoning Lily and agreed to do some anger management therapy. He looks like a fucking hero, and I look like a crazy, loose cannon. There. All caught up now. Your turn."

He wordlessly flipped the faucet handle back up and finished the dishes, his jaw clenched tightly. When she slapped the handle down a second time, waiting, he ground out, "I can't. Not yet."

He tossed the sponge in the sink. Right then, his eyes were so haunted when they locked on hers, Kit would have agreed to anything to make the look go away. When he traced her jaw with still damp fingers and asked, "Maybe you don't need or want the help, but would you let me, just until Monday?" she gave in.

"Sunday night," she countered. "Monday, I can drive myself to urgent care and work without your help. Because if I can't, I've got bigger problems."

Every time she wanted to step in, take over, send him away, he melted her heart either in real time or from a flashback to his bewildered, post nightmare face. That night, as he spooned her, he confessed to having nightmares almost every night and being unable to go back to sleep most nights afterward.

"Until last night," he mumbled, already half asleep behind her.

Kit closed her eyes, trying not to think that she was sleeping better, too, after just one night.

She woke before him the next morning, easing out from under his arm to find an unprecedented second day of rain falling outside the blinds. She turned at a rustling sound to find Thatcher sliding into his jeans.

"I'm going to stop by my place today for a few things."

She nodded, unable to renege on the permission she'd given the night before, however much she wanted to right now in the light of a new day…a day with her daughter fully present.

She crept into Lily's room to find her precious girl lying quietly in her crib, awake but not fussing.

"Hello, gorgeous!" she cooed as a smile lit up her baby's face and little hands reached upward.

Frustrated tears sprang into her eyes as pain shot through her when she reached back to lift her up and out of the crib. Thatcher eased beside her. Wordlessly understanding the problem, he slid a hand to the back of her neck and pressed a kiss to her temple before he eased Lily into his arms.

Still wide-eyed and curious, Lily reached for his face

again. He smiled as her hand patted his stubble, then pulled back from the prickliness of it.

"Hey, Lil' Miss," he said, jiggling her a little as she started to frown and reached for Kit. "I'll bet you need a diaper change."

Kit watched anxiously as he easily whipped off her pajamas and the soiled diaper.

"She showing any interest in potty training yet?" he asked, efficiently cleaning and diapering Lily as if he did it every day.

"A little. I can't keep her out of the bathroom when I go," Kit smiled. "And sometimes she comes to me and pats her diaper when she's wet or dirty. Not always."

"Only when she's had enough," he nodded. "You're about ready, aintcha?" He tickled Lily's tummy as Kit found a clean outfit for her and passed it over.

"You didn't get this training in the Army, Valiant, so how'd you learn all this?"

"Uncle Thatcher has a beautiful baby niece," he said to Lily, dressing her as effortlessly as he'd undressed her. "And her mama and daddy were all too happy to give me a crash course in Baby 101." He kissed Lily's clothed belly, blowing a raspberry just like Kit would have done. Lily's squeal of laughter told her she found it as hilarious when this strange man did it as when her mama did it.

She leaned in to kiss her, too, before hurrying to the door. "My turn to make breakfast," she announced, hoping he thought the rasp in her voice was just a remnant of sleep.

The hollow feeling in her chest when he left to grab more clothes alarmed her as much as it bewildered her. It wouldn't do any good to get used to this little slice of home and hearth. *Temporary,* she reminded herself, rolling a ball to Lily on her play blanket. *Just until Sunday night.*

The next few days were a tug-of-war between the part of her that still believed, deep down, that happy-ever-after was possible and the part that knew it wasn't. She ran hot and cold on Thatcher. She watched herself doing it as if from afar, kicking herself as he tried to navigate whichever version of herself she showed him. He didn't say so, but she was sure he must be thinking she had some kind of dissociative disorder.

Kit grew to hate each passing minute. She both loved and hated discovering late in the week that she could lift and lower Lily on her own. She could bend and stretch and reach with moderate but manageable twinges of pain. She really hated that once in a while, Lily reached for Thatcher, preferring him to her mother, whining and threatening to go full blown tantrum if she denied her daughter his male attention.

Late that evening, with Lily in her crib, Kit washed dishes while Thatcher dried them, remembering the way that her baby reached for him, fussing, until he, too, kissed her goodnight.

No good, she thought. *No good, no good. You have to stop this.*

CHAPTER FOURTEEN

"My folks are having a barbecue on Saturday," Thatcher said as they washed and dried Thursday's breakfast dishes. "Want to come with me? Lily can play with my niece, have a little interaction with another kid. It'll be great."

Kit heard hope and fear in his voice and flashed back to Phoenix Rise Grill and Artie's little side conversation with the staff. *He's having a little trouble with big groups, even family.*

He was scared. Scared to spend time with his own family. She remembered the white-knuckle hold he'd had on the steering wheel, sitting in the parking lot at his own father's restaurant, trying to draw enough courage to go inside. *Do you know, Kit, that being here, helping you, it's done more for me than sitting through group?*

Kit wondered what the answer was, whether it was okay in the short term to let Thatcher draw comfort from allowing him to fuss over her and care for Lily, or whether she should just rip off the proverbial bandage. Were they hurting him more, giving him space he asked for instead of pushing him past his comfort zone? How much was too much to ask of him?

Watching him limp, seeing him fumble things with his left hand sometimes, these were a visual reminder of something greater he'd suffered. Something he hadn't explained yet, didn't want to. Was it okay if he never did? Would he ever be at ease if he didn't?

She thought of Artie, of the eagerness in his little speech

to his staff. The hope in it struck her more as a "fake it 'til you make it" sort of thing. Thatcher wasn't really getting better every day. He was holding steady. He was hiding. He was begging off in group, giving just a tidbit of information each time, usually in the form of an empathetic agreement to someone else's problems. An *I've been there* without ever really saying just where *there* was.

Thatcher tangled her all up in his hope. He all but held his breath waiting for her to accept his invitation to the barbecue. She took the last of the plates from him and dried it and tried not to think about how much she wanted to meet the rest of them. Kit tried to remember all of their names. There was Parker, his wife, and the niece that had made him Uncle Thatcher. There was Greer, the one in construction. And Eden, who apparently owned the company that she'd bought her favorite battery-operated appliance from—not that she'd be mentioning *that* at the family barbecue. Payson and Page, the identical twins. To hear Thatcher tell it, you could tell them apart not only by their different hairstyles, makeup and clothes, but also strictly by their personalities. Sedona, who Thatcher said always had some insane story about her job as an insurance fraud investigator. And Kearny. Sure, she wouldn't mind fangirling over Kearny. Not one bit. She certainly would *not* bring his CD—yeah, she still bought CDs—in hopes she might get an autograph. That would be rude. But her purse was very large, and she had to carry *something* in it when she wasn't stuffing it with free food.

"Kit?" he asked. "Saturday?"

Fucking amber-eyed hope just oozing out all over the place.

She shrugged. "Why not?" A minute later, when he began humming a tune under his breath, she plunked the dried plate into the drainer and said, "Don't read too much into this, Valiant. It's a barbecue, not a date."

He stopped humming and threw the dishtowel he'd

slung over his shoulder down on the counter. "I know."

She had the distinct feeling that he didn't, though.

By Saturday, Kit was asking herself if *she* knew it wasn't a date as she stood in her closet wrapped in a towel and fussed over what to wear.

It's not a date. Put anything on. Anything at all.

When she chose a cute bra and panty set — one of the only matching sets she owned — that's when her inner critic really started shouting.

They. Are. Not. Going. To. See. Your. Underwear!

Put the dress back! Pants. Shorts. Either one. Not a damn dress. This isn't church. It's a damn barbecue.

But she slid into the dress and did a slow turn, checking her ass and wondering whether she was trying too hard.

Yes! It's not a date. Or an interview. Who are you trying to impress? Take it off and put on shorts and a t-shirt!

She didn't. She hadn't worn a dress since before her short-lived service with the Guard. It felt good to feel like a woman. It wasn't for him, no matter what anyone, including her inner critic, thought. The tropical print hi-low dress with its spaghetti strap crisscross back, fitted top and ruffled hem skirt was airy and fun. Although it begged for a pair of high wedges or platform heels, Kit chose a pair of low-heeled sandals.

There's still time to stop this ridiculousness.

She ignored the voice and switched off the light in the walk-in closet.

"Hey, gorgeous!" she smiled as Lily raced toward her in a bright tank dress with summer fruits on it.

Thatcher stood in the archway to the kitchen, just looking at her.

Shit. See? It's too much. He's wondering what the hell you think you're doing.

"I'm going to go change," she turned back toward the bedroom. He lunged forward and caught her wrist.

"Don't. You're…beautiful."

"It's too much. I don't get out often, so—"

"Kit, it's fine," he said. "Leave it."

"It's—"

He pulled her tight against him and tucked his lips close to her ear.

"The only thing wrong with it is I'd like to tear it off you right now, and since that would be totally inappropriate with Lily in the room, I'm going to grab the potato salad and her diaper bag and be right behind you." He kissed her neck and then gently bit her earlobe before releasing her. "Think you can get Lily into the back, or do you need me to do it?"

"I can do it," Kit said and smiled down at her. "C'mon, Lily Bug, let's go for a ride!"

Her lower back and hip protested, but it wasn't bad. Relief flooded through her as the silent clock stopped, the one that had been ticking the days off, testing the hours that slipped by against her improvement. If she could lift her daughter, she could wash dogs.

He'd moved the car seat to the Jeep. Kit bit back a complaint about doing it without asking and another about the fact that she was more than capable of driving. She'd agreed to his help until Sunday night, and she couldn't help noticing their time together would end in one more day.

How had he so quietly fit himself into her life in just six days?

By being his usual Valiant self. He's treated you like a damn queen this week, and Lily like a princess, and you have to ask yourself why you're a little bit sad it's almost over?

Kit threw on a pair of sunglasses, the perfect camouflage for her watery eyes, and watched him efficiently tuck the bag containing their potluck contribution on the floor behind her seat before plunking the diaper bag down behind the driver's seat. Lily was happily distracted by a stuffed toy alligator he'd shown up with after stopping by his house for enough clothing to last the week.

She watched the desert streets blur by against a vividly blue sky so unlike the hazy brown cloud she was used to. The two days of rain had refreshed the city, left it sparkling for a brief while, with greener greens and bluer blues and richer browns. The breeze through their cracked open windows was deliciously perfect…not too hot but not chilly.

His parents' house was a sprawling fusion of Mediterranean and Mission styles. Thatcher pulled into the half-circle double width driveway behind several other vehicles. Even though they weren't touching, she felt him tense. She tensed along with him. This wasn't *We own eight family restaurants* money. This was money in its own right. Old money. She'd been part of a wealthy family until the age of twelve. After that, things started going down the medical toilet, and the financial comfort slowly drained until they stopped shopping at high-end department stores. The home she lived in was an illusion. The car she drove was closer to reality…a fifteen-year-old symbol of frugality that bordered on clunker. Nerves clawed at her.

Kit glanced over at Thatcher. He drew a deep breath and popped open his door.

"Ready to have some fun in the sun?"

She nodded. "Why not?"

Artie met them at the door as Thatcher was opening it.

"Welcome to Phoenix Rise. Kit, wasn't it?" he beamed. Kit frowned. His face lit with understanding. "We named the grill after our homestead," Artie explained. "We call the grill the grill, and we usually call the house 'the Rise' for short."

"It's beautiful," Kit told him, taking in the sprawling great room, from a television nook to another seating area grouped around a gas fireplace, to a giant, intricately detailed dining room table and the kitchen behind it.

Behind a wall just wide enough to hold a huge wall-mounted television was a 90-degree staircase leading to the second floor. Next to it, an archway framed with more of the intricate wood trim led down a shadowy hallway that she supposed held some bedrooms and maybe a bathroom.

Kit suddenly understood Thatcher's nervousness when faced with a crowd of only his own family. As Artie led them through a set of arched doors onto a Saltillo tiled covered patio and turned a corner formed by those rooms off the little hallway she'd seen, they came upon the rest of the group. Between his siblings, their spouses or dates, and the baby, they were quite a bunch. She wished she could tuck her face into the bodice of a grownup's dress the way Lily ducked shyly against her chest upon entering the sizable back yard of the Rise. Kit picked her up and kissed her reassuringly, but she wondered if it was more to comfort herself or Lily.

"Thatcher!" a woman cried, hurrying toward them.

"Hey, Mom," Thatcher said tightly. Kit didn't miss the bleak look in the woman's eyes as they met hers just before she disappeared into her son's embrace. When they parted moments later, Thatcher stepped to the side and said, "This is Kit and her daughter, Lily. Kit, this is my mom, Della."

"Hi, Kit!" Della's smile was like sunshine, warm and welcoming. "Lily is just a little doll! Playing shy, I see, but no one can hold out against this family for long. We'll have her running all over the place in no time."

Lily tucked her face against Kit's shoulder again. The women laughed, and Kit felt the cold clutch of nerves drain away. She wished Thatcher fared as well, but he remained taut beside her as Della made the introductions, ending with Parker and Melody's infant girl, Hayden.

"Oh, goodness!" Kit crooned as Hayden gave her a gummy smile. "How old is she?"

Melody smiled fondly. "Just over seven months. And," she said as Hayden began a plaintive whining, "starting to teethe."

Everyone was friendly and relaxed, but Thatcher remained frozen beside her until it seemed she'd met everyone on the patio.

"Where are Janine and Kearny?" he asked.

"Next door, finishing up with the horses." The oldest brother, Parker, said, popping a grape into his mouth.

Kit blinked. "You have horses?"

Page shook her head. "Used to, but my horrible parents sold that part of the property to our neighbors, Marty and Jean. I'm never forgiving them."

"Page and Payson were horse crazy when they were little. Once they got boobs and boyfriends, they stopped taking care of them like they were supposed to, so Mom and Dad sold them and the east part of this property to the Lunds," his second oldest brother explained.

"Greer!" Della chided.

"What? It's true."

"True but—"

"But filter free, as usual!" Page complained, scooping strands of midnight black hair over her shoulder.

"Greer tells it like he sees it," Melody, Parker's wife, advised, bouncing their baby girl, Hayden, on her lap.

A wood and metal gate across the yard swung open and a woman in a fifties' style sundress, yellow with big red cherries, entered, followed by none other than Kearny Myers, frontman of Ashes Onward. Right there, on the other side of the pool.

Kit watched him follow the woman with the Bettie Page haircut as they made their way toward the patio. He tucked his hand around her elbow as they drew closer to the group.

"Baby bro," Thatcher greeted, his voice at ease for the first time since they arrived.

Kearny's face split into a wide grin. "Thatcheroo!" he cried, reaching a hand out as they hit the brick patio.

Thatcher took it and pulled his brother in for a hug.

"Janine," he nodded.

"Oh, I see. He's the only one who rates a hug?" Janine chided, lightly punching his arm.

"Well," Thatcher teased, letting her slide her arms around his waist for only a moment before pulling back.

She didn't seem the least offended, just popped her eyes wide and began fawning over Hayden before Kearny could trip over Melody's outstretched legs.

Thatcher squeezed Kearny's bicep and said, "C'mon, let's get you through the crazy maze. There's an open chair, but it's not in the shade. If you get too warm, we can move it later."

"Perfect. Lead the way," he answered, slipping his hand in the crook of Thatcher's elbow. "I could use a break, anyway. Those horses are a lot of work. Page. Payson," Kearny's voice rose as he followed Thatcher's leading arm to the arm of a chair and sank down in it.

"Yeah, yeah. No one twists your arm to take care of them when Marty and Jean go out of town," Page fired back.

Flitting around a large, horseshoe-shaped table no doubt custom built for the sizable Myers clan, her twin, Payson added, "And besides, I'm guessing that wasn't the only hard work you were doing over there!"

Janine laughed as Kearny's face reddened a little.

"It wasn't his fault." She laughed again at his mortified expression. "I got a little handsy." Turning her million-watt smile on Kit, she greeted, "I'm Janine, Kearny's fiancée."

As she reached for the woman's hand, Lily leaned outward and reached toward the ground, her way of asking to be put down. Setting her on her feet, Kit watched her sway a bit, then find her footing. Once on the ground, though, she seemed completely uninterested in exploring, preferring to clutch the back of Kit's skirt.

"Kearny," Thatcher said, reaching for Kit's hand, "I'd like you to meet my friend, Kit."

Kit carefully stepped out from the shadowy back porch to take the hand he offered. Aloud, she said a simple hello. Inside, however, she was swooning.

I'm shaking Kearny Myers' hand!

"Hi" He turned the wide grin on her, and she felt a little weak in the knees.

"Hi," she said again and rolled her eyes at herself as she answered Lily's tug of her skirt by picking her up again.

"Who's that you have with you?" Kearny's head tilted.

Startled, Kit said, "Oh! My daughter, Lily!" And then, thoughtlessly, she stuck her foot in her mouth. "You can see her?" Panic rushed through her. "Oh! God! I'm sorry, I—oh, Jesus, I didn't—"

Laughter rang out around her, and Kit wanted the ground to swallow her.

"I've got some light perception," Kearny explained, unruffled. "You blocked the sun, so I can sort of see that. It's kind of hard to describe to people, but I can sometimes make out blurry shapes. No definition at all, just a lighter shadow against a darker shadow or something like that. But the shadow shifted, and there's another weird small shadow down here—" he held a palm out beside his chair, right about at Lily's height, "—so I sort of assumed it was a who and not a what." He didn't seem in the least bothered by her idiocy, but she wanted to run and hide all the same.

"You almost can't offend him, Kit," Page said helpfully. "Not only has he heard it all before, but he's not easily offended to begin with, about anything."

Kit flashed her a grateful smile, rolling her eyes as Lily changed her mind, her body language asking to be put down again. She took a few wobbly steps, then stopped, looking around as if trying to decide if these people were something she wanted to engage with.

"Where did you get that dress, Kit?" Janine asked, redirecting the conversation. "It's gorgeous!"

Her face grew hot as every eye returned to her once

more.

“At Ross,” she said, wondering what kinds of stores a rockstar’s family shopped at. Probably way out of her price range.

Melody smiled. “I *love* Ross. I got this top there.”

“It’s pretty,” Kit said, studying the filmy floral print, startled when Melody leapt to her feet, dropped Hayden in Parker’s lap, and sprinted across the patio.

“Mom! Let me help!”

Della stood frantically clutching three large bowls, one of which threatened to fall to the patio floor.

The oldest Myers sister, Eden, rushed out of the house behind Della, juggling two different plates of buns and a slotted rack full of various condiments. She hurried to deposit them on the table, but Melody beat her to Della’s side, rescuing the teetering bowl.

Thatcher’s little sister, Sedona, hurried to grab another.

“Mom, you should have told us you were ready to set the table,” she chided, easing the bowl to safety. “You don’t have to do everything!”

Kit looked for Lily only to see her chubby hand land on Kearny’s knee. She didn’t realize she was holding her breath until Kearny’s face split into a grin.

“Hey, there,” he greeted, gently finding Lily’s hand and stroking it with a finger.

Kit bit back an *awwww* as Lily gave his knee a few soft pats and toddled to Thatcher.

Bit by bit, as his family buzzed and chattered around him, Thatcher seemed to unwind. He refused the offer of a beer from his dad, taking a seat between his father and Kearny at the table. Kit sat across from him, sandwiched between Della and Sedona, the insurance fraud investigator, who told a funny story about a tiny, older Italian woman she’d dubbed Mrs. Cosa Nostra.

“I’m sitting in her kitchen, my digital recorder’s rolling with her full knowledge and permission, and she’s sweet as can be, offering me coffee cake and something to drink. I start asking her about this diamond ring of hers that vanished, and she's giving me an incredibly detailed description. Old, European cut diamond that nobody does anymore, flanked by two smaller round cuts in this very detailed Art Deco filigree band, white gold, just over 3 carats total weight, excellent clarity and color and worth over twenty grand. Then she reaches across the table to a lazy Susan where she's got these amazing, ornate teacups face down in their saucers, and grabs one to pour herself some tea. And there in the saucer is a ring that for all the world looks like the exact ring she just described. She drops the teacup back down over it very quickly, obviously hoping I didn't see it. I pretended not to have, pointing across the room at an old painting on the wall and asking her a question about it. She grabs the teacup next to it and makes an excuse about the other one having a broken handle and not wanting to end up with hot tea in her lap."

Kit laughed. "What did you do then? Did you call her on it?"

Sedona shook her head and took a bite from her corn on the cob before answering. "Not right away. I had her go through all the details with me again, like 'Where did you see it last? Are you sure that's the last place you saw it? Do you have any other similar rings that might be mistaken for that one?' and she's emphatic that it was the only ring on the planet of its kind and dead certain she last saw it on her bedroom dresser in a little ring dish handed down from her grandma from all the way back in Sicily. She drags me down the hall to show me the ring dish, even."

"Sicily? Seriously?" Artie chuckled.

"Seriously, Dad. We make our way back to the kitchen, and that's when I drop the bomb on her. I reach out and lift the teacup, and I take a photo of the ring sitting there in the saucer. I ask her to explain the ring's presence there. She pretends to be surprised and thrilled to have found it and oh, she's so sorry she wasted my time. I've made an old Italian woman very happy, and she guesses we can just close the claim, all's well that ends well."

"Oh, man. She just gets away with it?" Chance, Greer's adopted teenage son, dropped his own ear of corn, partly amused and obviously partly disgusted, too, judging by the look on his face.

"No. Not at all. Because then I pull out a copy of some paperwork from the insurance company she was with before us, and here the same ring is scheduled for eighteen thousand, and they paid her for a total loss of the same ring last year in January. I show her the copy they sent me of the cashed check and the settlement letter and even a copy of the appraisal she provided them. Then I drop the appraisal she gave us on the table. Same one."

Eden's jaw dropped. "Oh, my God. What did she do when you showed her that?"

Sedona laughed. "She started making all these veiled threats. She knows my name. It's very unusual. She's got family she can 'involve' in this matter. People who threaten her, things don't go well for them."

"Jesus," Greer said, going a little pale. "Sed..."

Concerned looks bounced around the table like tennis balls at Wimbledon.

Before Kit could ask, Sedona waved it off with a chuckle. "Relax. Let me finish. I reach over for my iPhone, because the recorder is an app on my phone that saves the conversation in real time to my office hard drive. I can tell she's forgotten all about it, and I want to get it before she remembers and does something stupid. Or tries to. As soon as I tell her all of that, she bursts into tears and begs me not to call the police, not to arrest an old woman. She's sitting in a million-dollar home along the Camelback corridor, expensive artwork and furnishings all around us, and tries to convince me she's down to pennies on a fixed monthly income. I'm sitting there thinking, if you're hurting for money lady, why not sell all this stuff and the house? You'll be able to live comfortably for the rest of your life on the proceeds." Sedona shook her head.

Kit felt gutted. Would that be how they would look at her, living in her mother's half-million-dollar home? With derision? Would they scoff at her for hanging on to it when she could barely pay the electric bill?

"Maybe she is, Sed. Circumstances can change," Thatcher said. Kit suddenly felt a shoe nudge her ankle. He wasn't looking at her, but she knew it was him when the shoe nudged again.

"True," Sedona nodded. "But because I had had her sign a credit authorization prior to this interview and it came back with several accounts funded in the high six figures, it's pretty clear that hers haven't changed."

"And Cosa Nostra goes down!" Chance cried, fist pumping the air.

Laughter rang out around the table as Sedona nodded. "She'll be lucky if she avoids jail. We'll deny the claim for misrepresentation and send her file to the NICB—" looking at Kit, she added, "National Insurance Crime Bureau—but who knows what the other insurance company will do?"

The conversation shifted, hitting on each person at the table. Laughter and good-natured teasing were prevalent. The one thing the table lacked was space for a high chair, so everyone casually passed Hayden and Lily around, feeding them safe tidbits from their own plates using clean plastic spoons. Kit initially worried that while Hayden seemed accustomed to the baby passing, Lily would freak out at so many strange people. She fussed a little each time a new person took her, and shrieked when Thatcher passed her to his father, but amazingly, she settled quickly, pacified by little bites of food. Some potato salad here, some baked beans there. Juice cups followed each child as if tethered to their wrists.

Toward the end of the meal, Chance made a face.

"Ohhhhhh," he groaned, rising with Lily, a dark stain on his cargo shorts. "She's leaky."

Kit felt her face go hot.

Stupid cheap diapers!

Kit leapt to her feet, but Della took her wrist gently.

"Family tradition," she said. Calling across to Chance, she asked, "What's the rule?"

"Whoever has the hot potato when it leaks or stinks gets diaper duty," he said, grimacing.

"You don't have to do that," she said and tried to tug her arm free.

"Sit down," Della said mildly. "Chance knows the rule, and he knows his way to the nursery."

"He's an excellent babysitter, if you need one," Melody added. "Just make sure the fridge is fully stocked, because he's at that age."

"What age? There's no age," Artie laughed. "You kids are still eating me out of house and home whenever you're all here."

Kit hesitated. They all seemed great, but she'd never left Lily alone with a total stranger before. Thatcher gave her a wink.

"It's okay," he told her, finishing his lemonade and easing to his feet. "I'll supervise. Make sure he powders the right end."

She sat down as Thatcher grabbed the diaper bag she'd brought just in case.

Sitting back in her chair, relieved more than she wanted to admit, Kit listened to the light-hearted chatter around the table and rebuked herself silently.

Do not *start falling in love with these people. Do. Not.*

CHAPTER FIFTEEN

Late afternoon slid toward evening, the sun casting a brilliant orange light over the desert as it dropped lower in the sky.

Kit wanted to stay there on her comfy lounge chair forever, but Thatcher invited her to tour the pool house and his temporary quarters above it. Janine volunteered to look after Lily as she toddled around in the grass.

Kit stood in the doorway of the small bedroom that was the end of the short tour and held her tongue when it wanted to invite him to stay with her a little longer. She couldn't quite find the words to object when he pulled her into the bedroom and closed the door, backing her up against it and devouring her mouth.

"I've wanted to do that since we got here," he panted, rocking against her until she was incapable of coherent thought. Until she couldn't use their privacy to ask about his two lengthy disappearances into the main house, once right before lunch, and again just after the meal.

She felt uncomfortably damp under her dress and all too aware that the longer they waited to rejoin the party, the more people would wonder where they were and what was keeping them. And the more likely she'd be to give up and let him take her right there in his little bachelor pad. She didn't need any knowing looks or teasing innuendos like the one Payson had given Kearny and Janine earlier.

"You've done it," she said, kissing him one last time. "We need to get back before—"

He kissed her shoulder, cupping her breast. His tongue traced its way to her throat, sending shivers and a pool of heat downward. She pushed back.

"We've been in here too long, Valiant. Let's go back before someone comes looking for us."

"Not yet," he whispered huskily, dancing her backward onto the bed.

"Shit, you're good at that," she moaned as his fingers quickly found their way past her panties. "We need to—"

"Let me do this," he urged. And with that, he ducked under her skirt, tugged her panties down, and clamped his lips over her clit.

"Dammit, Valiant," she protested weakly as heat pulsed under his assault. It was growing harder to care what his family was thinking, whether they missed them.

"I want you to come," he murmured, his tongue flitting into her core. "I want you screaming on my bed."

"Not gon-na ha—happen," she stuttered, hips lunging upward. "Too loud. Someone might he-hear!" she exclaimed, then clamped her hand over her mouth at the volume.

"No?" he swirled his tongue inside her.

She grabbed a pillow just in time to muffle the scream he wanted, then tossed it aside because seeing the shape of him under her dress, feeling the delicious suction of his lips and tongue around her clit again, had her coming in hard, hopeless, breathless spasms.

And to her surprise, instead of plunging into her in search of his own orgasm, he pulled her panties back into place, smoothed her skirt with a rakish grin and offered her a hand up. The question must have been in her eyes, because he licked his lips and wiped his mouth and mimicked her words.

"Let's get back. Don't want them wondering."

Heading out the door and back down the steps on rubbery legs was tough when all she wanted to do was turn back, shove him inside, lock the door, and throw up her skirt again, this time to make *him* muffle his pleasure with a pillow. Quick and dirty. She shivered again and kept going back to the patio with nothing but sheer willpower to get her there.

No one seemed concerned about the length of their absence.

Della and Page were just bringing out several pie tins, paper plates, and a re-stocked cutlery caddy as they made their way back to the patio. Instead of using the large table again, they clustered on lounges and chairs. The key lime pie was light and fluffy and perfect for a mild evening outdoors. The phosphorescent light from the pool and the gentle lighting on the patio dropped the many threads of conversation to a low murmur.

Kit thought she'd faint dead away when, shortly after the dessert dishes had been cleared, Thatcher casually placed a guitar in Kearny's lap. A jar full of plastic poker chips made its rounds until Sedona placed it in her hands, whispering for her to take a chip and pass it on. Kearny picked out a few lazy notes, made a few adjustments, and asked, "What does the random number generator say?"

"Hold on, I'm still setting it up," Page replied, poking at her phone. "Eight!"

Kit glanced at hers. Six.

Della whooped and held up her chip.

"Hold on to that," Thatcher whispered. "He usually does three solos, and then everyone is expected to join in after that."

She gave Thatcher a questioning look.

"He loves singing and performing," he told her quietly, "but he gets so many demands, you know, when he's just trying to be Kearny. Any party he goes to, his friends want a concert. We didn't realize it was wearing on him until one time he kind of melted down."

Kit nodded. "So, poker chips and limits."

"Yep."

"Mom? You there?" Kearny asked, plucking the 'Jeopardy' theme.

"Oh, stop, you nut!" Della laughed. "I'm thinking. It's my *one* song!"

Kit glanced at Kearny, then back at Thatcher. "That's fair," she said.

"Yeah. And don't get me wrong. He does love it. But—"

"But it sucks to feel like the only reason people want you around is your music," Kit finished. The appreciative look Thatcher gave her felt like a cross between a deep kiss and a sucker punch. If she hadn't been seated, she'd have plopped backward, boneless.

"What'll it be, Ma?" Kearny asked, back to picking at random notes.

"Patience," Della answered.

"Sorry," Kearny teased.

"Guns N' Roses' 'Patience'!" Della laughed. "You're so incorrigible!"

Melody clutched her chest. "Ohhh, I love 'Patience.'"

Kearny's soft rendition gave Kit shivers up and down her spine and goosebumps along her arms. She was glad she wasn't the only one who broke into enthusiastic applause afterward.

"Next?" Kearny asked.

A voice called out toward the front of the house. "Wait, wait, wait! I want my chip!"

A pretty strawberry blonde in dress slacks and a nice blouse rushed into view and, in turn, kissed Chance on the cheek and Greer on the lips.

"You missed the first one, Shelb," Kearny called out cheerfully. "'Patience.'"

"Aw, damn!" she cried. "You know I love that one."

Kearny shrugged. "Maybe next time."

She sighed. "Can you wait for two minutes while I change out of these clothes?"

"Start the stopwatch," Greer joked.

"Whose side are you on?" she laughed, and Kit realized she had a noticeable baby bump.

Greer grinned and gave her a pat on the bottom. "Yours. Always. But you know Kearny will try to cut it short."

"Don't you dare," she shot back, pointing at Kearny.

Kit was glad she wasn't the only one who forgot and used gestures he couldn't see.

When she returned in a short floral dress, Kit shot her a look of appreciation. She *was* overdressed, though no one seemed to care. "Hi!" she waved at Kit as she situated herself on Greer's lap. He placed a protective palm on her swollen belly. "I'm Shelby. I was pulling clinic time."

"Doctor," Greer paused to kiss her deeply, "can you take a look at my—"

"Shut up," she laughed.

"Lucky thirteen!" Page called.

Thatcher lifted his chip and said so quietly she almost couldn't hear, "'Fantastic Four.'"

Kearny looked stricken. "You sure?" he asked softly.

The patio grew still, like the calm before a storm. Kit searched her mind for a Smoke/Fire/Ash song called "Fantastic Four" and came up empty. Was it his? Was it a cover? Was it something his new band, Ashes Onward, was working on? She didn't know. But the atmosphere had grown thick and leaden with something. Something not good.

"Yeah. Please," Thatcher said, swallowing so hard Kit heard it. He fumbled his hand into hers, gave a little squeeze and whispered, "This is the most I can say about…things. For now."

Kearny sat forward in his chair, fingers hovering over the strings, reluctant to begin. "Thatch…"

Thatcher rasped, "I want to hear it."

Kearny let out a deep sigh and closed his eyes, his brow furrowing. Kit thought he looked like someone being forced to play at gunpoint. Notes she didn't recognize rose slowly.

"Little boys playing hero
Always the brave
Always the strong
Death wasn't forever and
The good guys always won
Didn't know back then how it could all go wrong

Grew up...thought we knew it all
Invincible badasses headed for a fall.
Felt too much of everything
Out to prove ourselves...escape ourselves
Signed the devil's pact with a cheap ass pen
Kissed love goodbye until God knows when.

Started out strangers, but when shit hit fan
We were close as brothers, man to man
Was a long, hard fight, but we knew the score
...might not come back from this real-life war.
Marked the days with every bullet and bomb
In a hell where time stood still but the world moved on—"

Kearny's face twisted and his jaw twitched, but he shook his head a little and kept singing.

"And they all fall down...
—can't hear you, I'm screaming—
And they all fall down...
Wake me up, please tell me I'm dreaming

And they all fall down...
—can't hear you, I'm screaming—
And they all fall down...

Wake me up, please tell me I'm dreaming

In the silent dark I prayed
Could feel you one last breath away
But then we all fell down
—can't hear you, still screaming—
Wake me up, please tell me I'm dreaming
I don't wanna play no more
God, I miss you, Fantastic Four."

Kit sat frozen, tears streaming down her cheeks as the final somber note faded. She heard other sniffles but didn't dare look around. It was a sacred moment. When she came back to herself fully, she realized she was stroking the back of Thatcher's hand with her thumb. He broke the silence first, pulling his hand from hers to clap. The others joined in softly, golf clapping.

Kearny let out a little cough. "Page?"

"Um, yeah, one sec. Um, six."

"Me," Kit said quietly.

"What would you like to hear?"

Anything that will make me feel like I can breathe again.

"Do you know 'Brown-Eyed Girl?'"

"Van Morrison? Hell, yeah," Kearny grinned. Soft laughter bit through the shadows on the patio.

When he finished the song, he called for the sing-along to start. Kit learned that he always chose the first song. He chose "The Joker".

Several songs later, Kearny eased back into a soft tune she'd never heard. Before he began to sing, he said softly, "It's getting late, so these last few are for the kiddos."

Greer snorted, but his reply was quiet. "We're not at a concert. You don't have to announce what you're doing."

Kearny's voice returned to normal volume. "Shut up, Greer!"

He then proceeded to play a series of lullabies that had Kit half asleep, herself. At the end of the last one, his voice broke through her fuzzy drifting. "On that note, I think I'm going to ask my lovely almost-wife to drive us home. Now *I'm* tired."

"Awww, look. You put Thatch to sleep with the babies," Greer chuckled.

Kit looked over and, sure enough, he was out, Lily sprawled on his chest, drowsy but awake, her thumb tucked in her mouth. Her heart quivered in her chest at the sight. Was there anything so tender as a man, sleeping, cradling a child against him? Kit reached out and stroked Lily's soft cheek. One of Thatcher's hands slipped from her back as his muscles fully gave way to sleep, and it roused him.

Hearing everyone exchanging goodbyes, he sat up, clutching Lily carefully, cupping the back of her head in his palm. "Hey, Lil' Miss," he greeted, as if she'd suddenly appeared in his arms from nowhere. He kissed her temple. "You ready to go home?"

Kit fought a grin. *Someone* was ready to go home. She wasn't sure Lily cared one way or the other.

She stilled.

Oh, no. No, no, no.

Don't start.

She said her goodbyes, hugged all these new, wonderful people, and rode silently beside Thatcher, trying to talk herself out of a headlong drop into the last thing she wanted.

Love.

CHAPTER SIXTEEN

"Sunday night," Kit told him lightly. "Back to reality tomorrow."

His heart slumped in his chest. Or felt like it, anyway.

He reached over and settled the last dish in the drainer to the side of the sink. Tossing the towel into the laundry basket as he passed the utility room door, he sat down at the table in the breakfast nook, his heart feeling as creaky as the chair.

"I appreciate everything you've done this week, Valiant," Kit said, a goodbye speech if he'd ever heard one. She hesitated only a moment before stepping between his legs. One hand on his chest, Thatcher sensed she used it not for intimacy but for the opposite, thwarting his attempt to draw her in and kiss her senseless.

She didn't wipe away all the bad, didn't magically stop all his nightmares. No one and nothing could. But over the course of this week with her and Lily, he'd felt more settled. Less anxious. Less aimless. He'd had a task, albeit a temporary one, and he'd enjoyed doing it.

Kit filled an empty place in him he hadn't known needed filling. He wanted to tell her, but she held all the chips. Until now, he'd let her hold them. Holding them calmed her skittishness. But he wanted so much more of her than she'd been willing to let him have. Her walls were so high and thick, he thought he might never make it through.

"Hey," she nudged him with the hand on his chest,

"where'd you go?"

"Sorry, what?" he looked up at her.

"You've been great, Valiant. My house hasn't been this organized or my lawn so gorgeous in a long time. But I need you to ease up now. I feel much better. The bruises are fading, see?"

She turned and flipped her shirt up, hauling the waistband of her yoga pants down. Sure enough, the bruise at her hip was shifting from a deep, scary black to a mottled mess of browns, greens, and yellows. Still large, still having no goddamn place on her skin. But any illusion that she needed him as much as he'd come to need her, to want her, was rapidly fading.

He nodded, his heart aching in his chest. He'd truly hoped that he might put a crack in the fortress around her heart.

"I'm going to get a shower," she said, stepping back. "When the laundry's done, Valiant, it's time for you to pack up and head home."

He sat glumly at the table, knowing he should start packing his bag, start pulling his clean clothes from the laundry basket behind him, start untangling them from Lily's tiny clothes and silky things of Kit's that he'd only caught brief glimpses of. The second load of washing would be done soon, ready for the dryer. And then he'd have the rest of his clothes and no further excuse or stay of execution.

His eyes roved over the napkin holder she'd converted into a mail caddy. Fingering one of the envelopes idly, he wasn't terribly disappointed when it slipped out of the pile.

Past due! It screamed in red on a white background. He grabbed the rest. *Final notice. Due now. Urgent Attention Needed.*

Glancing down the hall, he rose from the chair to seek out his phone. Four of the bills allowed payment without any kind of login. Three others he shoved into the bottom of his duffel for later. He made it back into the chair, but he was still sliding the torn envelopes back into place when Kit's voice exclaimed,

"Valiant! Goddamn it, quit snooping in my mail!" She pulled the now opened bills from the holder. "What is it with you and this fucking savior complex?" She tossed them down in front of him, eyes flashing. "For the last time, I *don't* need you to save me! I don't *want* you to save me. I have to do this myself. What about that don't you get?" Anger and weariness warred with each other in her words.

"The part where in two days, Lily will be in a house with no power, no water, and where you won't have an active cell phone to call for help from if you managed to put your pride aside long enough," he told her flatly, considering it a win when she didn't pull her hands out of his and, in fact, allowed him to tug her between the cradle of his thighs. "Pay me back if you want. Just let me do this for you."

"Valiant," she half-sighed, half-screeched. "Why do you have to have such a thick skull about this?"

"Why do you, Kit?" he countered, his hands tracing her waist, taking in the impossibly soft fabric of what could only be an ancient nightshirt.

"Because, Daddy Warbucks, help is not free. There are always strings."

He held up his hands. "No strings. I promise."

"That's only reason one," she told him as he put his hands on her waist again.

"And two?"

"My prick of an ex."

"David? What does he have to do with this?"

"Everything. Whether he's a narcissist or just a total asshole, he took everything from me and left. Forgive me if I prefer to expect nothing from anyone. And maybe he hasn't given us a second thought, but I really can't stand thinking he might be out there expecting me to fall on my face without him. I'll be damned if that's going to happen."

Thatcher nodded. "Fair enough. But maybe I don't want you to fall on your face, either. So—"

"—so, you're the third reason, Warbucks."

"Me?" Thatcher dropped his hands from her waist, where they'd been absently stroking her, and crossed his arms in front of his chest. When she didn't answer, he slid his right hand up under the bottom hem of her nightshirt to trace the curve of her ass.

"You. I know what kind of money you make—or, made—Warbucks. Military pay tables are public information. I know approximately what kind of money you made." She looked away from him, her breath catching slightly as he cupped her whole bottom with both hands. "So, unless you're a trust fund baby, I—"

"I'm not," he assured her, moving his hands so one held her left hip and the other urged her closer to him. "I enlisted right after high school, the day after my 18th birthday, and except for the Jeep, some birthday and Christmas gifts over the years, a few incidentals on base, and the occasional expense during leave or between deployments, I saved or invested what I earned. I get a small portion of the profits from the restaurants also. Nothing I could live off of, but it was often enough when I lived on base that I used it for expenses. I can handle a few bags of groceries and a few bills, no sweat."

She sighed as he stood and settled his mouth over hers. He felt her begin to yield, but then she pushed him back.

"You can't just barge in here and steamroll over everything I have to say about it."

"I'm not trying to steamroll you. I'm trying to help."

"I know," she said huskily, leaning slightly forward to press her lips to his.

He kissed her deeply, tasting, longing, urging. Those little happy noises of hers that almost undid him started up, and he went from mildly aroused to rock hard, idly fingering the waist band of her panties under her nightshirt. She gasped into his mouth as he traced the delicate place where her thigh met her labia. When he lightly traced the seam of her, she backed up a step.

Blinking at him as if waking from a dream, she stumbled over her next words as he sat back down and coaxed her closer again.

"I'm not…" she drew a breath as he did it again, curving one slow finger against her, dipping a little inward, brushing wet heat that made his flesh throb forcefully. "I'm not trying to be a bitch or unappreciative. I need—" she moaned as he slid one finger inside her. "I need to do this on my o-own, Thatcher!"

He froze, his finger quiet inside her just as she dug her hands into his hair. Sensing the change, she looked down at him, her eyes smoky and dazed.

"What?"

"Say it again," he growled, thumbing her clit.

"What?" she murmured, kneading his shoulders now.

"My name," he said, sliding a second finger in after the first, pulling them toward him.

"Thatcher," she chuckled huskily, eyes closing as her hips rocked toward him. His name, uttered with desire, had his cock pressing so hard against the seam of his fly it hurt. "Thatcher!" It exploded from her as she raked through his hair, now, bucking eagerly toward his thrusting, twisting fingers. She swore softly, her head dipping back as she all but rode his fingers now.

He moaned, nestling his face against her belly.

"Thatcher!" she cried, urging with her voice and her hips.

He tongued her navel, rubbing his thumb over and around her clit with increasing speed.

"Thatcher! Thatcher! Thatcher!" she teased urgently, laughing and moaning before falling to wordlessness as he felt her wet heat begin to clench and unclench around his fingers. His cock jumped at the sensation, and he wanted to dump her roughly on the table and bury it deep, but instead, he slowed his stroking fingers to match the slowing of her hips. She sighed his name a last time, still clutching him tightly as the final little ripples of her orgasm coursed through her.

She stumbled as he withdrew his fingers. He guided her to sit on his good thigh. Her eyes regarded him with a softer look than ever before, roving over his lips before her fingertips traced them and her mouth followed. When she pulled back to catch a breath, her whisper stabbed him deep.

"You're really going to fuck me up, aren't you?"

He didn't get a chance to deny it before her mouth covered his again, stifling his protest. Before he could get enough of her mouth, she left him, tugging at his fly. He obediently lifted his hips, ignoring the angry sizzle of pain as he did so. Impatient, she only shoved his jeans and boxers to his knees before she latched that sweet, dirty mouth of hers around his rigid flesh.

The shocked sound that burst out of him only egged her on. Thatcher struggled not to blow in her mouth. Watching her come undone moments earlier, dropping that steely guard, he'd nearly come, himself.

Don't look. Don't look down, he told himself, tipping his head back in delirium, instead. If he didn't look down, he wouldn't see her spiky head bobbing fast. Putting that image to the sensations would be entirely too much. He tried not to hear those crazy, delicious happy noises or feel the vibration of them against his cock and all through him.

He flexed his hips a little, wanting to shove upward, to fuck her mouth, but it was tempered by the hot needles of pain sizzling down from his left hip into his leg.

Nope. Ignoring that.

He thrust up again, harder this time, and she circled the

base of him with her fingers, sliding a finger from the other hand under him, pressing it gently behind his balls. His hips pumped again, pain be damned.

"Kit," he begged, not entirely sure what he was begging for...for her to stop before he flooded her mouth or for her to never, ever stop. "Kit," he warned huskily, hips jerking again.

She made a choking sound, freezing as a wordless sound somewhere between agony and ecstasy burst out of him. He burned from the inside out, moving again, uncontrollably, but half-restrained by her forceful hand on his right thigh. He made the mistake of catching her eyes with his own and surged forth, unable to stop it from ripping through him as she locked eyes with him, riding it with him.

She lifted a hand to wipe her mouth.

Dirty.

Sexy.

Mine, his mind insisted.

All strength left him, the pain he'd earlier refused hitting him full force now, his left thigh and hip muscles spasming angrily. He put a hand on his upper thigh and stifled a different type of groan.

"Shit," she said softly, still crouched between his legs. Her eyes roved over the red, puckered, jagged appearance of his skin where, not terribly long ago, it sported hundreds of stitches and a few dozen staples. "Did I hurt you, Valiant?"

She didn't wait for his answer, just rose and grabbed a fistful of paper towels, dampening them at the sink.

"No regrets," he croaked, sliding downward a little so he could drop his head down on the back of the chair. It was useless to deny that he was hurting. Kit hesitated beside him, the clump of damp paper towels clutched in her hand until he took them from her gently, granting her silent permission to look away from the hideousness of his injuries while he clumsily cleaned himself up.

She disappeared from his view, busying herself as he tipped his hips, trying not to wince as he pulled up his boxers and jeans. The washing machine lid banged shut, followed by the dryer door. A dial turned noisily, and the sound of the dryer's drum covered the sound of her return.

He watched her, waiting with growing dread for her to thank him again, a subtle invitation for him to leave. Only the clothes still tumbling in the dryer stood between him and the departure he'd been dreading almost since he'd arrived.

She grabbed two bottles of water from the fridge, twisting one open. He watched her throat work as she swallowed and flashed back to her between his knees. A fresh wave of lust crested over him.

To his surprise, nothing in her face had changed. Her eyes were still full of all the fire and sass that made her Kit. Her appraisal of him was still guarded yet full of hunger, fully lacking the pitying disinterest he'd feared.

He stood as gracefully as the muscle fatigue would allow, one hand grabbing the second bottle of water as the other tossed the paper towels into the trash can with what he hoped was nonchalance. They stared at each other as he downed half the bottle.

"Ready for round two?" she asked as he wiped his mouth with his forearm.

"Hell, yes," he said.

CHAPTER SEVENTEEN

Good God.

She was somewhere outside herself.

Liquid.

Boneless.

Thatcher was…holy shit.

Kit whimpered loudly as he, lying on his right side, worked his way, kissing and licking and nibbling, from her mouth to her belly button to…lower. Magic freaking tongue.

Magic.

A hard, focused point just where she wanted it most, and a fluttery wisp in the next shuddering breath. He nipped at her inner thigh and she threw it wide in a silent plea.

Yes, please.

More, please.

Sweet Jesus.

That last thought she might have gasped aloud. Probably had, because he chuckled softly and the vibration of it against her swollen flesh had her hips doing her begging for her when her mouth could only find wordless nonsense.

Hard. Soft. Hard. Soft.

He was killing her with that mouth.

Those eyes, when she met them, unleashed her words.

"Now," she sighed.

He rose up over her, propped on his right elbow, and his head dropped.

"Shit," he groaned. "I don't have anything with me."

Fuuuck.

She didn't, either. She'd never imagined wanting anything to do with a man, at least not anytime soon.

"How many?" she asked, stroking the damp hair at the base of his skull.

"How many what?" he asked, contenting himself by tonguing her again. She tugged his hair, forcing him to lift his head or lose a handful.

"Partners, Thatcher."

His jaw clenched. She feared the number, picturing him notching his bedpost into sawdust with a reaction like that.

"Three," he finally answered, crawling up beside her. He must have seen the doubt she tried to hide.

His jaw twitched again. "Ten years in the Army, Kit. Two combat deployments of nine months and one for twelve, and three non-combat deployments for twelve months each. Not much time for dating or getting serious in between. One was my high school girlfriend, well before I enlisted. The other two were friends with benefits during dwell time. Always with condoms. Both of them ended things with me when they began seriously dating other guys."

She traced the muscles of his abdomen until he grabbed her hand.

"You?" he asked.

"No one since David," she told him, watching him lick his lips. She chased his tongue back into his mouth, kissing him until he pulled back with a soft groan. "Four guys before that, all with protection." She slid her hand downward along his abdomen, but he stopped her just short of the tip of him. "I'm on the pill, and we wouldn't be here if I didn't trust you. So, I—"

He silenced her with his mouth, grinding his hard length against her, teasing. Promising.

"You don't have to build me back up, Buttercup," she gasped as he nudged her again, his cock sliding along her folds.

He laughed, his mouth buried against her neck, his breath tickling her skin. And then he lifted those ridiculously sexy eyes to her, desire flaring, the flash point reached, and slid inside her.

Oh.

God.

The words panted out before she could stop them. He moaned in reply.

Thatcher bowed into her once, twice, three times, each thrust deliciously harder, deeper than the last, before his left arm folded under him, pitching him to her right side. The redness of his face, she realized with horror, wasn't from exertion.

"Off," she ordered softly, gently pushing his right shoulder, nudging his right hip with her own. He resisted, his muscles turning to stone. She slid one hand down his lower belly, circling there so that he pulled in a sharp breath. "Hey." Kit moved the fingers of her other hand to his temple. "Look at me," she ordered.

He met her eyes, his jaw clenching. She reached lower and stroked him, felt the wetness of herself on his length. He pulsed in her hand. She squeezed a little when he tried to look away.

"On your back," she whispered and felt the resurgence of his interest in her hand.

When she rose over him, those eyes flashed again, then slid closed as she sat up fully, rocking, and guided him to the quick rhythm she needed. "Eyes on me, Thatcher," she urged, and locked hers on those amber depths. "Touch me," she panted, reaching down to open herself for him.

He didn't disappoint. He met her with his fingers, following as she moved, back and forth, faster, faster. His nostrils flared, his eyes flashed and rolled back on a muttered stream of naughty words and delicious promises.

Kit jerked involuntarily as his hands found her hips and

the still healing bruise.

"Shit," he gasped, lifting that hand instantly. "Sorry. Are you—"

"Hush!" She brought herself down on him harder, faster. "Thatcher!" She felt it building, felt it at the base of her spine, tingling into her legs, making them weak as her orgasm rushed just to the edge of that tenuous cliff but not over it. And then his hips jerked, his breath caught, and she felt the pulse of him inside her, letting go. She began her own free fall, her body fluttering and clutching around him.

His hips bumped upward a last time. Kit leaned forward to ease off of him, but he growled and locked his arms around her, bringing her to a sprawl on top of him. She rode the rise and fall of his breath, drowsing there, half-tickled by the slow, light stroke of his fingers along her spine.

This was where she needed to open up her mouth and suggest that the laundry must be done by now, but the words drifted as she drifted, floating in the place where the rhythm of his heart under her cheek made more sense than the notion that either of them should move.

~~~

Monday's group was difficult for several reasons. First, because Kit seemed embarrassed to find their circle of chairs was now back on the theater floor instead of on the stage, which was something the group had arranged the week before in their absence. Second, because he and Kit agreed to keep their…whatever this was (Kit's words) to themselves, and the secret made his hands itch to hold her and his mouth long to taste her. He had to force his eyes away with increasing frequency. Last, because Kit joined the rest of them in trying to pull more of his past into the
~~~

light. The more they pushed, the more he instinctively shut down or pushed back. Inevitably, he'd begin to feel the stranglehold of anxiety reaching upward, tightening its claws around his throat. George would notice and redirect the conversation, to his eternal gratitude.

This time, George turned to Kit and told her she seemed to be doing much better.

"I am. I've got some amazing friends who took care of me all last week," she said. "I'm sorry I missed the sessions. I was pretty much under lock and key. My nursemaid had me riding the sofa, catching up on Netflix."

Terry grinned, smoothing his hands over his large gut. "What are you complaining about? Sounds like my kind of week."

Kit's transient gaze hit Thatcher low in the belly. Remembering how their time together had ended, he shifted on his chair.

"Speaking of amazing friends," Mike said, leaning forward in his chair, "some anonymous person pulled my ass out of the fire and paid my rent last week."

Thatcher inwardly winced at the thought of Jenny waiting for him to return, only to be disappointed day after day. He'd been so focused on Kit and Lily he'd completely forgotten about the rental. And now he didn't want to lock himself into anything.

"A silent angel," George offered with a smile. "That's good news."

"It's obvious, is what it is," Mike said, looking around the circle. "Which one of you did it? 'Fess up." When no one spoke, his voice cracked. "Well, thanks. Whoever it was. Or if you all pooled your money or something. Whatever. Thanks. You need anything, you ask me. I'll be there. Even you," he nodded toward Gil after giving Kit a quick look.

Gil snorted. "What makes you think it was any of us?"

"Because I don't go around telling people my

problems," Mike answered, looking around the circle again. "Except in here. My own mother doesn't know how close I came to getting evicted. But you all do."

Oops. Caught. Thatcher glanced around the circle. Perhaps because they were used to fighting much worse secrets, no one gave anything away. He wasn't registering any "tells".

Gil huffed. "Well, as many warm fuzzies as your story brings, I wonder if anybody thought about the fact that your rent is going to be due again in another month, and you're not gonna have that, either, if you don't get a job soon. You gonna cry again then, hoping someone will come to your rescue?"

Mike sighed. "Well, now I know who *didn't* save my ass. Thanks for ruling yourself out, Gil." Mike gave him the finger.

Thatcher bit back a laugh.

"Does it really matter?" George asked. "I think the thing to take away is that we should all help others when we can, whether with money or a shoulder or our time."

Mike nodded. "Amen." He looked at Gil again and said, "And for your information, Gil, I had another three interviews last week, and just this morning I was hired by that same insurance company that gave me the 'sorry, no dice' letter. Instead of the insurance section, I'll be working in the mortgage department. I guess one hand didn't know what the other was up to when it came to the letter, but I start next Monday."

"Whoopdeedo," Gil scoffed. "Now you can pull your big kid pants up and start paying your own bills."

Mike shook his head and rolled his eyes. "Whatever, dude."

Donnie nodded, too. "Seriously, Gil, I think I'll die on the spot if you ever say a kind word to anyone."

"Promise? 'Cause that sounds like something I could get behind," Gil folded his arms across his chest.

"Gil," George said mildly. Gil shut up but offered no apology. Turning back to Donnie, he asked, "Do you have anything you'd like to discuss, Donnie? It's been a while since you've had anything to share."

Donnie shrugged. "Things are the same. Nothing ever changes. I do good for a while, and then something happens and I go back to feeling like nothing matters," he shrugged.

Thatcher knew that feeling. He was in the throes of 'things are looking up', waiting for the other shoe to drop, himself.

"Something happens? Like what?" George asked.

Donnie shrugged again. It was like his signature move, those lanky shoulders lifting and lowering. "Anything bad. Car trouble, a fight with my wife, my kid having a bad day at school. One part of me knows this stuff is normal, these annoyances happen to everyone. But little things just knock me down."

"That's depression," George said. "Are you taking your medication?"

Donnie nodded. "I hate it, though. It makes me tired all day and then I can't sleep at night. And, you know, if I'm going to drop into a dark hole every time some little thing happens, what's the point?"

"Have you spoken to your doctor? Maybe it's time for a dosage change or a different medication."

Gil shook his head. "Man, that's big pharma nonsense. Have a problem? Take a damn pill and shut up. No one ever bothers to fix the problem. No. They just throw a layer of drugged haze over it and charge you fifty a pop for the pleasure."

"You're right about that, Gil," Donnie said. "That's exactly how it feels, anyway."

Gil seemed startled by his reply. He leaned toward Donnie, nodding. "You should read this book I'm reading. It's all about natural cures and how the media and the pharmaceuticals companies are in collusion, keeping

America sick when the cures are practically free. You can't make money off the things that really help, things no one can put a patent on, so they put all these lies out there and everyone stays sick and keeps making money for the legal drug cartels."

Jon laughed. "Oh, my God. You're one of those off-the-grid, doomsday prepper wannabes, aren't you, Gil? Full of conspiracies and big speeches but not much else, unless it's brown and it stinks."

Thatcher was almost sorry to see the shift in Gil. For a second, he was almost friendly. Jon's sarcastic remark shut him down, and he went back to his narrow-eyed, grumpy self.

"Well, when all you sheeple end up with cancer or Alzheimer's or needing bypass surgery after stuffing down all those hyped-up pills, don't come crying to me."

Thatcher gladly let the others argue politics and medicine and what George called the commonalities of PTSD. It kept them from asking him to talk more about the nightmares he'd grudgingly mentioned when George pressed him for something. It kept them from asking what they were about or lecturing him on how he might have fewer of them if he talked about what he knew was behind them.

George ended the session by asking them all to stay after for a few minutes for a quick round of one-on-one check-ins. "Gil, I know you have to leave, so let's take care of yours first."

When George returned to the room, instead of calling another person aside, he gestured them all back to their chairs.

"The one-on-ones were just a ruse so I could talk with you all about something serious involving Gil."

Thatcher eased warily down into his chair.

"I've struggled with how to do this," George said, "without violating Gil's privacy. But in some ways, we're a family. This group is a family. Conflicts between members exist just like in a real family. Bonds also exist. I'm going to trust that what I'm going to tell you won't leave this group, and I trust that you'll understand why I'm violating Gil's privacy."

They waited. Thatcher wondered if the others were as curious as he.

"Sometimes people who need the most kindness are the ones who show the least kindness to others," George said. "I believe Gil's one of those people. It's no secret he's here for anger management issues, and I'm guessing it's no secret he's not making much progress with those issues. Sometimes there's just so much unrelenting stress in a person's life they can't let go of the anger. If they do, they might come completely apart."

Kit checked her watch. "Look, George, spit it out. None of us have time for this dancing."

Donnie snorted. "Especially where Gil's concerned."

George nodded. "Fair enough. Gil has a fourteen-year-old son with severe asthma. The boy's lungs have collapsed, one or the other or both at once, six times in the last four years. Two weeks ago, I happened to give Gil a lift home, and I think I've discovered the reason. His house is falling down around his ears. The roof is so old and leaky, I'm surprised it hasn't fallen in on them. There's mold on most of the walls, near the ceilings. In some parts, the ceilings were so saturated by water that they fell in and there are just holes and bits of insulation hanging down where the drywall used to be. His homeowner's insurance lapsed last year, and he hasn't been able to afford the premiums to get another policy in place. He owns it outright, such that it is, so there's no mortgage company forcing insurance on him."

When no one offered a response, George steepled his hands against his chin. "I know Gil has alienated pretty much everyone in this room, but I've made a number of calls to veterans organizations and some other charities, and I've secured some free services on his behalf… a structural engineer to give us a ruling on whether or not the place can even be saved, and if it can, a hygienist to verify the extent of the mold infiltration, an abatement company to remove it, and several building supply stores to donate whatever materials are needed to make the place habitable if it isn't a total tear down. What I still need is a lot of bodies…a large group of volunteers to provide labor, not unlike a Habitat for Humanity project. I'm waiting on a response from several organizations that could potentially provide the manpower needed to fix his home, but it's possible I won't hear back in time. We have a limited window of opportunity. In about a month, Gil will be out of town for five days tending to his father, who will be having minor surgery. There's no way the work can be completed in that little time, but if we can get things started while he's gone, he'll probably let us finish. He's made it pretty clear he doesn't want anyone's help, and no one has managed to convince him otherwise. His sister has been helping me sneak all of these experts over to the house during group. I'm told if it isn't a tear down, the work will take about four weeks, but it'll never get started to begin with if he's home when the first crew arrives."

When no one broke the silence that followed, George rose from his chair. "You all have my number. If you'd like to help, please send me a text or give me a call. I'd post a signup sheet, but Gil would see it, and that would defeat the purpose. I don't want anyone to feel pressured to participate. Maybe I'm doing something inappropriate here, even asking. But I appreciate you giving me your attention. Please help yourself to the food at the back, as always, and I'll see you on Wednesday."

"I'm in," Mike said as George turned to leave. "I meant what I said earlier. Anybody in this group needs something, even Gil, I'm there."

George nodded and clapped him on the back. They walked out together.

The others grabbed food and cleared out without sharing their opinions. Thatcher wondered if any of them would sign on to help. He wouldn't blame them if they didn't. He felt for the guy, but he wasn't sure whether he'd be any use where that sort of work was concerned. He knew a little about construction from lending Greer a hand when he was on leave between deployments, but his injuries might slow down their efforts more than speed them along. He could certainly do some work, but certain tasks would be out of the question. Whether it made him an asshole or not, Thatcher wasn't sure he wanted to help the guy who'd thrown Kit from the stage and put marks on her body that still hadn't completely faded.

Once he and Kit were sitting side by side in folding chairs, chewing on untoasted bagels with schmear, she asked, "What were you thinking about earlier? When Donnie was talking about how nothing changes, your face got weird."

"I'm not ready to talk about it, okay?" He glanced at her, at her pursed lips and solemn face.

"No," Kit shook her head, looking around before putting a hand on his thigh. "It's not okay anymore, Harpo. You're the only person who can't see that your silent routine isn't doing you or anyone else any good. Those people we hung out with on Saturday love you to the moon and back. You're lucky to have them, that they're still there even when you block them out."

He snorted. "Kettle. Black."

She tossed the rest of her bagel in the trash and snatched his out of his hand, sending it after hers. Then she pushed her way between his knees, put her hands on his shoulders, and bent until they were nose to nose. "I said baby steps, Harpo, not zero steps. I may have these walls you keep going on about, but you've slipped past them from time to time, in case you haven't noticed. My kitchen. My *bed.* You've held my daughter, changed her diaper. That's *inside* the walls, Harpo."

"You heard the song, Kit."

The words floated between them and crashed to the floor.

"There's more to that story, Valiant, than a few song lyrics." She stepped back and grabbed her purse from the floor beside her chair. "Time to start putting your money where your mouth is, Warbucks. I'm not going to wait forever."

She waited, but true to her word, she didn't wait forever. "It's your turn to lower the drawbridge, Valiant. Let me inside those castle walls."

She left him sitting alone in front of the table full of bagels and schmear, considering his own fortress.

CHAPTER EIGHTEEN

After spending the morning at urgent care getting clearance to come back to work and then at group, Kit was glad to arrive at work. She made the mistake, however, of recounting the events of the week with Nanette.

"You're falling for him!" Nanette smiled as though she'd won the Powerball lottery.

Kit shook her head. "He's a good guy. A good friend. And his family is really nice. But—"

"Hold up. His family? You met his family?" her boss' eyebrows lifted.

Kit waved her away with one hand. "He asked me to a barbecue on Saturday. It was more for him, I think, than for me."

Except the part where he gave you an amazing orgasm in his room and then went back to the party without even asking you to reciprocate. What guy does that?!

Nanette studied her silently for a moment. "You're in deep," she declared, turning back to the mutt she was trimming.

"Am not," she shot back, leading Scotch, a young Boxer, back to the washroom.

Liar!

She let the rush of the water in the tub mask anything else Nanette had to say.

It was Monday afternoon, and she was already counting the minutes until she'd be off work. Somehow, when she read a text from Thatcher during her last break asking if he could swing by with a pizza, she'd agreed, even though she'd told herself it was time to take a hearty step backward. It was just pizza and a little television, no big deal, but she felt like it was never going to be three o'clock. Suddenly, he was essential to her day. She wanted to joke with him at breakfast again. Do the dinner dishes while talking about anything and nothing. Tuck Lily into her crib.

Shit. Back out. Now. Call him and cancel.

She gave her inner-self the bird and buckled Lily into the car with a wide grin.

"Ready, Precious?"

Lily thrust out the stuffed alligator Thatcher had gotten her and smiled, as if she sensed their evening would include her new friend.

She made it home in record time, settling Lily in front of the television with a cartoon before tossing her damp, dog-hair covered clothes directly into the washer. When his knock sounded on the door, her heart leapt like some lovestruck schoolgirl's. The critic was oddly silent as she pulled open the door and Thatcher entered, clutching a very large, square box.

"That's not pizza," she joked, stepping back to let him inside.

He gave her a wink and said, "Let's see what Lily thinks of this."

Why the hell did the sight of a kiddie potty make her want to cry?

Lily's excitement over the shrunken toilet, a replica of the real thing, pushed her over the edge. "Lily potty!"

"That's right, baby," she sniffled.

Thatcher just winked at her again and headed to the main bathroom to set it up. By the time she peeked in the door, Lily was already tugging at the tapes on her diaper.

"Off!" she demanded.

Thatcher pulled the tapes. No sooner than the diaper fell, Lily put her little bottom on the potty and started tinkling.

Kit clapped her hands over her mouth in shock, laughing and sobbing both at once.

"Way to go, Lil' Miss!" he grinned. "I've got some pull-up diapers in the Jeep, too," he said, straightening up from a crouch with a wince. "I'll go grab them."

She squeezed his bicep as he passed. "Thanks, Valiant."

Kit wiped her eyes as Lily stood up and crowed, "Lily potty!"

She laughed, more tears spurting out of her eyes. "Yes, you did! Lily's a big girl now!"

It punched her in the gut, this rite of passage. Had she been in denial about Lily's readiness? Lily clearly knew what the thing was for and just what to do. Had Nanette and Crystal been working with her? She'd never seemed inclined here at home…

Pride and sadness warred as Thatcher returned with the transition diapers.

"I'll let you do the honors," he said softly, setting them on the counter and thumbing her tears.

She nodded and without thinking, pecked him on the lips. With Lily in the room. She leapt back from him as if he'd taken a match to her. He took the hint.

"I'll go order the pizza," he called over his shoulder.

Smiling down at her daughter, who was now peering in the bowl at her urine, Kit grabbed the pull-up diapers and sing-songed, "I've got some big girl underpants for Lily!"

Her excitement over the milestone reached, she reasoned, was how she managed to let him hang around until Lily was in her crib in a pair of pull-up diapers for the first time. Cracking her door closed, Kit whispered, "I'm such an idiot. She could have been out of diapers a long time ago!"

Thatcher shook his head as they moved down the hall together, away from the sleeping toddler's room. "She'll have a few accidents before this is all over, even once she's in regular undies during the day."

Kit gave him an amused smile. "Is that so, Uncle Thatcher?"

She lost her teasing smile as he pinned her to the wall at the end of the hallway and kissed her deeply.

"I veto that nickname," he said huskily once he let them both up for air. "It's creepy, especially right before I kiss you."

She nodded. "Agreed."

Kit ducked out of the hall and into the living room to clean up a night of toy-scattering, pizza-eating fun. When he stopped her in favor of making out on the sofa, she hit the pause button without a second thought, letting his wicked mouth take her away until her phone rang. Because David had isolated her from most of her friends and her focus on the Guard had effectively distanced the rest, Nanette and Crystal, the folks at group, and Thatcher were the only ones still calling her, she pushed him away to answer and would later deeply regret not checking the screen of her phone first.

"Hello?"

"Kit?"

David.

Oh, my God, it's David.

"Why the fuck are you calling?!" she blurted loudly, putting Thatcher on full alert. It was endearing, really, how his body went as rigid as hers.

"Kit…" the voice on the other end of the phone set her teeth on edge.

Kit met Thatcher's eyes as she said, "Why are you calling me, David?" She leapt from the sofa and paced, panicked, into the kitchen, but then her legs started to feel shaky and weak. Thatcher rounded the corner into the kitchen as she plopped into a chair at the dining table. He eased into the chair across from hers, his brows drawn in concern, and her heart melted a little more.

David's silence on the other end caused Kit to hold her

phone out to see if the call had dropped. "Why?" she repeated.

"I…it was a mistake, Kit. I never should have handled things the way I did, and I'm sorry."

Sorry for what? For moving me to Texas only to start freezing me out, make me wonder what I did wrong? Why you didn't love me anymore? Or for dumping our daughter on a woman who was on her deathbed? Or, hey, how about for refusing to look after Lily for a few days until I could do it myself?

"Kit?"

"No," she said. "I don't accept your apology. Goodbye." But before she could poke the button that would disconnect the call, she heard him shout.

"Please listen, Kit!!"

"No," she told him again.

"I cut you a break, Kit. I could've had you thrown in jail. I could've. You know it."

That's the David I remember.

"What do you want, David?"

"I want to see her."

"Lily?" she shot to her feet, laughing incredulously. "Fuck, no. *No*."

Thatcher stood, too, his face drawn in worry. She held up a hand, took a step back even as he stepped toward her.

"Please. Kit, for God's sake. We were so new, ourselves. I wasn't ready to even think about kids. But you got pregnant, and I got scared. I didn't handle it well."

"Damn fucking right you didn't. And you're not getting another chance at it either. Not here. Go knock up someone else if you want to give fatherhood another go, David."

"Kit," he said, his words spoken so calmly that she froze.

What if he's recording this? What if he's recording this to show how nice and reasonable he's being, and meanwhile you're flying off the handle and talking like a trucker?

"Lily is too important, David. You walked away from her like she was nothing. You want to walk away from me, fine," she said, voicing what her heart had been saying for just over two years. Hell, more than three, seeing as how he'd gone distant on her almost from the moment she told him she was pregnant. "You walked away from our daughter. You signed your rights away. That's it. The end. No second chances. No do-overs."

"Kit, whether you want to acknowledge it or not, whether I signed a paper or not, I'm her dad."

"You're her sperm donor. She doesn't have a dad. Not the way she should." *Thatcher is more of a daddy than you are, you useless bag of shit!* She bit her tongue to keep from saying it out loud.

"Let me *be* her dad! You can punish me, keep me away from her. I know the court would see your side over mine. But someday, when she's grown, I'll reach out to her. You won't be able to stop me. And I'll tell her flat out the mistake I made as a young idiot and how I knew I'd never win back my wife, that she'd never in a million years believe I still loved her. But I do, Kit. I've been thinking about it, and you, every day since the social worker found me. I've regretted it every day, too. And one day, I'm going to tell Lily all of it. How do you think she'll feel knowing I wanted to see her, *begged* to see her, and you kept her from me?"

Fury rose like bile. She shook her head. Everything shook, whether or not it was visible to Thatcher's searching gaze. Her knees. The hand she still held up between them like a force field. It wouldn't keep him at bay much longer, she knew. Especially now that the fury spilled from her eyes as tears. She was *not* hurt. David did *not* just destroy her with his words. She was blindingly, mind-numbingly furious. She wanted to find him, wanted to hunt him down and beat the holy hell out of him. So much it scared her.

How dare you make this my *fault?*

She didn't realize she'd said that aloud until she heard herself repeat it.

"How *dare* you make this my fault? Sitting on the other end of that phone playing the victim. Poor heartbroken daddy just wants to see his little girl. Well, you're right about one thing. If you try, if you even think about court action, I promise you *your* actions will speak louder than any of the shit words you're saying to me right now. No, David. The answer is no. Don't call me again."

This time she really did hang up. Didn't care what he might be shouting through the phone.

She and Thatcher stood frozen, like a movie-of-the-week on pause, for an eternal minute.

"My ex wants to see Lily. The dirt bag who discarded her like trash wants to see his daughter," she said slowly, her voice sounding hollow in her ears.

"Yeah, I gathered," Thatcher said softly, gathering her up in his arms.

The way he did so, silently, not trying to fix it or talk her down from the ledge, it put her back together in a way nothing spoken could have done. Her heart overflowed with love for him, a love she knew she shouldn't feel and didn't want to feel. Every wall she had crumbled to dust at her feet as he stayed there, holding her, saying nothing, until suddenly he was kissing her gently, hands stroking up and down her back.

Pulling her mind away from thoughts of her jerkwad ex…this was the excuse she gave herself later for letting Thatcher pick up where they left off, starting in the kitchen and stumbling back to the living room, where things escalated so quickly that he took her, exhilaratingly, bent over the back of the sofa so she was left helplessly clutching the cushions.

The chemical effects of the amazing orgasm rendered her mute, unable to send him home. She tugged him to her bedroom, turning the tables, lavishing him with all the love she felt but didn't want to express, making him as helpless against her tender assault as she was against his.

Maybe, came the whisper from the depths of her mind.

Maybe things can be different with him. He's not David. He's so very obviously not David.

These were the things she told herself as she dropped off, cradled in the curve of his body behind hers.

His moaning —not the good kind — woke her a couple hours later. He mumbled what sounded like, "No. Please, man, don't…" as Kit reached out and switched on the bedside lamp. She met his sleepy, confused eyes. He came back to himself, to her, and sat up, swinging his legs over the edge of the bed with his back to her. Even with six inches of space between them, she could feel him trembling. Her heart quaked, and she reached for him.

Rubbing his right shoulder gently, she let him sit in silence for a few minutes, scrubbing his face with his hands. But when he offered his usual nothing, Kit flung each of her legs on either side of him, as if on a motorcycle, flattening her chest against his back and sliding her arms around his waist. She kissed him between his shoulder blades, trying not to think about the tenderness in the gesture or what it meant.

"Valiant," she said softly, "this isn't working."

He stiffened under her, his back going rigid.

"Remember George's motto? Forward motion?"

His reply was muffled by his still-scrubbing hands.

"This isn't forward motion," she told him, idly rubbing circles into his skin. "It's standing still."

"Kit, another—"

"No," she answered, sliding one leg across his back and rising from the bed to face him. She crouched at his knees. "Tell me. Now. No more 'later'. No more, 'I will, just not yet.' No more deferring to songs. Tell me."

She tried to take the sting out of her words by stroking

his thighs.

"Jesus," he sighed, giving his face a final scrub before stilling her hands with his own. "What will it help? My leg," he pointed. "My shoulder. There. All caught up."

"There my ass," she snorted, rising. "You're killing my knees with all this talking around the subject."

"I'm not talking around it. I damn near got myself blown up. It hurt. It scared the hell out of me. I didn't think I was going to make it, that my family's last experience with their son, their brother, would be guys in dress blues on the door step, telling them I was killed in action." He let out a shaky breath.

Kit turned her palms over to clutch his hands. That he let her, that he squeezed back, it opened a door. "The devil's in the details, Valiant," she squeezed again. Too far. His eyes darkened. He tugged her hands out from under hers. "How'd it happen?"

He gave her a sentence about a mission gone wrong, catching bomb fragments all through his shoulder and from hip to knee.

"Just you?" This, so softly she thought he hadn't heard.

"You already know that one, Kit," he said dully. "The Fantastic Four, too." His voice cracked. He blinked furiously, ducking his head.

"I don't know everything. But I know it's never just the physical. Tell me the rest. All of it."

"I'm tired, Kit. I'm so fucking tired."

She wasn't sure if he was trying to beg off or starting to give in. "Well, no wonder," she said, taking his hands again. "Carrying all that stuff around, refusing to put it down, refusing to share the load. No wonder," she repeated.

"Kit," he sighed and pulled his hands back forcefully now, rolling away from her toward the center of the bed.

She stood, feeling hollowed out by his dismissal. She rounded the bed, turned out the light, and slid in beside him. Reached for him one last time. And he rolled away, onto his left side now, though she heard the hiss of his discomfort. It felt so much like the inexplicable, sudden distance between her and David, her eyes watered. Stung, she sat back up and told the darkness, “Get your clothes on and go home. I’m tired, too.”

He didn’t move.

“Start talking, Harpo, or go home. I’m serious.”

It was a gamble, this ultimatum.

When he slid out of bed, disappointment leaked out of her in tears she hoped were muffled by the sound of him struggling back into his clothes. Kit flashed back to all the times she’d tried to re-engage David, to get him talking, to tell her what she’d done to make him stop loving her.

“Kit…” he tried again, his voice quiet, pleading.

It’s not the same.

It feels *the same.*

“It’s not going anywhere, Valiant,” she said drowsily, suddenly as weary as he’d claimed to be. “Until you’re ready to get the thorn out of your paw, it’s going to keep festering, spilling poison all over your waking life and your dreams. I’m not going to enable your silence anymore. When you’re ready to pull that thorn, you know where I am.”

Silence. He didn’t move, didn’t leave. She could feel him waiting, trying to wait her out.

“Go home, Thatcher.” No nicknames. Nicknames were for people inside the walls.

He crept wordlessly out of her room. Kit bit her fist to stifle the sob that ripped through her, unable to silence the critic now as it all but cackled in her head.

Stupid! What did you think would happen? Some cathartic admission, then everybody’s all better? It’s better this way. You let him get too close. Better he walks away now rather than later. Less far to fall.

She rolled into his spot and clutched his pillow against her. A poor substitute, but it fooled her into the comfort of him, that still-warm spot that smelled of him. Kit let it fool her right to sleep, the only place she could hide from the loss of him.

CHAPTER NINETEEN

Thatcher drove home on quiet streets, nearly turning back a million different times. But every time he convinced himself he could survive the telling, his airway seemed to swell until he was gasping, his hands slippery with sweat on the wheel of his Jeep, his heart hammering so hard he thought this might really be a heart attack and not a panic attack. He pulled over three times as anxiety clouded his vision with dark spots. Those were the worst. Those were when he came closest to wheeling the Jeep around and back to her house. Because what if she was right? What if stuffing it all down inside was like a spring-loaded trigger that fired everything into his nightmares? What if his nightmares would, if not vanish completely, lessen significantly if he talked about it instead of clamming up as instinct told him to?

He stared at the ceiling for what felt like hours, wondering if she'd ever speak to him again.

Not until you tell her, a little voice inside him said.

Just as loudly, another whispered, *I can't.*

One stupid dream he didn't want to talk about, and he'd ruined any chance of spending time with her and Lily. Worse, he'd hurt her. She might have thought he hadn't noticed, but he heard her crying in the darkness as he left her room like a coward.

The nightmare that followed was the worst yet. Not because it was particularly bloody or horrifying, but because it hit him right in his aching heart.

"Bro?" Kyle asked as they patrolled the empty fields at the edge of a district long ago reduced to a rubble of burned-out houses and looted storefronts. "Seriously. What are you doing?"

Thatcher tried to get him to stop walking, knowing they were about to step into a series of buried IEDs. But he didn't know what Thatcher knew. He still believed a sweeper team had already been through, that this was just another late afternoon under a blazing hot sun, keeping the perimeter secure as the rest of the battalion convoyed out, closing up shop in the area, on their way to a new field post. Their platoon would bring up the rear after everyone else was out.

He tried again to get Kyle to stop.

"Dude, don't worry. The sniffers cleared this field already," he replied, using their nickname for the bomb squad and their dogs.

"Kyle..."

He finally stopped walking. Thatcher's heart began to beat again, only to stop once more as Kyle squinted into the orange light of sunset.

"Thatcher, I don't have any more chances to fix all the stupid shit I should have."

Kyle spontaneously became his final self—bloodied and singed. He stood there, rivers of red flowing freely down to pool around his boots, and clapped Thatcher's suddenly also bloody shoulder.

This isn't right. He should be on the ground. I've got to stop the bleeding!

From the corner of his eye, Thatcher saw the med unit touch down, saw shadowy shapes scatter into the field, knew what they would encounter...Paul and Sam, bodies torn apart, almost unidentifiable. Mikey facedown, almost completely unscathed, yet somehow dead. Turned over, however, they'd understand. Unlucky bit of shrapnel through the eye, into his brain, after the first blast blew off his protective eyewear.

Kyle shook his head as the blood continued to run. "Wendy and I had so many ridiculous arguments, and all that stuff was just left hanging when I died. She's going to feel guilty for the rest of her life about some of the shit she screamed at me during those fights, and I'm telling you, brother, none of it mattered. There's no score card. No big prize for all the times you thought you were right. No punishment for being wrong, either, except what you do to yourself."

With that, Kyle crumpled. Thatcher dove after him, picked up his seeping, broken body, cradled him though it lit his arm and leg on fire. He'd pushed through it then, and he pushed through it again, fueled entirely by adrenaline and panic. "No, no, no!" he begged. "You were fine just a second ago!"

Kyle stared up at him, eyes losing focus. "Stop thinking this was all your fault. We knew, all of us, what we signed up for…how it could end."

"Kyle!" he screamed and, knowing all was lost, still shook him, same as last time, knowing it wouldn't come out any differently, but hoping, anyway. "God damn it, Kyle…"

He woke bawling. Unlike most times, he didn't try to stop. He let it pass through him instead of trying to force a burst dam closed.

After, he stared at the ceiling, the pillow case hot and damp on either side of his face. He turned each way, trying to find relief from the crushing pain in his chest. A few greedy gasps later, the pain eased, but it didn't go away.

3:45 a.m.

A mere two hours after Kit sent him home. Less than one since he'd tumbled into bed, thinking he wouldn't sleep. Of course, he'd rather not have.

He thought of her behind him, fitting herself against him, kissing him between his shoulder blades, one side scarred, the other clear. Night and day. Before and after. She didn't seem repulsed or dismayed by the puckered skin like he was. Those scars…his thigh, his shoulder, his bicep. What he could see made him ill. Not because he was vain. Not really. It was the other things he saw in his mind when he looked at them. The carnage. The wasted lives. The looks he imagined on the faces of those left behind, without husbands or brothers or sons.

Thatcher watched the ceiling, following the shadows cast by the moon shining through the branches of the back yard tree. It was soothing, and he needed soothing.

Any ground he'd gained with Kit…lost. He was certain those walls were being fortified as he stared at the ceiling. He should have tried to tell her. He could feel her frustration, her impatience…her worry. But he couldn't push the words out. He was too busy pushing the images back, like trying to close double closet doors on a towering, disorganized hoard.

He drifted like a zombie through Tuesday, barely sleeping.

On Wednesday, he didn't go to group, but he replied to George's texts so the man wouldn't send out the cavalry.

Don't feel well. Maybe Friday.

George's reply was almost instant, as if he watched eagerly for Thatcher's reply. Then again, with a PTSD group, maybe he *did* watch closely. Just in case.

Feel better, man. You're missed. Everybody asked about you.

He didn't know how to respond to that. It didn't surprise him, really. He'd come, in a short time, to care about his fellow group members. Even, to an extent, for Gil. Such as he was. He'd even been kicking around the idea of signing on to help with Project Gil.

When Thatcher walked into his PT session that afternoon, Cesar frowned.

"Uh-oh. What happened, Mano?"

"What? I'm fine."

Cesar laughed, clutching his belly. "Lies, Mano! Lies. Last time, you came in here all loose and relaxed, and today you're like a freshly wound up top ready to spin right off my table. Face down, Sergeant. We'll loosen you up again."

Doubt it.

To his surprise, Cesar began with less of a PT stretch and something closer to a massage, and he found himself giving Cesar a highly abbreviated version of the events on his last day in Iraq. Or at least, the last day he remembered.

To his embarrassment, as Cesar ended the massage and fluidly switched to the usual PT exercises, he realized as he rested his face in the face ring of the table that the moisture plopping on the floor under the table wasn't sweat.

He was crying.

Cesar continued on with the usual face-down stretches, easing Thatcher's lower leg upward into a 90-degree angle, then pressing gently so his heel grew closer to his buttock, stopping when Thatcher issued a soft grunt of protest. A hand came to rest on his back.

"That's good, Sergeant. I'm going to give you a couple minutes. When you're ready, flip face up so we can finish the stretches. I'll be back."

On his way out, Cesar placed a warm towel across the back of his neck, something he'd never done before.

~~~

"What's going on, Kit? You're quiet."

She swept the grooming floor in silence until Nanette switched off her clippers and waited.

Kit sighed. "I'm fine."

Nanette snorted. "Okay."
~~~

She didn't want to talk about it. Him. Thatcher. About the fact that he hadn't called or texted on Tuesday and hadn't shown up at group on Wednesday. About how it was radio silence since she'd kicked him out of the house Monday night. Or about the fact it was now Thursday, and she felt like she was dying.

See? This is why you don't get attached. It's been less than seventy-two hours since he walked out, and you feel like you're never going to stop aching.

"Kit…"

She looked up at Nanette, leaning against the broom.

"Something happen with Thatcher?"

She rolled her eyes.

"That's a yes." Nanette left her alone for a few minutes. A few minutes she spent hoping was the end of the conversation. But, no. Of course not. Not with Nanette. "I'm waiting," her boss prompted.

"Keep waiting," she said, sweeping again.

Nanette barked out a laugh. "C'mon. You'll feel better."

"Doubt it," she muttered under her breath.

"What?"

"Nothing."

Nanette's quick hand snatched the broom right out of Kit's. "Stop. Talk to me."

Kit sighed again. "He's so closed up when it comes to his past."

Nanette's sharp laugh irritated her. "Kettle. Pot."

It reminded her of Thatcher's similar accusation.

"Yeah, but I told my story to the group, and you know what? I'm feeling better since I did. Not perfect, but better."

"Glad to hear it. But answer me this. Could anything on this planet have made you open your mouth before you were ready?"

Kit snatched the broom back. "Oh, shut up. Don't be so damn reasonable."

Nanette laughed again. "Is it that he won't talk in group or that he won't share it with you?"

Ouch.

Kit cursed her boss silently for her perceptiveness. And didn't answer.

Nanette switched the clippers back on, apparently having decided she'd gotten her point across. Or not. She switched the clippers off again almost instantly. "You know thinking you can save someone or, I don't know, fix them, is the road to disaster, right?"

The clippers began humming again, and Kit was left to sweep and to ponder.

Ponder and pout.

She did both for the rest of the work day, sulking all the way home with Lily. Throughout the evening, she checked and re-checked her phone to make sure she hadn't silenced it or turned down the volume or missed a message while she gave Lily a bath or when she took her own shower after Lily was in bed.

Call him.

No.

Text.

No!

She stopped short of throwing her phone across the room after checking it yet again. Barely. She knew her stubborn streak wasn't exactly a virtue, but the longer the silence stretched between them, the more she resisted being the one to break it. Besides, she'd meant what she said. She wouldn't enable his silence any longer. Extending the olive branch would be giving him permission to remain closed up and stagnant.

So, no. She wouldn't call or text. She'd sit miserably on her sofa trying not to remember their frenzied lovemaking right there against the back of it on Monday night before everything went to hell.

Except…why should she suffer?

She stared at her phone. It remained as stubbornly silent as she.

CHAPTER TWENTY

He barely slept Tuesday or Wednesday, then crashed hard on Thursday, sleeping most of the day. But when he woke, his first thought was of Kit.

He'd told Cesar, his physical therapist, so why couldn't he tell Kit? Why did he have to let her down?

Guilt. He knew, logically, what it was. Survivor's guilt. The feeling he should be dead instead of the others. Not Kyle, who left behind a wife and son. None of them should be dead, but especially not Kyle.

He also knew, logically, he wasn't to blame. A terrorist cell was…one-hundred percent. The knowledge didn't magically cure him of his guilt or stop the nightmares.

George texted on Friday. ***Will you make it to group today? Need anything?***

He stared at the text for a long time before declining.

I'll be back Monday.

Another PT session with Cesar and a shower later, he sat in the Jeep wondering whether to pop in on Kearny or check into some more apartments.

Instead, he killed the late Friday afternoon checking out a project of Parker and Greer's that they'd been bugging him about since he returned home.

"Welcome to the crash house," Greer said, leading him inside the warehouse.

Parker waved at them as they passed further into the building.

Thatcher's eyebrows lifted. "Wow. You weren't

kidding. It's a house. Inside a warehouse."

"And you're in luck. No one's here today, which is rare. We've been booked pretty solid since we opened."

Greer showed him the fake-but-real house, built with multiple purposes: to teach damage investigations to insurance companies and cause and origin to forensic investigation students as well as serve as an urban search and rescue training module.

"Everything slides and locks," Greer said, showing him how the exterior siding could be popped off and a fresh piece popped back on in seconds.

"Cool." He felt edgy as a yellow light began to spiral overhead.

Warning!

Warning!

"C'mon," Greer gestured.

Thatcher limped after him into a seating area behind plexiglass. Greer handed him a set of earplugs. Thatcher took his cue and tucked them into his ears. Shortly after, a loud buzzing sounded, followed by an unholy blast. Thatcher grabbed Greer and threw him to the floor, covering him with his body, his heart jackhammering. When he next became aware of anything, it was Greer's voice, edged in panic.

"Thatcher! Jesus, Thatcher, c'mon, it's okay. I'm sorry. Thatcher, it's okay. We're okay…"

Thatcher blinked as Parker's voice joined Greer's.

"Yeah. That's it…look at me." Parker's concerned face stared at him. "Give me your hand." Slowly, like moving through thick mud, he reached up for Parker's hand, and realized as he did so that something —the ground? —underneath him was moving.

"Take it easy," Parker encouraged. "Just follow me over here. Everything's okay. Everyone's okay."

He blinked again and took in his surroundings. Plexi-glass. The swirling yellow light abruptly stopping. And

Greer. Greer eased up from his face-down position, moving slowly. His face, too, when he turned toward them, was drawn in worry. And it was sheet white, which was saying something for a guy with Greer's all-year-round tanned skin.

"I'm sorry, Thatch," he said hollowly. "I didn't…"

Parker guided him to a chair. "Sit. You, too, Greer."

Greer ignored Parker, but Thatcher obeyed, largely because his legs felt incapable of supporting him. Jelly legs. Not once had he had that sensation overseas. Not once. Absently, he watched Parker hurry away. Moments later, he was back with two bottles of water. "Drink."

Thatcher gazed at the rubble remaining where the house-within-a-warehouse had stood.

A simulation.

Fake.

Not real.

Everyone's okay.

He heard Parker and Greer as if from a great distance. He looked down at his hand. Water. That…yes. He wanted a drink. Water would have to do.

"Should we call someone?" Parker's voice filtered to him, seemed to flow into his ears even as the water flowed down his throat.

"No. Just give me a few minutes." Reality hit him then, like he'd been somewhere beneath it and was now breaking the surface. "Sorry," he croaked. "I…it…the explosion." He shook his head, blew out a long, shaky breath.

His brothers flanked him instantly, sitting in the chairs on either side of him.

"Dude, I am so sorry. I didn't think. I—" Greer's mouth gaped open and closed like a fish for a second. "Jesus, I didn't think, Thatch. I'm sorry."

He nodded, but he didn't know what to say.

Gingerly, as if he might come up swinging, Parker eased a hand to his right shoulder. "Are you okay? Do you need us to call someone?"

"I'm okay," he said slowly. "I'm sorry I…"

"No. Don't be sorry," Greer said, still not quite himself. "*I'm* sorry."

"Are *you* okay, Greer?" Thatcher asked, remembering now that he'd pretty much body-slammed his older brother.

"I'll live. You?"

He nodded again. "But I think I'm going to go."

"Let me drive you," Parker said. "We can come back for your Jeep later."

Thatcher sucked down the rest of the bottled water. "I'm good now."

"Thatch…"

"Really, Park. I'm okay." He tried to keep the edge out of his voice and failed miserably.

Both of them tried again to stop him. They followed him out of the warehouse to his Jeep, Parker standing at the driver's door and Greer looking pained on the passenger side. He could all but feel their eyes on him until he'd turned out of the parking lot.

He drove home numbly, on auto-pilot, grateful to make it to the pool house apartment without his mother popping her head out of the kitchen door to say hello.

~~~

Though he tried to distract himself with movies and TV, a light workout, and by cooking the most complicated meal a one-burner hot plate and a microwave would allow, he remained restless. Sleep wouldn't find him. He had no idea how many hours he stared at the ceiling trying to turn off his brain.

He ignored the voice that said he should wait, that it was too late—or early, now— to turn up on Kit's doorstep.

Thatcher pulled some fresh clothes on and moved quickly to the Jeep. Drove without a single idea of how he
~~~

was doing it. Couldn't remember any part of the drive once he climbed out of the Jeep again.

Didn't remember ringing the bell, but suddenly the door swung open and there she was, her pixie hair sticking up at odd angles and pillowcase creases on her face, peering out at him.

"Hey," she whispered. "You're shaking. What's—what time is it?" She waited for him to speak, but he made sure she didn't wait long.

The words spilled from him like rain, almost before he stepped over the threshold, starting with the background stuff: how he met the guys, how over the years he'd ended up on four different deployments with Kyle, and three with Sam, Paul and Mike. How three of his six deployments had been to combat areas. He told her how the Fantastic Four insisted it was the Fantastic *Five*, and how he insisted it was Four. He was their boss, after all. No playing favorites. How he'd been closest to Kyle, though he'd have eaten a bullet for Paul, Sam, or Mike—or any of his army brethren—just as readily.

The recounting of their actual last moments was mechanical, robotic. He only vaguely realized she'd led him to her bedroom and had him sit on the edge of her bed. He spoke without looking at her. He couldn't.

Going numb was the only way he could get through it. Somehow, as he spoke, he'd started to undress. He found himself sprawled across her thighs as the last of the words broke the wall, the one that held back the worst of the pain.

"He fucking died in my arms, Kit, I stared into his eyes and watched them go empty, watched Wendy and Matty lose every goddamn thing right there in that fucking hole of a field…"

Vaguely, he heard her murmuring random nonsense, felt the stroking of her hand at the base of his skull. Didn't understand a word of it, couldn't. The poison gushing from him drowned the meaning right out. The guilt that he grieved harder for the Four than for the two other fatalities in his own damn squad, though their deaths were no less unfortunate. He told her how he'd visited the graves like a coward to slip quarters onto their headstones, unable to face the grief of the squad's loved ones. And about getting unlucky with the last one, the hardest one. Having to look Wendy in the face as she caught him sobbing, his back propped against Kyle's coin-littered headstone, a year too late for the funeral. Matty perched on her hip, staring at him with those eyes, so much like Kyle's. Accusingly, he thought. Fatherless, he knew. Kit heard it all spew out of him.

Empty, he began to notice things again. Her nightgown, wetted by his tears. The blued light of pre-dawn at the window. *Had he been talking that long??* The whisper of the ceiling fan. Her hand still stroking the back of his head. The hot drip of moisture on the side of his head. Her tears, he realized, and locked his arms around her, his cheek on her thigh. Her indecision as Lily began to cry down the hall.

Just as he opened his mouth to tell her to go, she slid out from under him, pulled the sheet up around him, and whispered, "Sleep."

He was happy to oblige.

When he woke, alone, in the brightness of midday, Thatcher wondered what she was thinking. He only vaguely remembered telling her everything, holding nothing back, the memory of it hazy as though he'd been drugged. He wondered how to face her as he showered. Wondered what it meant, Kit keeping her distance. Was she simply allowing him to come to her when he was ready? Or had his story changed how she felt about him?

He wondered and worried for nothing. Built it up over nothing. When he crept down the hall, he saw her on the blanket with Lily, watching her flip through a puffy book about the alphabet. Lily noticed him first, beaming, hopping to her feet, running at him.

"Hey, Lil' Miss," he greeted, settling her against his right hip, dropping a kiss on her temple. "You learning your ABCs?"

"ABC!" she agreed.

"What's next?"

"ABC!" she cried again.

He chuckled. "No, but we'll get there."

Kit rose slowly, came to him slowly, and stopped in front of him with a question in her eyes. He didn't know how to answer, so he gave her a kiss, too, at the temple, right over the edge of her scar. He pulled her tightly against his side and kissed her again, lacking the right words. She put a hand on his chest, smiling hugely at Lily.

"We'll get there, too," she told him. She took Lily from him, asking, "Are you hungry, my precious? Let's have some lunch."

CHAPTER TWENTY-ONE

Emptied out and quiet, Thatcher seemed mellow as they moved through the week together. Even Kit's critic couldn't find a reason to send him away. Not one she'd listen to, anyway. It sputtered the usual things: *Don't let Lily get too attached.* Too late. Her little girl lit up at the sight of him. He was already as firmly wedged into her little heart as he was wedged, unexpectedly, into Kit's. *Don't fall for him. You fell for David almost as fast, and look where that got you?* He was nothing like David. Not in the bedroom or anywhere else. She'd only thought the sex was good with David. But if it was, what word would be enough for sex with Thatcher? She'd never had so many dirty thoughts, so many wanton desires. She felt like a horny teenager, always turned on, always ready. *Say the word, buddy, and let's go.*

She loved Lily to death, but bedtime was her new favorite time of day. Any place but her daughter's room was fair game. The kitchen table. The bathtub. Up against the washing machine. The floor of her bedroom when they couldn't quite make it to the bed. The lounge chair on the patio where Lily's fever had interrupted them before. The pool, though still very chilly. Or, really, the deck. And not intercourse, that time. Just Thatcher's head between her thighs, doing delicious things until she had to bite her own hand to stifle her cries.

Six days of domestic bliss, Saturday through Thursday. Breakfasts, lunches, dinners. Parks, restaurants, an outing with Kearny and Janine, a playdate for Lily with Parker's daughter, Hayden. Though Hayden was younger than Lily, the girls babbled nonsense to one another, playing games only they understood. Everything she'd imagined with David but never got.

Thatcher was more settled in group, even offering up a few more bits of his story. He'd told them about Gabriela, his high school girlfriend, and how her death shattered him. How he couldn't stay in Phoenix, no matter how much his family loved him. He couldn't handle their concern, their worry. How his breaking point, the thing that led him to enlist and escape, was the fact that Gabby's family didn't resent him. It was their concern, their love, their visits and calls that caused him to flee into the relative anonymity of the U.S. Army. She understood and didn't push when he couldn't share the rest of his story, because she understood he needed time to recover from telling just that part.

As group let out Friday afternoon, Thatcher nodded at her as he asked George to wait.

"I want to volunteer for project Gil," he said.

Surprise and warmth coursed through her. She'd already told George the same. It was something she could give back to someone who hadn't been beside her, exactly, but who'd, in a sense, been there, anyway. She didn't have to like him to help him.

"Are you sure?"

Thatcher nodded. "I am."

Kit nodded when George asked if she was still interested as well.

"Okay. I'll text you the details."

Thatcher eyed her. "You didn't have to volunteer just because I did."

She swallowed the bit of sandwich. "Groceries, first of all, I volunteered before you did. Second, do I look like the kind of person who does things just because other people do them?"

He fought a grin. "Nope."

"Well," she said, rising from the metal chair, "there you have it."

As she threw away her sandwich wrapper, her phone buzzed.

Nanette.

Fridays and Saturdays were Kit's days off, and Nanette typically never called unless she was trying to convince Kit to let her and Crystal babysit so she could "do something fun with someone. Anyone."

"What's up, Nanette?"

"Hey, Kit," she said, "I'm sorry, but I'm going to have to close the shop next week. I've already re-scheduled everything we had on the books."

Panic rose in her for many reasons. "What's going on? Are you alright? Is Crystal?"

"We're fine. Sort of. Crystal's dad passed away. We have to fly to South Carolina."

Nervous energy had her pacing between the food table and the group's circle of chairs, now abandoned. "God, I'm sorry. Are you sure you don't want me to take care of the appointments?"

"No, hon. Thanks, but you don't have enough expertise with the show clients, and this place is impossible to run all alone." After a short pause, Nanette said, "Don't worry. This is a paid vacation for you. Have a little fun for once. We'll be back a week from Sunday. You can let yourself in on Sunday for the cleaning. Just remember to lock up."

Kit moved on to stacking the empty paper plates and wadded napkins into the mostly empty pizza box. "Call me if you need anything, Nanette. I mean it."

"Will do. Have a little fun, please. I'm begging you. Take that man of yours and—"

"Bye, Nanette!" she nearly shouted, hitting the "end call" button quickly.

Thatcher frowned when she told him the news. "I'm

sorry to hear that."

"Yeah," she sighed. "Me, too. But I'm not sure how Crystal feels, going back to her hometown. Her father basically disowned her for being gay. I mean, she said he sent her Christmas and birthday cards and called once in a blue moon, but they used to be really, really close. Her mother died and her father raised her on his own."

"Wow."

"Yeah."

Thatcher slipped up behind her, tossing his own trash in the receptacle before snaking his arms around her middle from behind.

"This might be a bad time, but I've got a surprise for you," he said, looking around to make sure they were alone before kissing her.

"A surprise? What surprise?" she grinned at the mischief in his eyes.

"Even before Nanette had to close the shop for next week, I had a conversation with her and got her on-board."

"On board for what?"

"I had her give you a long weekend. She was actually going to call you today, anyway, and tell you to take Sunday and Monday off. Parker and Melody will be keeping Lily this weekend. I thought we'd sneak up to the family cabin in Greer this afternoon and come back on Monday in time for group."

Kit's heart fluttered in her chest. She trusted Parker and Melody, but…all weekend?

Reading her mind, he smirked. "She'll be fine, Kit. You've never had a weekend to yourself since she was born. It's time."

It is. This is what the normal humans do.

Remembering her thoughts of a carefree vacation while waiting in the Jeep in the Safeway parking lot, her heart fluttered again, this time with excitement.

"Okay," she found herself agreeing. "Let's do it!"

A joy she hadn't felt in a long time bubbled up inside her as they rushed home to pack for the weekend. Now, as they drove east, windows down to the warm, mid-April breeze, chasing a bank of storm clouds to the north, she felt excitement and contentment rise in her chest like bubbles. When she fussed, worrying if they'd hit bad weather, he shrugged.

"I can handle just about anything, babe. Relax."

"Have we reached the 'babe' point in our..." she trailed off.

"Relationship?" he finished, winking at her. It made her crazy when he did that, hit her down low in her belly. "We have, whether you want to admit it or not. *Babe*." He grabbed her hand and kissed it.

She rolled her eyes but smiled out the window, into the current of air.

"Whhoooooooo!" she called into the breeze.

He laughed. She did it again just to hear him laugh a second time.

They grinned at each other like conspirators.

Kit relaxed into the seat, into the ride, watching the desert give way to scrub pines and then her ears were popping from the altitude. She took the gum he offered, the world blurring by with the afternoon. By the time he bumped the Jeep along a dirt road, the sun had set and lightning flashed in the sky.

The headlights settled on a large A-frame structure with floor to ceiling windows that reached up two stories, all the better to take in the gorgeous views of the forest. As he popped open his door, the air hit her and she shivered.

"Oh, God, it's cold!" she laughed. "I'm not dressed for this at all!"

He smiled. "You brought warmer stuff than you're wearing. You'll be fine in a minute, when we get inside and get a fire going."

"Mmm, a fire. That sounds like fun."

He nodded. "So, get a move on. Unlock the door, will you?" He tossed her a set of keys. "I'll get our bags."

They had the lights on only long enough for Thatcher to stow their bags in the bedroom upstairs in the loft and to light the fire he'd promised. They had a quick dinner of Subway sandwiches they'd gotten at their last pit stop.

After a lazy lovemaking session, they stared into the fire from a pile of soft blankets and large throw pillows. Snuggled against her, keeping her backside warm, Thatcher kissed her neck. Kit floated somewhere between wakefulness and sleep, half-convinced she'd died and gone to heaven to be here with him, like this, on the first vacation she'd had in years, since even before Lily.

"I love it up here," he sighed, idly stroking along her ribcage. "I love *you*, Kit," he said, kissing her neck where it met her shoulder again.

She was sure he must have felt her go rigid under his fingers, against his lips. But she pretended to be asleep, and he didn't call her out on it.

You love him, too, chicken.

I do not. I like him. A lot.

You love him.

I love his body. I love what he does to me with his body.

You love all of him. His eyes, the way they look at you, his heart, so fucking generous, even his pain. His family. Everything.

No.

Yes. You do. But go ahead. Be a chicken if that's what you want.

His fingers slowed; his breath grew deeper.

Kit opened her eyes, stared into the fire.

Shit.

There it was.

She felt it.

Love.

~~~

"That's dirty pool, dude," Kearny laughed. "You took her to the cabin, got her all toasty warm in the forest, and dropped the L-bomb on her?"

Thatcher glanced toward the bathroom, heard the water still running. "It's not like that. I mean, it is, I love her, but I didn't orchestrate this trip to butter her up or anything. I just saw the opportunity, and I took it. She didn't have to work for a few days, we didn't have group, so why not, right?"

"Why not take a trip, sure. Why not tell her you love her? Was she ready for that? How did she react?"

"She fell asleep. Or faked it," he admitted.

Kearny laughed at the dismay that was obvious in his voice. "Bro, give her and yourself a break. She's mama bear, remember? This is a big deal for anyone, but she's got a kid. Now it's her kid's heart, too. You break her heart, fine. Not fine, but you know what I mean. She'll live. But you break her kid's heart, just try hiding. There won't be a safe place on the planet. You'll gut her kid, and Kit will gut you."

He chuckled in spite of himself. Janine's voice burst onto the line as Kearny's protest rang out in the background.

"Thatcher, she'll come around. She's head-over-heels for you, too, but Kearny's right. She's got a lot at stake if things don't work out."

He felt like such a girl as he leaned forward in the dining room chair, eager for her input. "Think so?"

"You haven't seen the way she looks at you when she thinks no one is paying attention. You'll just have to take my word. It's love. It is *so* love."

He couldn't help grinning like a fool. Levity gave way to panic as the water cut off. "I have to go. Big love."
~~~

He didn't wait for a response before hanging up, though it was several minutes before Kit emerged from the steamy bathroom, letting out a cloud of humid, steamy air.

Jeans and a thermal never struck him as sexy before, but as his eyes roved over her curves, they caught him that way, now.

"Mmmm," he growled against her neck, nipping her in that place that made her shiver.

"Stop," she laughed, shoving him back onto the couch. "I want to say I did more with my vacation than roll around on the carpet in front of the fireplace."

"Why?" he joked, reaching for her again. She ducked away, and he gave a half-hearted chase, mentally cursing his leg. But there was no time for regret. "Okay, time for a Myers family tradition. A picture by the front door of the cabin, selfie style. Every new person to walk in the door has to do it for our celebration wall."

He pointed at it, the long expanse of wall next to the front door, stretching through the informal dining area all the way to the kitchen counter. Dozens of frames, various sizes, cluttered the wall. A large frame with eight spots contained pictures of Thatcher and his siblings. Two larger frames high up on the wall held portraits of Artie and Della. Other smaller frames held Parker's wife, Melody, alone and with their daughter. Shelby and Chance had their own spaces, as did Janine. Various other men and women, both friends and former girl- or boyfriends, reached upward toward the ceiling and below the chair rail, inching toward the floor.

"What are you going to do when this is full? Take some down?"

Thatcher shook his head. "Never. We'll make a new wall."

"Does anyone ever get taken down, like if a relationship ends badly?"

"Nope," Thatcher told her, pointing to picture high on

the wall of a brunette, outdoorsy woman. "That's Lexy, Parker's fiancée from five years ago. She couldn't handle the unpredictable hours of search and rescue work, so she broke things off six days before they were supposed to get married. He thought they'd patch things up, get married. He refused to cancel any of the arrangements, most of which he paid for since her family wasn't doing well financially. He was convinced it was just cold feet and that she'd have some eleventh-hour change of heart. Forced us under the threat of death to show up. We did. She didn't."

"Oh, God." Kit steepled her hands in front of her mouth.

"Yeah. He went a little nuts and had a bit of a meltdown in the church. Told us if we knew what was good for us, we'd sit down and eat the reception dinner and the cake and make sure it didn't go to waste. 'Have yourselves a fucking party,' he said. 'I'll be fine, but I'm going to go.'"

"Did you really stay and eat and dance and all that?"

"Hell, no. My folks and my sisters boxed up the food and dropped it off at a homeless shelter, struck down and returned all the rented decorations and chairs and tables and stuffed five vehicles full of gifts to be returned to the givers. Greer, Kearny, and I hauled ass up here after him to make sure he didn't do anything stupid."

"He came here?"

"Place was brand new then. Parker and Greer built most of it. Kearny and I pounded a few ceremonial nails while I had some leave. Lexy was the first of the significant others, and she pestered Parker about how she should be up on the wall, too, since she was about to be family. We pulled it off the wall that weekend, but the next time any of us made it back, we noticed he'd put it back up."

"Wow."

"He said, 'Not all memories are good memories, but all of them are important.'"

Thatcher pointed out Greer's ex-fiancée, Shannen. "She and Greer applied and were approved to be foster parents together. None of us understood their relationship. She was warm and wonderful one minute, and the next she'd freeze everybody out. He loved her, though. Thought she loved him, too, but one day he came home from work and she'd cleared out the house and their joint bank account. Not a damn thing left except for his clothes and shoes and personal stuff like family albums. Everything else was gone. How the hell she managed that in the ten hours he was gone, no one knows. No note, no trace of her. Just vanished like she'd never been there to start with."

"God." Kit stared at the picture. "Why would he want to keep her face up there to sneer at him?"

"Memories," he repeated.

"Was she ever found?"

"Yeah. She'd either had a drug habit all along and hid it, or she'd fallen into it just before leaving and cleaning him out."

"Poor Greer."

Thatcher nodded. "He was so unruffled by it, it scared all of us more than if he'd freaked out. Parker and I and all of our sisters, hell, everyone at one point or another, have tried to grill him about it. Everybody's sure there's more to this story, but he holds fast that there's not. He says he wasn't more upset about it because they'd reached the point where you knew it wasn't going to work. Right after they were approved as foster parents, she started icing him. He thought maybe she was having second thoughts, thought maybe it was more his idea all along, you know, to foster, and that maybe she'd gone along with it but wasn't into it and got scared."

"Did she walk out on Chance, too?"

"No. Chance came to us later. About a year, year-and-a-half or so after Shannen. Greer found him squatting in a home he was building. Skinny, half-frozen and half-starved. Reminded him of himself. Greer, he came to us when he was eight. Drugged out mom, scarier and scarier series of boyfriends. Same thing for Chance. Eventually the kid figured living on the street was safer than hanging around with some of the dudes his mother brought home. Pretty amazing kid. He's got a lot of baggage, but it's like he doesn't live it. Carries it, but that's about it. It's like he saw his mother's life very early on and made up his mind to be different in every way. Quiet, respectful, honest, good. Shit," Thatcher laughed, still looking over the wall, "Greer's got rougher edges than Chance does."

They went through the wall together. He pointed out different friends and a few of the more memorable of his sisters' boyfriends. He stopped when he reached Kyle's photo. Coincidentally, they'd both had a week of leave at the same time the year before Kyle met Wendy. His folks had been on a cruise in Mexico, so he'd had no place to be. Thatcher brought him to the cabin for some fishing and relaxation.

"This is the life," Kyle had sighed from the hammock tied to two trees to the right of the front deck. "Makes me want to go AWOL. Just give the army the finger and stay right here."

He hadn't meant it, of course. But he'd talked about that trip a lot in the years that followed. Thatcher blinked as Kit's arms slid around him. He hadn't realized he was talking out loud.

"What about your exes?" she asked.

Thatcher was grateful for the change in topic. "You're the first woman I've brought here," he told her, watching her face as it sunk in. Surprisingly, she didn't give much away, just turned back to the wall a last time for a final look.

"Okay," she said lightly a few minutes later. "Where do you want me, Valiant?"

Anywhere. Everywhere.

Thatcher shifted, forcing his dirty reaction to her innocent question down.

"Front door," he gestured, "like all the rest."

She'd tried to talk him into taking the picture. He reminded her it had to be a selfie.

"You can email it to me. I'll make sure it gets developed and onto the wall."

She took seven or eight pictures before she liked one. He couldn't for the life of him see a difference in any of them, except for one exposure where her eyes were closed.

Kit insisted on taking one of both of them by the door.

"Not for the wall," she agreed, though she tried to talk him into it. "Just for me." He turned at the last second and kissed her, which annoyed her. "I want to see your eyes," she complained. He crossed them as a joke, and she snapped a photo.

"Delete that!" he laughed.

She refused.

He chased her out onto the deck and down the steps and several feet into the forest surrounding the cabin before deciding it wasn't going to end in his favor. Instead of cursing his aching knee and hip, instead of sucking down a beer to numb his disappointment in what might be permanent pain and disability, Thatcher returned her mischievous grin and grabbed her hand.

"C'mon. There's a hiking trail about three miles from here and a lake for fishing. We'll go get some supplies up the road and spend the day there."

"Okay," she agreed happily, stretching and breathing in deeply. "I love being out from under the brown cloud."

"It's polluted here, too, unfortunately. Sorry to burst your bubble."

"Not as bad," she argued, sticking her tongue out at him.

He chuckled, loving her playful side. "Not as bad," he agreed.

Kit out-fished him, bringing in three trout to his one. To his great surprise, she was already cleaning the fish for dinner by the time he'd stepped out of the shower.

"Marry me," he joked, slipping his arms around her from behind. He was only half-kidding. Though he'd never brought a woman to the cabin before, he was certain that none of his former friends-with-benefits would have been the gutting type.

"If that's all it takes, Groceries, you're way too easy." She let him nibble at her neck for only a moment before lightly jabbing him with her elbow. "Off. Go make us a fire."

He did as she asked, then contented himself watching her cook when she wouldn't let him help.

"Sit," she said, lightly elbowing him when he tried to stir the rice. "My turn to take care of you a little."

And take care of him she did. From one of the best fish dinners he'd ever had to loading the dishwasher to turning him inside out on the fireside nest they'd made. Watching her move astride him by firelight was a whole new dimension in pleasure. Even her happy noises were different here. Louder. Freer. Less hushed. Her orgasm ripped through her with a wild abandon he felt through hands that clutched her hips. It quaked all the way up into his arms and shoulders and then shot straight down to his groin, igniting his own climax.

But no matter how hot that particular fire burned, how crazy it drove him, it was the soft, pliable warmth of her body tucked against his afterward that hammered him harder than any sexual release ever could. He needed her there, right there, for the rest of his life. Her soft breath, her sleepy babble about nothing at all. Her "I should call and check on Lily, but I know she's fine. And it would require getting up. Which I never, ever want to do," was like a blanket for his soul. Her trust, that's what killed him. It was the ultimate reward. The lottery won. He held back the words he wanted to offer up again, not because he didn't love her, but because he knew that even if she didn't say them back, she loved him, too.

CHAPTER TWENTY-TWO

"I don't want to go home," Kit moaned as they packed up the Jeep. The smile Thatcher gave her in response set off a fluttering in her chest. It was exhilarating and horrifying at the same time.

Play time is over. Back to reality.

Kit sighed. The critic was right. Time to go. Time to get back to normal.

It was still dark as they hit the highway. Getting back in time for group was important. The fact that Thatcher acknowledged it and didn't try to talk her into leaving in the afternoon, instead, meant a lot.

David might not be watching, but she wouldn't miss any other group sessions. She'd grudgingly taken the week off after Gil tossed her from the stage, and she'd worried the whole time that somehow David would know, that he'd call and threaten her. He'd called, but he'd made no mention of group. What he *did* mention was worse. Either way, she was determined not to miss any more sessions.

They fled the sunrise, heading west and then south, managing to avoid the worst of rush hour in Phoenix. She was surprised by how relaxed, how loose she felt. Like something had come unknotted. Was this what it was like for everyone, getting out of town for a while? It had been so long since she'd even taken a day trip that she couldn't remember. Kit knew she must have felt carefree at some point in her youth, before things with her mother got bad. But when she poked at them, all her memories were tinged with shadows. Whether they'd been there during the actual events or were added by revisionist history, she didn't know. But a thick layer of bittersweet coated every memory she had of her mother now, and that included the few vacation memories she had.

Thatcher, too, seemed wrapped in the same easy contentment. He tapped the steering wheel, occasionally muttering a chorus or two, cracking a grin when one of Kearny's old Smoke/Fire/Ash songs or a song by his new band, Ashes Onward, popped up on his playlist.

"I love that one," she said when her favorite Ashes Onward song played.

He gave her a fond look. "Me, too," he said, wheeling onto her street.

If his stomach sank a little, also, he didn't let on. But by unspoken agreement, they sat and sang along to the song before reluctantly exiting the Jeep.

There wasn't time to do the laundry, but they stood in the utility room tossing two days' worth of clothes into baskets for lights and darks. She emptied her toiletries from the rolled kit and zipped up her wheeled-suitcase. He tucked it back into the top of the closet for her, though he winced a little as the motion challenged his left shoulder. But just like when he pulled it down, he shrugged off her protest.

"Want to get a quick bite before group?" he asked, checking his phone.

And that's when it hit her, really hit her. Fun time was over. Back to mommying and…life.

Lily wasn't the problem, though. Kit ached to hold her daughter, wanted to blow raspberry kisses against her little neck with every fiber of her being. It was everything else. Living hand to mouth. Worrying every moment, waiting for the next financial disaster to sweep her away. For the food to dwindle. For the bills to rise. For the ever-present voice at the back of her mind to resume clamoring, *sell the house.*

Get out from under this albatross before you land your ass in the street and have to live in your damn car!

Shock coursed through her as a new voice whispered back, *Groceries would never let that happen.*

Thatcher glanced at her, frowning. "Kit? Lunch?"

It was like there were little microscopic masonry experts hiding inside her. She all but felt the frantic shoring up of her defenses, the fortification of her inner fortress.

"I've got plenty of food, Groceries," she said lightly, opening the fridge as if to demonstrate. "Let's grab something here." As she ducked further into the fridge, she called over her shoulder, "And we'll have to drive separately to group. I've got some errands I need to run after I get Lily."

"Kit," he started, clearly lost.

She tossed him a smirk as she dumped sandwich makings onto the counter. "Thanks for this weekend, Valiant. It was just what the doctor ordered. But time to get back to business, right? I'm sure you've got stuff of your own you need to do."

She didn't look his way again, but she felt his puzzlement like the beat of wings at her back, as if his confusion were a seagull in search of a snack, waiting for the right moment to swoop in front of her. Only he'd search her face for answers instead of food.

This time the silence was awkward, full of questions she knew he wanted to ask but didn't know how to. Kit could all but see them spinning through his mind, see his mental rewind of the past several hours spent driving home, working through those moments in search of an answer for her abrupt distance.

Idiot.

You can't give him time like this and then just walk away.

He's done nothing wrong.

Don't shut him out.

This is how you end up alone forever, stupid.

She came close to chopping her finger instead of the onions.

How had her inner critic gone from its usual refrain to this? Seconds ago, it was reminding her that she was back. Back to her life. Her impossible life with her one saving grace—Lily.

David. David is how you can walk away.

Kit felt the rustling of a million protests, a million comebacks stirring inside, trying to form. But the tiny masons shoved bricks at every last one. And they held.

~~~

The thing about happiness was that the moment you were trenched in it, rolling around in it like a dog in garbage, that was the exact moment everything went to shit. If she were honest with herself, Kit figured she'd been waiting for this moment since that last night at the cabin. Maybe not this particular shitty thing, but *some* shitty thing. She'd never have guessed it would come in the form of a damn phone call the following Saturday morning of quasi-domestic bliss with Thatcher and Lily.

"Hello?"

"Kit?"

She nearly dropped the small bowl of Cheerios before she could set it in front of Lily at the table. Another thing she'd been blind to…Lily's readiness to sit on a booster seat instead of in the high chair.

"Kit?" David's voice hardened. "I'm not going away. I want to see my daughter."

"No."

"I'm trying to be nice here. If you're telling me to lawyer up, I can do that."
~~~

Lawyer. Oh, God.

He knows I don't have two nickels to rub together. He knows I can't afford this fight.

"Fuck off!" she all but screamed into the phone, forgetting her daughter's little ears listening right next to her. Her hand shook as she poked the 'end call' circle on her phone.

Thatcher didn't have to battle past her hand to close the distance between them. She let it fall. She didn't fight him when he tucked an arm around her and muttered,

"Let's go in the other room for a sec."

She was shaking too hard to speak, fury rumbling through her like hellfire.

"Lil' Miss," he said over his shoulder, "eat your Cheerios. Your mama and I are going to be right back."

Valiant understood the living room wasn't far enough away. He led her all the way to her bedroom and eased the door almost closed. Then he just watched her and waited. When she didn't say anything, just stood trembling with fat tears sliding down her boiling cheeks, he said more than asked, "David still wants to see Lily."

She nodded.

He waited. Kit was too afraid of screaming to open her mouth yet.

Thatcher stroked her tears with his thumbs. A fool's errand, for sure, as they were readily replaced with more. "Are you scared a judge might force visitation?"

She shook her head. "He signed away his rights. He can't take that back."

At least she didn't think so. She wasn't really afraid of that. The prick knew just what to say to scare her, though. "Last time, he said someday, when Lily's grown up, he'll find her and tell her that I kept him from her, and she'll hate me."

Valiant, ever the mind reader, tucked her against him. Now the hysterical sobs came. The terror. The little *what-*

ifs screeched, wheeling in her mind like vicious birds. What if he did? What if he found Lily, played the victim, and turned her precious girl against her? What if he did lawyer up and by some miracle, a judge blew past the fact that he'd signed away his rights and granted visitation or— oh, God—*joint* custody?!

Though violent, it didn't take long for the crying jag to pass.

Thatcher kissed her tenderly at the corner of each eye, making a final swipe at her tears. *Oh, God, this man.* Her heart wobbled in her chest.

And then he opened his mouth and ruined everything.

"Maybe you should let him see her."

She felt her eyebrows lift, felt her mouth drop open, but the words were stuck.

Thatcher coaxed her back into his arms. Kit didn't want to admit how much strength she drew from his embrace. The warmth of him where she'd gone ice cold, the solidity of his body against hers, shoring her up when she wanted to fall to the floor in a heap. How tired she was of doing it all alone, and how she hadn't known it until he'd come along with his goddamn groceries and his *being* there. And how she didn't want to do it alone again now that she knew what it was like to have that support, that help, that…*love.*

Don't. Not again. Look where love got you last time.

But it wasn't love, and you know that now. What you felt for David...that doesn't even come close to what you feel for Thatcher.

"I can't," she finally said. She said it to both Thatcher's suggestion and his feelings for her, though he didn't know that.

"Okay," he agreed.

She eased him back as Lily's shout from the kitchen pierced the air.

"Mama! Down!"

Kit hurried from the room, worrying that Lily would

hurt herself climbing down from the booster seat. She broke into a relieved smile at the sight of her daughter trying with all her little might to push herself back from the table. Thankfully, the chair holding her booster seat was too heavy and she'd been pushed in too close.

"Okay, Lily Bug, okay," she chuckled as her daughter grunted from her final attempt to do it herself.

"Down!" Lily hollered.

"Inside voice, Lily," she said mildly, kicking the chair back with one leg and lifting her out of the booster seat.

"Down," Lily repeated more quietly. "Pease!"

"That's my good girl! Please!" she laughed, kissing Lily's neck. Blowing a raspberry against her soft skin, Kit set her gently on her feet.

Lily veered around Thatcher as he stepped into the kitchen. He grinned after her, amused, and helped Kit warm their cold breakfast plates.

The light Saturday morning mood was broken, however. She pushed rubbery scrambled eggs around on her plate, poking at them listlessly. David wouldn't leave it alone for long. He wasn't the type to take no for an answer. She'd tried, when he'd asked her out on that first date. He'd worn her down. At the time, that persistence was much to her delight. But now, she'd like nothing more than for him to have truly grown up the way he claimed to have, to have grown out of that dogged persistence.

Kit remained uneasy as morning slid into midday. She waited for the phone to ring again as she worked through her usual piled-up chores and cleaning. Being his Valiant self, Thatcher refused to just sit idly by while she worked. They changed the sheets together, she dusted, he vacuumed, she mopped, he threw in a load of laundry. She ran out of chores before she ran out of worry. The other shoe, waiting to drop, hovered over her head as they walked with Lily to the neighborhood park.

"He's not going to just accept it," she said suddenly,

watching Lily bounce and rock on a spring rider shaped like a bee.

Unphased by the out-of-nowhere comment, Thatcher nodded. "Probably not. I think you'd be better off letting him see her for an afternoon. Satisfy his curiosity," he shrugged.

"No," Kit frowned. "He—"

"I know what he did, Kit," Thatcher said solemnly. "I know he tore your heart out."

"He did not. He walked away from his daughter, that's what he did!"

"And you." His unruffled tone bothered her more than if he'd raised his voice right back at her.

"He—"

"Hurt you," Thatcher insisted quietly. "And I'd like to gut him for that. But he did a better job of it, himself, judging by your reaction to him."

"Fine. He hurt me, Valiant. So, what? What matters is that he hurt Lily."

Thatcher shook his head. "Still you. She doesn't know the difference, Kit. She's too young to understand who he is. He's a stranger to her."

Right. And it's better that way. She doesn't have to feel like this. Like me. Wondering what I did wrong. Why he didn't want me anymore, out of nowhere.

"It's not your decision, Valiant."

"Nope," he agreed.

The silence between them was just as easy as the rest of his words had been, without malice or agenda. She knew he was waiting, though.

"Do you think he's right? Do you think she'll hate me someday for keeping her from him?"

He shrugged. "I think all girls pass through hating their mothers for something or other. My sisters did, sometimes. Or they acted like it, if the screaming matches were any indication. And guys butt heads with their fathers. Social order or realizing your parents don't know everything or something."

"That's different."

"Is it?" Thatcher smiled at Lily's gleeful squeals as she rocked and bounced the springy bee harder. "See? Testing her limits already." He lunged forward as the bee sprang a little too wildly. "Whoa, Lily Bug!" he laughed and kissed her in spite of her yowling protest. "Take it easy on the bee. He's getting tired." He sat her back down on the bee after using his right knee to still the out-of-control riding toy. "Be gentle, Lily." Satisfied that she wasn't going to rocket headfirst into disaster, he slid his arms around Kit. "I don't know the future. I do know that family is just about the only thing that matters. Whatever you call family. Blood, friends. Brothers." His voice grew thick. "You have to decide who family is and who they aren't. And then you have to let the chips fall where they may."

She sighed into his neck then kissed it to make up for what she was about to say. "Then I choose a family that doesn't include David."

"Okay," he said easily, stroking a lazy hand up and down her spine.

"You don't think I'm making the right choice," she sighed. She could all but feel the disapproval spilling off him.

"I don't. You might never regret it, but you might spend every day torturing yourself over what the right thing is, whether you made the right choice. Especially if he follows through on his threat to brainwash Lily against you."

"He could walk away again. In one day, in ten days, in two weeks, five years. And then I'm the horrible witch who let him back in. And if I don't, I'm the horrible bitch who never let Lily have a chance to know her father."

"Yep." She moaned into his t-shirt. His arms tightened around her. "It doesn't have to be decided this second, Kit."

"He's not going to just go away."

"Probably not," Thatcher answered.

They both stepped toward Lily, both reaching and restraining each other as she fumbled her way from the riding toy to the sandy bottom of the playground.

Kit smirked at him. "I wish you were her father."

The look on his face as she clapped a hand over her traitorous mouth was priceless. This man, this soldier who'd looked death in the face, this person who'd been to hell and back, he melted. His jaw tightened. He blinked fast and swallowed hard, his eyes flitting to Lily, full of hearts as she sat running sand through her fingers.

"I wish it, too. But I'm not, Kit," he said roughly, cupping her face in his palm. "So, you're going to have to figure out what to do with that."

She nodded.

"You're outraged on Lily's behalf. I get it," he said, wrapping his arms around her again from behind. "How dare that son of a bitch not feel all the love you feel for that little girl? How could anyone not feel it? She's adorable. Just remember, she's a blank slate. She's not feeling any of that, I don't think. I doubt she remembers him at all. But when she sees you, her face lights up. Her arms reach out. You built that over time, Kit. You met her needs, and you loved her into that place. She doesn't have that with David. She could, if he earned it back. If he's worthy of it. But she's too young to decide for herself right now, so you're going to have to do it for her. One way or the other."

She nodded again, unable to speak. He was right. Lily didn't seethe with anger toward David. Didn't want to rip him to shreds every time she looked at him. She didn't *know* him. She didn't know whether to reach up for him with a smile and a happy squeal or hide behind Kit's knee.

Fucking Valiant. Always making sense and valid points.

It bothered her all the way back to the house, Lily's tired little body tucked into her side, reminding her that the future was wide open, undetermined. A blank book waiting for words, memories, thoughts. Decisions.

Her heart still screamed “no”. But the logical mind Thatcher seemed to have awakened was still open, still wondering what the right thing was, which decision would garner the best possible of all possible futures.

She wondered through dinner, through Lily’s bath and her story. She wondered as she settled Lily into her lap on the rocking chair in her nursery for her bedtime story. She wondered as she rocked after the story ended, Lily’s body heavy and warm and asleep against her. She wondered as she lowered Lily into a crib that would soon give way to a big girl bed, same as every other recent big girl rite of passage.

She wondered when her phone rang just as she’d snuggled into Thatcher on the sofa in front of Netflix for their own pre-bed ritual.

“It’s him,” she sighed, showing Thatcher the screen.

Thatcher just kissed her temple and waited.

She didn’t say hello, just opened the line. David pled his case again, same as before. With coaxing and then threats when the coaxing didn’t seem to sway her toward his favor. Same as he’d always fought, first with charm, then with might. *Asshole.*

When he wound down to silence, she closed her eyes, wound up her courage, and said, “A week from tomorrow. Four p.m. You can visit for *one* hour. No more. Then we’ll see where it goes from there.” She hung up on his thanks, didn’t want them.

Thatcher kissed her temple again, took the show off of mute, and locked her in his arms. Tightly, the way he knew she loved to be held.

CHAPTER TWENTY-THREE

"Thatcher? George."

"George. One sec." Thatcher lifted his head, glanced at Kit's bedside clock. Seven a.m. Wednesday morning. He glanced at Kit to see if his phone had woken her, and he eased out of bed when he was satisfied it hadn't. In the hallway, he asked, "What's up?"

"I'm sorry for the lack of notice. Unexpectedly, Gil's father's surgery got moved up. He left Monday morning, which was why he wasn't at group. I'm sorry I didn't say anything then, but I was in panic mode scrambling to get started. The mold guys came out yesterday morning and tore almost the entire place down to the studs. Yesterday afternoon, the contractor replaced some rotted parts of the frame and an engineer was in to inspect. We're cleared to start building the place back to what it was. Are you still up for helping out? I'm only asking because yesterday, I cashed in pretty much all of my favors to get those guys to drop everything, and now I'm scrambling for bodies."

He stifled a yawn. "Sure. Today?"

"If at all possible. But we'll take any volunteers we can get all the way through Saturday evening. I've called the others, told them if they'd like, we can skip group today in favor of a little sweat equity. If not, a colleague of mine will host the session, same place."

"I'm in. When? Now?"

"As soon as you can make it here. The professional volunteers, you know, like the roofers and such, are already there working. But they'll be ready for some unskilled labor by eight. Nine at the latest, if we're going to get anything substantial done before Gil makes it back home late Saturday night. Then we just have to convince him to let us finish."

"What's the address?" He hurried to the kitchen table and scrawled it on the back of one of Kit's napkin-holder envelopes. "I'll be there. Want anything? Coffee? Donuts?"

"Bring yourself a large container of water. We've already got quite a spread laid out under a tent in the driveway."

"Great. See you soon."

He stepped into the shower, intending to wait until after to wake Kit, but he heard the door open behind him. She'd taken to hopping in with him, sometimes for utility, sometimes for other reasons. He grinned into the spray, wondering what sort of visit this would be. She wasted little time in letting him know, sliding a soapy hand down his belly and flattening herself against his back so that he felt her nipples jutting against him.

"Hello," he greeted huskily, tipping his head back as heat shot through him and his cock leapt to attention in her hand.

"Hi," she kissed his shoulder.

He turned toward her, ducking to tongue one of those hard nipples. She sucked in a breath. He tugged hard, ripping a moan from her, sending her hands into his still-soapy hair. They'd learned the hard way he wasn't quite up to sex in the shower, but a few bruises taught them where the limits were. Thatcher let Kit push them, felt her heel digging into his ass. He tested them, himself, leaning on his left arm for a bit as he moved to lavish attention on the other nipple and cupped her with his right hand, stroking her with his thumb, easing two fingers inside her.

She whispered naughty suggestions as he drove her higher, wanting to follow those happy noises of hers to their usual shattering conclusion, but she tugged gently on his hair, drawing him upward. He let her scrub the shampoo out of his hair. He stood against the wall of the shower while she hurried to shampoo her own, her eyes promising *soon, soon.* He stroked himself lazily a few times because he knew she liked to watch him pleasure himself. Saw her eyes go dark as she watched him, sliding her hand down to her folds to torture him in return.

She turned off the tap and danced him out of the shower. A quick towel-off later, she danced him into the bedroom, onto the overstuffed chair in the corner.

"Jesus, Kit," he groaned as she settled her mouth over his cock. "Yesss," he hissed, clutching the arms as she devoured him, licking and circling, sucking and blowing. "Right there," he moaned, unable to stop himself from cupping the back of her head, from lifting just a little, though his hip protested as always. He ignored it. As always. Lifted again. Sucked in a breath that was both agony and ecstasy as he felt his balls tighten, felt the shivery tingling at the base of his spine that signaled the onrush of orgasm.

With a wicked gleam in her eye, she lifted her head, climbed up onto the chair, knees beside his hips, and sank down with a cry she muffled with her hand. He buried his face between her breasts, filling himself with the soapy, warm scent of her as she ground hard against him.

"Fuck," she gasped, her chin lifting as she rode him, her eyes rolling back in her head the way that made him crazy. Her sounds, those crazy hot sounds, they grew louder and higher pitched as she rolled her hips. He caught them in his hands, held her tightly against him as he came in hard, jerking spasms.

"Kit," he curled forward, moaning into her chest as she fell mindlessly into her own orgasm. Her heart raced against his forehead.

They came down together, slowly, content to lean

against one another for several long minutes. He felt the clock ticking, his promise to George looming. He told her about the call in a hushed voice.

After fretting over leaving Nanette in the lurch for two days, Kit frowned. “What will we do with Lily? I can’t ask Nanette and Crystal to watch her. They work the shop together if I can’t be there.”

“Let me see if I can find someone,” he said, looking up at her as she pushed against the circle of his arms.

“I have to call Nanette to let her know I won’t be there. I have to get dressed. I have to get Lily dressed,” she said, kissing his throat. He let her go with a sigh.

He had the pleasure of watching her dress as he called Melody to ask who she used for her girls. Ten minutes later, he was dressed and in the kitchen with Lily as Kit finished readying herself for a day of hard work.

“Melody’s sitter can take her,” he told her as she skidded into the room in jeans, t-shirt, and socks. “Do you trust me?”

Her eyes went soft. “I do, Valiant. You haven’t steered me wrong yet.”

He dipped down to reward that praise with a kiss. She didn’t let him linger. One quick kiss, and she was back to stuffing Lily’s diaper bag with pull-ups, spare outfits, snacks, and a few small toys.

“Kit, the sitter’s got supplies of her own.”

“Over-prepare, Valiant.”

~~~

Speaking of preparation…he should have been prepared for the sight of Gil’s house after everything George had told them, but he reached for Kit’s hand and just stood at the edge of the sidewalk, unblinking, jaw dropped open.

“Jesus,” Thatcher said, shaking his head, “there’s no way this is all getting done by Saturday night.”
~~~

"We don't have to get it all done," George's voice startled him as he came up beside him, juggling four boxes of donuts and a box of coffee. "We just have to get far enough along that he gives in and lets us finish."

Kit grabbed two of the boxes, and Thatcher eased the coffee out of his hand, following him to the tent in the driveway.

"I've forgotten how much hungry dudes can eat," George joked.

Thatcher stopped so short he felt the corners of Kit's boxes poke the center of his back.

"Greer? You're the contractor?"

"Thatch," Greer smirked, sipping from the coffee he'd just poured himself, lifting the lid of a box as quickly as George could set them on the table. "These look great. I'm starved. I let the guys go first so I could send them to work."

"You're the contractor?" he asked again in disbelief. "How'd you even know about this?" From the corner of his eye, he saw Kit duck into the house.

After swallowing a huge bite of maple bar, Greer grinned and clapped his right shoulder. "Kismet, I guess. Chance saw a post on Facebook with a crowdfunding link, and he showed it to me. Said we needed to help a veteran in honor of Uncle Thatcher."

He was glad he hadn't bitten into the sugar donut he'd chosen. He'd never have gotten it down. "Is he here?"

Greer grimaced. "Yeah. I let him play hooky. Don't tell his school."

Thatcher laughed. "Mum's the word."

Kit wandered back out of the house.

Greer nodded at her as she chose her own pastry. "Hello, again."

She smiled. "Hi."

Both of them stared after her, dumbfounded, as she dropped her donut on a napkin on the table and ran out toward a group of volunteers unloading another round of supplies from a storage container.

"What's she up to?" Greer asked bemusedly as they watched Kit gesturing and pointing and making wide, sweeping gestures between the storage container, lawn, and the shell of Gil's house. Thatcher had no idea, except the guys who had started to unload supplies from the container changed course, seemingly at her direction. "I'll be damned," Greer laughed, shoving the last of his breakfast into his mouth before charging across the lawn to intercept her.

Thatcher wasn't close enough to hear their words, but something Greer said prompted her smile to bloom so wide and bright that a ridiculous little shock of jealousy pinged him in his gut. She shrugged, turned toward the house with Greer, gesturing again in those big, sweeping movements, then jerked a thumb over her shoulder toward the storage container before pointing at the house again. Unable to contain his curiosity when Greer reached out and shook Kit's hand, Thatcher moved toward them only to catch sight of a suspiciously familiar SUV wedging itself into one of the only open spaces left on the street.

His suspicions were confirmed when Parker slid out from behind the wheel and Melody rounded the back of the truck to open the cargo hatch.

Torn between which mystery to address first, he stood frozen on the lawn for a moment. When Parker turned to help Melody, he contented himself with catching up with Greer and Kit as they stepped into the house.

His heart began to jackhammer at the sight of bodies everywhere, flowing into and out of rooms, squeezing past one another like a colony of ants.

"What's all the pantomiming about?" he asked, trying to narrow his focus to only Greer and Kit, surveying what was probably the living room.

Kit's smile hit him low. "I'm just—"

“She’s just filling in for my supply coordinator, Tracey, until she’s back from maternity leave. She saved about three hours of work in a single conversation.”

It was a little bit like listening to a foreign language as Greer explained about work flow and construction trades, but the gist was a few suggestions from Kit about when to unload the supplies and where to place them had streamlined the entire volunteer project.

“If I’d been paying attention, I’d have done the same, but I was talking with you,” Greer shrugged. “Kit doing that told me she’d be an asset for us.”

“You gave her a job?” Thatcher grinned.

“A temporary job,” Kit’s smile didn’t waver with the concession. “And then maybe I can work into another position when Tracey comes back.”

“Wow. I couldn’t even get Greer to hire me when I got back from Walter Reed.”

Greer shot him a look. “You weren’t ready,” he said flatly. “If you’re ready now, I—”

Thatcher clapped his shoulder. “Relax. It was a joke. Let’s see if I’m capable of hanging drywall first. Just point me to the top priority.” He took a deep breath and swallowed hard, hoping his anxiety would taper off once he was focused on a task.

Greer paired him with a guy named Devon to start the sheetrock on the north and east facing walls of the living room. Thatcher glanced up, glad to see the ceiling was finished. He wasn’t sure he could hold up drywall, and he didn’t see a lift in the room. He had two teams assigned to each room of the house. The goal was to get all the sheetrock up and the tape and first layer of mud up in a single day.

“Tall order,” Thatcher commented.

Greer snorted. “You’re telling me. It’s a wish, not a promise.”

“Starburst stomp on the ceilings?” Thatcher asked. It

was generally done to mask imperfections with lumber and the sheetrock work itself…which was almost a guarantee with unskilled volunteer labor.

Greer nodded. "You won't have to worry about it, though. I've got you on walls only. You remember how to do this?" Greer asked. Studying him closely, he put a hand on Thatcher's right shoulder. "You okay to do this?"

Thatcher gave him a look. Greer held up his hands and backed away. "Ok, fine. Have at it."

"Didn't electrical want to re-wire the wall boxes?" Devon asked, halting Greer's retreat.

"Already done and inspected. You're good to go."

The chaos ramped up, frenetic pounding and the sound of drills in the bowels of the house muffled by the disposable ear plugs Greer gave him. He and Devon worked in companionable silence until they'd completed the cuts and the hanging of the drywall on the north wall.

Greer passed through, eyeing their work. "Nice. Take a break."

He didn't need to be told twice. He was already feeling the burn in his left side. An impossibly short twenty minutes later, he and Devon returned to find the south and west team had finished their portion and were pitching in to finish the east wall. Another two guys entered to tape and mud the ceiling. Thatcher's heart kicked up again. Too many bodies. He took a few measured breaths and pictured the house when they'd arrived, skeletal and sad. Devon seemed to notice he wasn't moving.

Devon leaned toward one of the ceiling guys and yelled over the noise, "Why don't you and the other two do the tape and mud in here, and we'll do the bedroom?" At the guys' nods, Devon lifted his chin toward Thatcher. "I'm going to measure for the front bedroom's wall cuts. Join me whenever!" Then he gestured with a toss of his head toward the entry door.

Thatcher followed the gesture and saw Parker headed

his way. His sister, Page, peeked at him from behind Parker. "Wow. Hi. You're here, too?" Page ducked out from behind Parker, giving him a grin. "Page?" he repeated.

She shrugged, looking tiny in her over-sized Greer Myers Design & Built shirt. "Yes. Obviously, I'm here."

"Here?" Parker laughed. "Are you kidding? She practically mobilized the entire crew that's working this project, including me and Melody. We couldn't have done all this without her."

"Really?" Thatcher lifted his eyebrows. Her cheeks reddened. "How did you do that?"

"Later," she said, gesturing toward the hallway, where Devon was poking his face out of the bedroom. "Go back and help him."

Reluctantly, he helped Devon with the measurements and wall cuts, wondering what Parker meant about Page being responsible for the success of the project. Would project coordination be the thing that might finally settle their impulsive, "from one thing to the next" sister? Or would it be just another of her fly-by-night passions that would fall by the wayside?

Soon, he forgot everything but the steady work of…work. Except for the occasional discussion about tricky drywall cuts and a little grunting while positioning the sheetrock around the (thankfully) perfect cuts, he and Devon worked silently together, surprisingly in sync for two guys who'd never worked together before. Two of the super speedy living room guys, who turned out to be professional drywallers, joined them in the bedroom. Anxiety kicked up again, his heart jittering and panic telling him to *Get out! Run!*

His muscles protested. He ignored them. They twinged. Then ached. Then shot angry daggers of electric pain all through his left side. That was when he finally stopped to rest and chug more water. He stepped out into the hall just as Kit crossed the living room.

"Nice," she said, grinning at the progress. "We've just finished in the master bedroom. Let's break for a very late lunch."

Thatcher checked his watch, stunned to find it was nearing two o'clock.

Greer called a time out on the work for a short speech on the lawn.

"You guys have been doing an amazing job. Thank you, all of you, for coming out to support a veteran in his time of need. We're going to take a thirty-minute food break, and then before you get back to work, we need to stick together out here for a quick group photo. I also want to thank my sister, Page, here, for organizing the volunteers and rounding up a large portion of our donated supplies."

Thatcher caught her eye as she sidled up to Greer. Classic Page nerves had her fiddling with the end of her long ponytail as the group applauded her efforts.

"Enough of that," she said, blushing. "Let's eat and get back to work!"

Thatcher fought off several more anxiety attacks as the afternoon wore on. At one point he found himself fighting for breath in a smelly portable toilet, the only place with any privacy. His shoulder felt like it was on fire, and his knee had faltered twice as he and Devon had moved on to taping and mudding the front bath. He felt like shit for not carrying a full load. He felt like shit for giving in to this ridiculous panic over a little loud noise and a crew of only well-meaning volunteers. And yet he couldn't fully catch his breath because there were only two toilets, and someone knocked on his door.

The good news about portable johns was no one wanted to make eye contact, whether coming or going. He ducked under the refreshment tent, grabbing a bottle of soda from the cooler, hoping a sugary caffeine boost would help, and focused his eyes on the empty yard next door. Void of bodies, it was just a few scraggly brown weeds and dirt. Still, he jumped out of his skin when a voice sounded behind him.

"How you holding up?" Greer asked.

He wanted to lie, but he couldn't find the energy. "I'm wrecked, man. I feel like I'm about to fall down." He couldn't look at his brother. Didn't want to see pity there, or defeat. Or maybe it was only his own disappointment. No matter how many workouts he'd done trying to get his body back into shape, it felt like it was all for nothing. He couldn't even work a single full day of construction.

Greer gestured to a lawn chair, taking the one beside it. "When's the last time you worked for nearly nine hours?"

He shrugged, leaning on the right arm of the chair.

"Thatch, you're expecting an awful lot out of yourself. What's your PT been? One hour a day? Two?"

He didn't answer. He knew Greer was right. He'd done more today than ever before. But seeing guys his age still scurrying around the job site, amped up on Red Bull and their own youth did nothing for his ego.

"Don't be so hard on yourself."

He glanced at Greer, relieved to see him looking back with nothing close to pity on his face. Matter-of-factness, sure. Greer's usual filter-free expression, sure. But no dismay. No concern.

"I guess," he nodded. "Anything I can do for you right here in this chair?"

Greer shook his head. "We're getting ready to call it a day. We're losing too much light, and we need to run the heater all night to make sure we're ready for the second coat tomorrow. The night security team will be arriving in about thirty minutes. We're going to start up again tomorrow around seven and see how far we can get. If you're up to the second round of texturing drywall or some paint work, feel free to stop by. If not, that's ok."

Thatcher shrugged again. "Not sure. Way I feel right

now, I'm not sure I'll even be able to move."

"No big deal. We're not hurting for volunteers, as you can see. Page is pretty persuasive."

"How much was Page, though? How much was you nagging at your guys and Parker talking his search friends into it?" He'd sure seen his share of guys he recognized.

Greer flashed him a smile. "Maybe a little. But she did a lot of calling around, too. She scored at least half of the materials and while she did that, she helped your buddy, George, score the fast track to our inspections and the engineer."

"No kidding?"

"Not even a little," Greer shook his head. "Maybe Page has finally found her groove." With that, he stood up and stretched. "I'm hurting, too, Thatch. It's not just you. We're just getting older. Maybe I can talk Doc Shelby into working the kinks out."

Thatcher laughed. "TMI, dude."

"Night, Thatch. Thanks for coming."

"Thank *you* for coming. Coincidence my ass!"

Greer just shrugged again and sauntered off, slinging an arm around Chance as he happened by. They stopped in the yard for a brief conversation, then Greer slapped him on the shoulder and teasingly shoved him back toward the front door in time to collide with Kit. The two of them steadied each other, smiling. Every time he'd seen Kit that day, she'd sported a huge grin. The guys traded barbs with her like they'd been working with her for years. No doubt her salty mouth helped her to fit in.

He grinned, suddenly hungry for a taste of that salty mouth, himself, and rose to claim his prize only to have his left knee buckle, toppling him back into the lawn chair.

Fuck.

Face burning, he shifted into a more comfortable, less accidental position, a shaky feeling coursing through him. He took a furtive look around and found the yard and driveway mostly empty. No one appeared to have seen him falter.

Damn it! Why hadn't he taken more breaks? Because he was trying to prove himself. To Greer, after that remark about his readiness to work. To Parker, after he pulled him aside during lunch to ask if he was holding up okay, if he needed a longer break. To Page, who cornered him during a quick late afternoon break to ask if working on Gil's house was taking an emotional toll. As if he were going to break at the mere thought or mention of anything military. To himself, wondering if he'd have the stamina to work a full-time job in any capacity other than some boring desk job. Not that it necessarily had to be construction, or even a job that was physical all day long.

Kit found him working up the nerve to try standing again. Leaning down, she kissed him in a way that said she'd missed him, too. "Ready to blow this popsicle stand, Valiant?"

"If I can manage to get up," he groaned, forcing a laugh.

She studied his face, reaching for his hands. "Up. We need to get Lily, and I need to get home and into a warm bath if I have any hope of doing this again tomorrow."

"Can I join you?" he joked, relieved when he stood and his knee held.

She tossed him a heated look over her shoulder that sent a sizzle of interest straight down to his crotch. "That's a date, soon as we get Lily fed and to bed."

He limped heavily but quickly after her.

CHAPTER TWENTY-FOUR

After four days of grueling volunteer work, Kit wanted to pull the covers over her head and sleep for a week. Thatcher would no doubt be amenable to that. He'd been so exhausted by the fourth day of volunteer work on Project Gil that he'd left at noon to pick up Lily from the sitter, missing all the drama when Gil, himself, arrived home at just after five.

Kit wouldn't soon forget the sight of Gil standing gape-mouthed at the curb next to the rideshare car for a long minute before charging into the yard, grabbing the first guy he saw, shouting, "What the *fuck* is going on here?! What are you people doing to my house?"

Behind him, a younger version of Gil climbed out of the shuttle. His son apparently knew already, because he broke into a wide smile, grabbed Gil's shoulder and talked in his ear for a few minutes. Gil released the wide-eyed volunteer and called out,

"Who's responsible for this? Who did this? C'mon out right now!" When no one stepped forward, he kicked his own suitcase and yelled, "C'mon! Grow some balls and explain yourself!"

Gil didn't have to wait long. Kit froze as Thatcher's sister, Page, stepped forward, dwarfed in her three-sizes-too-large Greer Myers Design & Build shirt, and—bravely, Kit thought—stretched a hand out for Gil to shake.

"Page Myers," she said, her ponytail flipping over her

shoulder.

Kit didn't hear the rest of her conversation with Gil because Page, unlike Gil, wasn't hollering at the top of her lungs, and the volunteers were returning the tools and materials to the storage container for safekeeping until the next day. But she didn't miss him rubbing his face with one large palm, over and over, and she definitely didn't miss him folding Page into his beefy arms for a long moment. When they separated, Page held out something to him in the dark and pointed at a car. Then she tucked Gil's and his son's bags into the hatchback, closed them in the backseat, and drove away with them. Crisis averted.

Since Nanette didn't care when she let herself in to Waggy Waggy on Sundays to do the weekly deep clean, she let herself wake naturally without an alarm. Thatcher didn't so much as stir when she slid out of bed, so she left him to rest. Even Lily slept in. It wasn't until she was about to leave that she heard Thatcher talking softly to her girl.

Kit poked her head into the nursery to find him dressing her for the day.

"You don't have to do that," she protested.

He grinned. "Why not? I know you've got to get going."

"I do," she agreed. "Mama has to work, Lily. Be good."

Lily fussed a little after Kit kissed her, but Thatcher was quick with a distraction.

Five hours later, the house was tomb quiet when she stepped into the laundry room. No television. No raucous sounds of Lily playing with Thatcher in the living room.

"Guys?" she called, plopping her purse onto the top of the dryer. After hastily removing her sweaty, hairy clothes and plucking clean ones from the nearby laundry basket, she went looking for them.

Kitchen, empty. Living room, empty. Lily's room, empty. The spare bedrooms, hall bath, and the master bedroom were also empty. Her heart began to hammer.

"Thatcher?"

She hurried back to the living room to peek out the window into the back yard. Pool, empty. Thank God.

"Thatcher?" she called again, this time not missing the panic in her own voice.

Why did you leave him alone with Lily instead of taking her to Crystal and Nanette's?

Where the fuck are you, Groceries?

She tried not to panic. Her phone had no missed calls, no messages. His Jeep was parked at the curb. She rushed back through the living room, looking for clues. She found one, finally, on the kitchen table. A piece of construction paper full of scribbles and the words, *Playing at the park with Lily. Home soon.*

Relief had her plopping backward onto a kitchen chair.

"Jesus, Valiant!" she cried into the empty room.

Home soon, her brain reminded her.

Home.

Kit tried to feel angry at his use of the word. Or afraid. Too familiar. Too assuming. Too…accurate.

Don't.

Don't read into it.

And don't…

She stilled.

Don't like it so damn much.

She made it out the front door and down the steps before she saw them coming down the sidewalk from the neighborhood park, Thatcher bent to the right so Lily could reach his hand, letting her toddle beside him because she'd no doubt thrown a fit at being carried. She'd been doing so a lot lately. First the big girl potty, then the booster chair, and now she seldom let anyone carry her anywhere unless she was too tired to care.

Kit's eyes watered at the sight. She told herself it was because her little girl was suddenly growing up so much, so fast. It wasn't at all because the man beside her was letting her do it, letting her assert herself and take the world on her own terms, even if it had to be killing his back.

She made a show of running down the street to them.

"Lily Bug, my big girl!" she cried, crouching down to give Thatcher a rest. "Hi, gorgeous! Did you have fun at the park?"

Lily nodded and let Kit snuggle her for a moment before she squirmed free and ran ahead toward the house as fast as her little legs would carry her.

Kit rushed after her. "You have to hold hands next to the street, Lily Bug."

Oh, that face.

Kit bit back a laugh at the defiant expression and fixed her own face to be stern, holding her hand out for Lily to take. Lily ignored it and ran ahead again. Kit let her go a few steps, then jogged around and in front of her.

"Miss Lily," she said firmly, "you have two choices. You take mama's hand, or you get carried home."

She held her hand out to Lily again, fighting back a laugh when her big little girl's expression went from defiant to furious defiant. When Lily ignored her hand again, Kit finally felt the first kick of irritation. Scooping up her little rebel of a daughter, she took one look at Thatcher's amused face and laughed. In response, Lily began to scream and kick.

"Stop," she said mildly, locking her arm around Lily to keep her from squirming her way free.

"And so it begins," he joked, catching up to them.

"I guess so!" she called over Lily's hollering.

They didn't try to keep up a conversation, just walked the short distance back to the house.

Inside, Kit took Lily to her room and deposited her firmly in her crib. "Tantrums mean Miss Lily needs some nap time," she said, ignoring her daughter's forceful chorus of "No, mama! NO! NO! NO! Down! Down!"

"Night night, Lily Bug," she said, though her spine had gone rigid. She fought the urge to look back as she left the room. In the hall, Thatcher opened his arms and took her in. "Where did my sweet little Lily Bug go?"

He chuckled at the desolation in her voice. "Still in there somewhere. She'll settle down in a minute."

"I hope so," she moaned against his neck.

He rubbed her back consolingly. "Come on. Let's let her work it out. She'll wear herself out eventually."

They cuddled on the couch until Lily's cries eventually slowed and then stopped.

They'd barely finished a very late lunch when a knock sounded on the door and memory flooded into her.

Shit. David.

The very sight of him on her doorstep had her lunch threatening to come back on her. David's smile froze in place when he caught sight of Thatcher behind her.

"Hi," David's voice was cool. He turned his eyes to her. "You didn't tell me you were involved with someone."

"Because it's none of your business."

A long beat of silence followed.

"Can I come in?"

She nearly said no and shut the door in his face, but looking at his expectant face made her remember what he was capable of. A lawsuit he wouldn't win but which would take her back to eating ramen seven days a week at the very least. Wordlessly, she stepped back.

"She just went down for a nap, David. You can see her from the door of the nursery, satisfy your curiosity."

"Kit, that's not fair," David protested, squaring on her.

Thatcher inserted himself between them. Kit was torn between laughing and melting. Gently, she pushed him aside.

Oh, Valiant. I can handle this asshole.

Aloud, she said, "And it was so fair of you to dump her in my mother's lap as she was dying. It was fair of you to refuse to watch her for even a few measly days until I recovered enough to take over."

"Kit, I'm sorry," David said, reaching for her.

Kit stepped back against Thatcher, who slid a hand to her waist.

"I don't care about your sorry," she shook her head. "This was a bad idea."

"I'm not leaving without seeing my daughter."

Kit laughed. "Fine time to get all proprietary," she shot back.

"Kit," David warned now.

She felt Thatcher stiffen behind her, and her heart did a giddy little flip.

See? This. This is a man, David.

"You go in there and you bring her out to me, Kit. I have a right to—"

"Seems to me you signed those rights away," Thatcher said easily.

"You stay out of this, whoever the hell you are!" David thrust a finger in the air, closer and closer to Thatcher's shoulder.

"Settle down," Thatcher said mildly. "Seems to me you're not in a position to bargain. You take whatever first meeting you're offered. Then maybe, just maybe, you'll get a second."

Kit nodded. "Come to the nursery and look at the little girl you tossed aside and then get the hell out of my house."

"Fine," David spat. "Let's go, then."

Kit led the way down the hall. She walked backward slowly toward Lily's door. Her lunch did the rumba in her stomach, threatening to erupt all over David. Everything in her was opposed to letting him near her precious little girl, let alone hold her. Thatcher stood a few steps away, watchful but giving them space.

Kit eased the door open and peeked inside. Lily had cried herself out and was sleeping on her back, one fist curled on either side of her messy hair.

Great. He's going to think you just let her run around

like this.

She stood next to the crib and motioned for David to step into the room.

He stood looking at his daughter for the first time in just over two years, saying nothing. After several minutes of staring, he turned his face toward her and said, "She's beautiful."

"Yeah," Kit nodded. "It's a lucky thing. She doesn't resemble you at all."

He didn't answer. In a quick motion, he reached down and plucked her out of the crib. Horror and snide laughter warred as Lily, so abruptly woken, found herself in a stranger's arms and began to scream bloody murder.

Kit snatched her out of David's arms. "What's the matter with you? She doesn't even know who you are and you just grab her! What did you expect to happen?!"

David shook his head and had the nerve to reach out and chuck Lily under the chin. "I'm your daddy, Lily."

She just screamed louder at the intrusion.

Kit jiggled her in her arms and kissed her temple. "It's ok, Lily Bug, it's ok."

David stood there helplessly. Kit swept past him, calling over her shoulder, "Ok. You've had your look. Now it's time to go."

"That's not—"

"Fair?" Kit challenged over her daughter's wailing. "Who are you to talk about what's fair?"

Kissing Lily again, she lowered her to the play blanket on the living room floor and handed her the toy alligator Thatcher had given her. It never failed to soothe her.

"Turning her against me, though? Her own father?"

Kit laughed. "I didn't have to turn her anywhere, David. She doesn't know you from a hole in the ground. That's how she reacts to people she's never met who put their hands all over her like she's some doll in a toy store instead of a person!"

Except Thatcher. She never cried when he picked her up. Looked at him funny, but never cried.

Thatcher stood calmly in the hallway arch but Kit could feel him, ready, waiting to jump in if needed.

David hitched his thumbs in his pockets in a way she'd once found sexy. Now she narrowed her eyes at him.

"So, what now?" David asked.

She could have suggested that he sit down on the blanket and pick up a toy and sit quietly beside Lily for a while, let her get acclimated to the new person in the room. She could have joined them there, grabbed her own stuffed toy, and found a way to engage the three of them in a game with the toys. Instead, Kit did nothing but shrug.

"Figure it out, David, like I had to figure everything out. Alone."

David snorted. "I'm hardly alone. You're watching me like I'm some kind of monster."

She fought a smile. "If the label fits…"

David's eyes narrowed. "You're determined to do anything to ruin this. If you'd just help a little, maybe—"

She rolled her eyes. "*I* didn't have any help."

He sighed heavily. "I jumped in, Kit, and you and Lily both freaked out. I'm asking what to do, and you won't help me. Make up your mind. Because I'm going to know her, Kit, whether you help or not. Whether you like it or not. She deserves to have her father in her life."

"She does," Kit nodded. "Or she did, once. I wouldn't do that to her now, subject her to the likes of you."

"Poisoning her mind isn't going to help her any," David shot back. "Making me out to be the bad guy at every turn, Kit, that's real classy. People make mistakes."

"Yeah, and they learn from them. I learned the one that said Lily's father is just a guy who provided a little sperm. Then he walked away and didn't look back for two years until some freak attack of conscience bit him on his sorry ass or whatever. Just because you've suddenly decided you want to be a dad doesn't mean I have to let you. That little girl is my mission in life, and I'm not going to let you hurt her."

"I don't *want* to hurt her. I want to know her."

"Why?" Kit challenged. "Why now? Why all of a sudden?"

"Not all of a sudden," David denied, stepping toward her again. "I told you before, Kit, I've regretted what happened almost from the moment it happened. I told you that when we talked on the phone." He glanced toward Thatcher. "I still love you, Kit, and I know I'm too late for that. But how can it be too late to love my daughter? Could it ever be too late for you? No. Because she's your daughter, and that is a love that doesn't end. Mine might have been late, but it's never going to end, either."

Oh, you're good. That's the David I fell in love with. The one that could turn a phrase into some kind of romance book declaration.

Only her memory was moved. Kit, in the present, felt nothing.

"Well, that's a shame for you, because you're going to have to carry that love around unrequited for the rest of your life." When he didn't answer, Kit clapped her hands. "This has been a productive afternoon, but I've got things to do before work tomorrow, so it's time to call it a day."

"When can I come back, Kit?" David asked as he reluctantly turned toward the door.

"I thought that was pretty clear, David. Never. You've seen Lily, satisfied your curiosity, and now that's all done. Time to move on. Go back home to Texas and do whatever it is you've been doing since you abandoned your daughter and landed her in foster care."

"Kit, I'm going to come back. Next Sunday, same time. If you keep blocking me, I'm going to get a court order."

The only reason she didn't claw his face off was because she was all too aware of Lily playing nearby.

"Well, David, you do whatever you want. Personally, I think a court will laugh right in your face, but I'm not too worried. You're not exactly the king of follow through, after all, and that much will be as apparent to any judge as it was to me when I woke up and found out my baby was in state custody because her sperm donor just could not be bothered."

He flipped her the bird on the way out the door. Kit watched him from the doorway, Thatcher's comforting warmth pressed up behind her, until David squealed away from the curb and roared off down the street.

When she shoved the door in the direction of the jamb and turned into his arms, he welcomed her with a deep, hungry kiss. The sort that sent your mood from basement level to rooftop in a matter of seconds. Then he tenderly stroked her cheek.

"You handled that well, Kit."

"No one died," she agreed, pressing her forehead into his chest with a frustrated groan.

"Give it some time to cool off," Thatcher said, "and maybe try again in a couple weeks."

Kit drew back to check his face for a cheeky grin. Sarcasm. It had to be. But it wasn't. He was serious.

"Are you insane?" she choked. "No. No way. This is over. He can sit and spin. He wanted to see her. He saw her. Done. Over."

"I know a little something about how kids wonder about those missing parents, Kit," he said quietly. "Payson and Page came to us as infants, abandoned when they were just a few days old. Both of them asked and asked our mother growing up why they didn't 'match' the rest of us. When Mom and Pop explained how they were adopted, they asked and asked why their mommy and daddy didn't want them."

Kit tried not to imagine them as little girls asking questions.

"Even though they love our parents more than anything, the hole is still there, wanting to be filled."

"Don't," Kit shook her head. "Don't do that. This is different and you know it."

"People fuck up, Kit. Don't you think I wish every day that I'd stayed sober, that I'd driven Gabriela home instead of being too drunk to drive?"

"So *you'd* be dead instead?"

"Maybe not, though," he countered. "Different weights, different heights. Different impact. Whatever. The point is, don't you think it's possible for a person to regret their actions? Don't you believe in second chances?"

"It's not the same, you aren't the drunk driver who hit your pickup. You didn't kill Gabriela, even if you feel responsible," she protested. "A drunk driver did that. He changed lives forever. Yours. Gabriela's. Her family's. Your family's."

"But I played a role. No one can say what might have happened if I'd been driving instead of Gabby."

"It's not the same," she said again, stubbornly. "He left our baby alone in foster care. And now he grows a conscience or what the fuck ever, and wants to play house? No, Valiant! Hell no!"

"Kit—"

"No. Stay out of it. Lily's *my* daughter. It's my decision."

His face changed. He looked like someone had reached into his chest and yanked his heart right out, still beating. "I don't get any say in this?" He asked. "No opinion?" He reached for her. She retreated.

Kit felt her own heart stutter, part regret for hurting him and part gaping wound of her own. "No. Why would you? You're not—" And she heard it with his ears, too late.

He stilled, his hand dropped, no longer reaching to hold her. "Not family," he said dully.

She'd never seen those amber eyes look anything less

than lukewarm, hadn't thought it was possible. "Thatcher, that's not—"

"So, all that talk about wanting Lily to have two parents. About a real relationship being a partnership. That wasn't really true. You don't really believe any of that."

She couldn't exactly deny the accusation, not when she was insisting on being the only one to decide Lily's future. Thatcher tried again, though, God bless him, from a different angle.

"He's a jackass, Kit, but what motive would he have to come here begging to see his daughter?"

When it came to David, she couldn't muster up any mercy. The wound was still too raw, too gaping. The words Thatcher said made perfect sense to her brain, but they'd never make sense to her heart.

"I don't care if he met Jesus or had a near death experience. I don't care what brought his change of heart. He lost his rights forever when he signed away his rights to his daughter like he was selling a fucking car."

Damn him. He waited. Just waited, knowing nothing he could say would sway her. So, he waited, letting her feel her own refusals, letting her see it in his eyes that he didn't agree. Letting her see his disappointment. In her. She knew it made her a jerk, that someone as inherently good as Thatcher was disappointed in her. Good God, that look in his eyes was unbearable. Like a wounded animal, she couldn't respond to his kindness with anything but fear.

"Stop judging me, Thatcher! Go the fuck home to your own family and stop passing judgment on mine!"

"Kit…" This time he reached for her, and that wounded animal fucking cowered and snapped.

"GO! Get the fuck out!!"

She pointed at the door until he used it.

CHAPTER TWENTY-FIVE

After working the morning at Waggy Waggy, Kit drove to group alone, kicking herself for pushing Thatcher away. She wondered whether he'd even show. Last time they'd fought, he'd stayed away. He'd told George he was sick, but she didn't believe it for a second.

Her eyes automatically honed in on his empty chair, and her heart sank. She didn't want to be the reason for his healing process stalling. She noticed another empty chair…Gil's.

Though Mike had been the only one to instantly agree to help with Project Gil, the others had all shown up on one day or another, and they must have been as worn out from the volunteer work as she and Thatcher had been. There was none of the usual quiet chatter.

The door creaked open, and Gil shuffled in, head down, and took his seat without making eye contact with anyone. She tried not to feel disappointed that the person to come through the door wasn't Thatcher. She spent the next few minutes wondering whether Gil would have anything to say after his outburst on his front lawn Saturday night.

The next time the door opened, her heart rose and fell again. George, arriving to start the session.

Hope and anxiety warred as she caught sight of Thatcher limping inside behind him. He glanced her way but looked away quickly. Her heart fell. He eased into his chair, saying nothing. Even Gil was silent until George opened his mouth to begin, and then Gil stood.

"Before we get going, George, I just want to say thank you. I know I'm a grouchy old bastard, and I know a lot of things I've said and done in this group are unacceptable. You, in particular, Kit. I should be up on charges for what I did to you," he shook his head, his voice rough, "but you were there. Thank you." Gil glanced briefly around the circle at the others, unable to hold their eyes for more than a second. "The fact that most of you turned up to help with my shack of a house…" Gil shook his head and put his hand over his heart. "I'll tell you, it means more to me than I can ever say. I can't promise I'll be some sweet pussycat all the time, but I'm going to try to keep my yap shut if I can't find nicer words to say than what I normally would." He eased back into his chair, pulling a wrinkled bandana from his pants pocket and dabbed at his eyes with it.

"We take care of our own," Donnie said, "No matter what."

Gil nodded.

Group moved on.

"Thatcher?" George asked. "Why don't you tell us a bit more about your story?"

His eyes flickered to Kit's. She didn't miss the barely restrained panic in them. She nearly interrupted, almost dove into her recent issues with David to spare him, but he looked away quickly, as if his glance had been purely accidental …something he regretted. She swallowed hard as he began to speak.

"Well, so I already told you I joined up to get away from Gabby's folks and, you know, my family. All their pitying looks. Well, not from my folks. Those were from Gabby's. My family, they're…supportive. But they don't coddle. Not much, anyway. But they sort of go overboard with checking in. I was…suffocating. I didn't know how to be around our group of friends without her. She was just this big, gaping hole that we were all hyperaware of, yet no one would say her name. Anyway, the army was the most dangerous safe place I could have chosen, but I chose it. And I kept on choosing it after my original enlistment contract was up because I still didn't know how to come home and face…everything. Stupid, huh?"

Kit shook her head along with everyone else.

Though he got deeper into his history, time was up before he reached the horrifying last day of his squad. No one seemed to want to redirect him as he rambled on with seemingly aimless stories about the Fantastic Four and how they came together and how they fought like but also goofed around like brothers.

When George gently interrupted him to end the session and asked Thatcher if he wouldn't mind continuing on Wednesday, Kit felt a kick of pride when Thatcher swallowed hard again and nodded. The pride quickly gave way to sadness and regret but also stubborn anger as he skipped his usual visit to the food table and limped away as if someone were chasing him.

She tried not to cry. She tried not to kick herself for letting another man into Lily's life, only to see him walk away.

Except he didn't walk away. You pushed him away.

She ignored the food table, too, though she'd be back to purse smuggling in no time, and slumped out of the building.

~~~

The text messages began on day five. Kearny was the first.

Thatcheroo, where r u?

Clearly a coordinated effort, Parker's message followed soon after.

Should I send a SAR team after you?
~~~

When he didn't answer that one, his filter-free brother, Greer, took a shot.

Ok, so something happened with Kit. Don't use that as an excuse to hide in the pool house, or we'll come over and bust down the door. I can fix it before Mom and Pop even notice.

He sighed heavily.

Dude, enough. I'm fine, but I don't want to talk.

Word must have gotten around, because ten minutes later, Kearny pinged him again.

I'm coming over. Me and Janine.

Shit.

Don't. I'm leaving in about 20. Talk soon. Promise. Just not now.

If Kearny answered, he didn't notice. Thatcher climbed into the shower, reluctantly making good on his words. He'd skipped group on Wednesday, but it was Friday now, and he could at least pretend that was where he was headed. He wasn't going to actually go there, despite the prodding texts George sent. He'd stayed away, fearing that if he went, Kit wouldn't. He knew she feared David was somehow keeping track, ready to sic the police on her if she didn't complete the six-month program George ran. He wouldn't get in the way of that, even if he ached to see her. Even if she wouldn't answer his calls or texts. Even if Nanette gently refused to get in the middle of things when he sent a quick text to ask if Kit was okay.

Telling himself he had no actual destination in mind, Thatcher packed a bag with a few pairs of clothes and got in the Jeep. The Jeep somehow ended up outside Kit's house. He knocked, but she didn't come to the door. If she was showing up at group, she was already gone.

The Jeep circled the parking lot at group, pausing behind Kit's old Honda. The Jeep could, he reasoned, park itself outside Waggy Waggy. She'd have to pick up Lily from Crystal's care at some point. She didn't work Fridays, if she still worked there at all and not for Greer yet.

He didn't know where she'd be if she was working for Greer. He texted his brother to ask when she was starting, and he got exactly the response he expected.

As your brother, I'd love to tell you. As her potential employer, it's none of your business.

He didn't blame Greer. Recognizing that he was bordering on stalker, Thatcher wheeled the Jeep out of the lot and drove aimlessly, or so he told himself. But he found himself on the 51, then the 202 to 87. He pretended he didn't know exactly where he was headed until he hit the 260, stopping in Show Low for gas.

When he arrived at the cabin in Greer, he was surprised to find a familiar white pickup already parked in the rudimentary driveway. Speak of the devil.

Shit.

It was too late to go back. Greer was on the deck nursing a beer.

Resigning himself to Greer's style of tough love, he eased out of the Jeep, tugging his duffel from its place on the passenger floorboard. Another thing the army taught him: always have a "go bag" with a few days' worth of clothing and other necessities… just in case. I thought sure you were already here," Greer said, taking another swallow.

"I hoped I'd be alone," he shot back.

"Well, if you'd answered anybody's texts sooner, you might have been."

He had no valid answer for that, so he just clomped up the stairs, dropped the bag inside the door, and made his way to the empty deck chair beside Greer's.

"How long have you been here?"

Greer held out a beer as he sat down. That was a good sign. The offer meant Greer was more annoyed than angry.

"Just about an hour. Took a three-day weekend."

"You should be home with Shelby."

"You should answer people when they're obviously worried about you," he retorted.

He nodded and slapped the cap off the beer on the arm of the chair.

"She won't talk to me," he said, swallowing beer in hopes it would clear the lump from his throat.

Greer said nothing, just waited for the story.

Thatcher stared out at the pines and gave him the Greer version. The bare facts, just the way Greer liked it. His logical mind was better with hard facts than with feelings, though he could be careful when it mattered. Like when Thatcher finished and a rare measure of audible emotion tumbled out with Greer's reply.

"That's a tough one, Thatch. I can see both ends of it. It isn't fair to shut you out of the situation, not if you guys were headed the way it seemed like you were. But when you've felt all alone for so long, it's hard to let someone else in."

Thatcher knew Greer was talking as much about himself as he was about Kit. More so, he thought, about the wary kid he'd been when he'd arrived as a foster child in the Myers household than about the mechanics of his relationship with Shelby. But it translated the same.

"I don't know the answer to this one," Greer admitted a few minutes later.

"Yeah. Me, neither. I call. I text. Nothing. I tried her boss, but she wouldn't offer up any information."

"Privacy," Greer shrugged.

"I know." He sighed.

They sat watching squirrels run up and down the trees to the boxes Greer had made in hopes of keeping them from choosing the cabin as a nesting place. Feeder boxes and habitats were mounted to a half dozen trees within view of the deck. So far, they seemed to be serving the purpose and lending entertainment value as a bonus.

"Give her time."

Thatcher nodded as though he agreed. As though every day that passed without Kit in it was any more bearable than the unbearable day before. As though her refusal to answer the phone or his texts didn't drive the stake deeper and deeper into his chest. As though the fear she'd never let him back in wasn't growing exponentially day by silent day.

He knew he needed to find a way to move on, or at least *begin* to plan for the possibility that she'd never come around. Stop spinning his wheels and dig out. He'd come to the cabin, the refuge of the heartbroken. The regrouping destination of choice since Parker's initiation.

They fished. They hiked. They sat on the deck watching the squirrels by day and inside watching things blow up on DVD by night. They seldom spoke. Seldom needed to. The church of nature did what it always did for the Myers men. Thatcher caught a reluctant but firm second wind. Greer relaxed from watchful big brother mode back to about-to-be-a-biological-father-mode, swapping a few texts with Shelby Saturday night into Sunday morning.

Late Sunday morning, they closed up the cabin, slid into their respective vehicles, and headed back home. His phone, while not barren of texts or missed calls, held nothing from Kit. Since hers was the only call or text he wanted to see, he turned the phone off for the drive back and selected a way too emo playlist for the drive.

In Payson, he stopped off at his namesake sister's favorite place, the Tonto Natural Bridge, hiked down into the rocks just below the falls, and had a fellow hiker snap a photo, which he sent to her with a message that said,

Just clearing my head, sis. Spread the word that all is ok if Greer hasn't already. TTYL.

He had lunch in a popular local Mexican place before heading back to the pool house. He ached inside, wishing it could be Kit's place he was pulling up to. He missed her. He missed Lily, too. He'd fallen every bit as much in love with that sweet little girl as he had with her mother. Wanting David to have a shot at fatherhood, despite his actions, was an extension of his love for Lily. For as much as Kit wanted to protect her girl, Thatcher did, too. He wanted to spare her the hole he knew his sisters, Payson and Page, carried every day. The question mark of, "Who were they? Why didn't they want me?" Kearny carried a different emptiness…the emptiness of parents he'd known, parents he'd loved, parents he'd lost. Different but the same. And Greer. Greer held yet another emptiness that would never fill. The emptiness of a mother who loved drugs and catting around with a carousel of different men, chasing the next high, next man, next thrill, treating her son as an afterthought or a punching bag as the whim arose. And sometimes not treating him at all.

He didn't know whether one was worse than the other, but he always suspected that at least if you knew who they were, you could make some sort of peace with your parents, good or bad. The question that would never be answered seemed worse to him. The faces that would always be shadows seemed harder to bear. But what did he know, really? He had two parents he'd always known, always loved, who'd always loved him.

He'd no sooner tossed the duffel on his bed in the pool house before he whipped out his phone.

Do you think it's worse to know who your folks are than to never know where you came from?

He sent it to Kearny first. Debated whether to wait to send it to Greer before Kearny answered or after. Debated whether to send it to Payson or Page at all. In the end, he copied what he'd sent to Kearny and texted all of them, without waiting, then put his phone aside and unpacked the duffel and cleaned the pool house before checking for replies.

Greer was first.

I don't know. I knew my mother, and she sucked.

Thinking about her sucks. The twins didn't know either parent, and it follows them, but only they can tell you how that feels. There's no answer that's right or wrong.

Kearny was next.

Don't know. Can only speak 4 myself. I still miss them. I think even if they were a*holes I still would. Sometimes.

Page just sent question marks.

Payson's reply was short and surprisingly, more Greer-like than Greer's.

This is about you and Kit, not about any of us. Talk to her, dummy!

"I'm trying!" he shouted at her text. "She won't talk to me!"

~~~

Kit stood in Waggy Waggy, surveying the little grooming shop for what felt like the last time. It wasn't, really. She'd still be dropping Lily with Crystal five days a week. But it felt final. Her two-weeks' notice had both flown and crawled. They'd flown when she was in the shop, focused on the dogs, and as she and Nanette chatted back and forth. Realizing she wouldn't have Nanette to chat with every day anymore made her sad. But when she thought of Thatcher…

Just pick up the phone the next time he calls.

Except he'd stopped calling. Stopped texting. It had been four days now with nothing. He could be waiting for her to come to him, or he could be…

Just thinking about it made her ache deep in her bones.

Serves you right if he's moved on, if he's seeing someone else.

Even George and the others at group stopped asking where he was, after the first week.

Lily missed Thatcher almost as much. She'd taken to running to the door whenever there was a knock or the bell.
~~~

Kit's heart leapt every time. Whether that was from hope or from heartbreak, she didn't know. The end result was the same. Lily kept looking for him, and she'd even looked up at Kit last night at bedtime with her big green eyes and whined,

"Tasher?"

She was surprised that Lily even knew his name, considering she was always holding him at a distance with nicknames. But Thatcher always called himself Thatcher when speaking to Lily, and he'd spoken to her a lot. It hit her then just how often he'd been around, how ingrained he'd become in their lives.

Her heart was still bleeding on the floor somewhere. There was a giant invisible hole in her chest. Her throat felt raw from the sob-fest she'd had in her room, where the inner critic had torn her further apart.

See? This is why you don't get involved. This. Lily. That little pitiful look. That sweet little voice wondering where her—

Kit's eyes flooded with tears.

Where her father is. The man who should *be her father, but isn't. The man she probably* thinks *is her father.*

She ducked into the washroom, hoping Nanette's focus had been on Biscuit, the sweet little mix dog whose fur was exactly the color of her namesake.

This. This was what Thatcher meant all along. What if Lily asks who her daddy is someday? What if she gives you that *look again?*

She could never bear another glimpse of that look. Half puzzlement, half pure longing. Lily missed him, this man who'd been more of a father to her than her own father. But what if she asked, someday, about her father? What if Lily gave her the "Tasher" look, but gave it to her while asking about her daddy?

And that's exactly what Thatcher was trying to get you to understand. That exact look. The one you never want to

see again.

"Why don't you just call him, Kit?"

Nanette's voice from the doorway made her jump. Sniffling, Kit wiped her eyes.

"This isn't about him," she lied.

"Bullshit," Nanette shot back flatly.

"I'm going to miss this place," Kit said, hoping since that was a true statement, Nanette would believe her.

"Maybe, but that's not what this is about." Nanette swept into the small space, a room that already felt as though it lacked air, and folded Kit into her arms.

She couldn't speak. Denying it was useless. Agreeing, however, was also useless. It wouldn't bring him back to her, and she didn't have a right to ask. Not when the idea of letting David see Lily was still a firm, screaming *NO* in her heart.

Kit cried harder. The more she tried to stop, the less she could.

"Okay," Nanette said softly, rubbing her back. "Okay."

Minutes or possibly hours later, Kit cried herself out and Nanette eased her back, hands on her shoulders.

"Kit, I love you to death, but you are *the* stubbornest pain in the ass I've ever met. Once you get something in your head, you're like a dog with a bone. Growling whenever anyone tries to take it from you. But you're missing the damn point. Whether you're right about this David thing or Thatcher is doesn't matter one iota. What matters is you and your little safe castle that no one can penetrate. You just pull the drawbridge up and you sit in there, all alone, letting nothing and no one inside. He can deal with your feelings about David, Kit. He can agree to disagree with you. He can think you're dead wrong. But he can still love you. He *does* still love you. I've seen the love all over that man's face, and I've seen him less than a dozen times."

"Stop, you're going to get me going again," she choked,

wiping a fresh batch of tears from her cheeks.

"Well, too bad. Guys like him, those are the ones you let inside. Drop the drawbridge, kill the crocodiles. Let him in. Not just until you have a disagreement. Forever."

She shook her head. "You don't understand. It's not that I don't know he's making sense, you know, about David. I just can't. I can't forgive him. And I can't let him have Lily. Fine, I'm a bitch, and I'm unreasonable and I'm cruel. But I can't."

Nanette blinked at her. "Girl, am I talking to air? Did you not hear me say just seconds ago that this is so not about David? This is about you letting Thatcher *in.* Letting him feel whatever the heck he feels but instead of pushing him out the door, just letting him sit with you in that disagreement. I mean, did he walk out when he accused you of bullshitting him about wanting an equal partner?"

"No. But—"

"But nothing. He was in it. He wasn't going anywhere. You kicked him out. *You* left *him*, Kit. Plain and simple."

Nanette's words stung, but they rang true. Kit sighed heavily.

"It's Friday, Kit. You're not even supposed to be working today. You're starting on a new, much better paying job on Monday. Take your last week's pay and go do something special for yourself. Lily will be fine here. If you need the whole night, just call us." Nanette pulled a wad of cash from her pocket and held it out to Kit.

"I don't care what you do with it as long as you don't spend it all on bills. I want photographic proof that you did something purely for yourself. Preferably something that screws your head on straight. Now, get the hell out of my shop before I cry, too."

Kit watched her storm back into the grooming area and duck to open another kennel. Grabbing her purse from the shelf for the last time, she stuffed the cash, uncounted, into her pocket and slipped out the door.

CHAPTER TWENTY-SIX

There was no putting them off again. No sooner than he returned from Greer Sunday afternoon, his family began the text spamming, driving him nuts all through the week, pestering him about a game night. Texts blew up his phone at all hours. When he was sleeping, when was showering, when he was packing his meager belongings into boxes. All he needed to do was make it back over to that apartment complex on the west side and see if the receptionist, Jenny, had anything available for immediate move in.

His time in the pool house apartment was over. Kit or no Kit, it was time to move on. With Kit would be infinitely better, but that was a thought for another day. Thatcher texted a reply to Page, the latest of his siblings to wheedle about game night next Saturday night.

Why not? Not like you have anything else to fill Saturday nights anymore.

Sighing heavily, he thumbed a reply. **I will be there. Spread the word. Stop the madness!**

He put a smiley emoji after it so she wouldn't go and get her feelings hurt. Page was sensitive like that. Her confidence was shaky at best, a thing he'd always secretly attributed to "the hole". The one she and Payson carried in their own ways. Payson had a tendency toward anger, particularly on her birthday. Knowing you were left in a dumpster behind a church like a bag of trash rather than safely delivered inside like a treasure did that to a person. Page got shaky in other ways. If there was a test at school, she'd bomb it. She'd spend the day doing that thing where you instantly apologize for anything and everything, even if you weren't at fault in any way.

He taped another box, then tossed the tape on the coffee table and checked his phone for the billionth time.

God damn, it, Kit. Why the hell won't you just pick up the phone, answer the door?

He sighed and stretched out on the floor to run through a few of Cesar's latest PT exercises.

Because she's Kit, he thought as he grimaced his way through some leg lifts.

He smiled in spite of himself. He couldn't help it. Thinking of his sassy, stubborn Kit hurt like hell, but it also never failed to make him grin. For every whisper that suggested it was over, to give up, another whisper flashed through every memory he had of her resistance.

Harpo.

Groceries.

Valiant.

Daddy Warbucks.

Every nickname another fruitless attempt to keep him at a distance. Every nickname a reason for him to try harder, to push at the walls. And damn it, they'd crumbled. They *had.*

But now.

Now, they were back to square one. Square minus one.

When was it time to call the loss? When was it time to call time of death? Were they already there?

Jesus. He hoped not.

He didn't know what else to do, though. Call? Go by the house again?

Thatcher wondered about it as he showered off another frustration driven workout. He wasn't ready to give up. Kit was off today, at least if she still worked for Nanette. He simply needed a plan.

He hadn't come up with one by dinner Saturday night.

Sitting out on the porch with everyone, he couldn't help but think of the last time he'd been seated at the horseshoe table with his family. They obviously couldn't, either, because every last one of them avoided the subject of Kit until their avoidance was like an elephant in the room. It felt like Gabby all over again. No matter how many jokes went back and forth, no matter how much of a good time he was actually having, he could feel Kit like a ghost next to him, behind him, inside him.

He waited for the anxiety, for the panic attack. And while panic edged up on him a few times, he managed to fend off a full-scale, hide-in-the-john attack.

It was the baby passing that got him the most. He missed Lily as fiercely as he missed Kit. Holding Hayden on his good knee, blowing a raspberry on her neck, it stabbed him in the gut. He loved his niece, but he was glad to pass her to Shelby. Shelby's little one, thankfully, wasn't going to make an appearance until around Thanksgiving.

He drifted through the evening, acting as unaffected as he could. He grinned and he laughed and he talked. He fidgeted until Greer told him to put Kit aside and chill out with his family for a couple hours.

"You can go back to moping later," Greer smirked.

They passed the poker chips, and Kearny played the usual number of songs. Thatcher had him play a much less awkward song, Ashes Onward's, "Going Under". His folks got both of the other solo chips and had him do two of their favorite oldies, "Wild Horses" and "Hotel California". When the sing along finished, he joined them inside for a game of Scattergories, and he managed to make it look like he was fully tuned in to the game.

He wasn't. Not by a long shot. He kept sneaking glances at his phone, which he'd obligingly set to silent mode after Eden got a lecture about her phone blowing up with non-emergency work junk.

Or thought he was sneaking glances, anyway.

"Dude. Almost everyone who calls you is in this room, so you can stop pretending you're not acting like a total chick waiting for your girlfriend to call."

He flipped Greer the bird.

His mother frowned at him, then laughed. "It feels just like family game night again!"

Sedona, sitting on his left, nudged him lightly with her elbow. "Yeah, complete with rude gestures."

He gave her a noogie in reply.

"Knock it off and get ready for the round," Parker teased, holding the timer up for a half-second before flipping it over and announcing, "Go!"

Several more rounds passed. Thatcher fought the urge to check his phone now that he knew they were watching. Kearny made them laugh with his "B" list of "Sports". Tongue in cheek, his answers were "blind" this or that.

"And doubles on the baseball and basketball! Suck it, Greer!" he teased as Greer's balled up play sheet bounced off his nose.

"Disallowed!" Greer booed him. "No playing the blind card!"

"Allowed!" Kearny shot back. "Disabled rights violation!"

"Disabled my ass," Greer retorted. "You've never been disabled a day in your life, kid!"

"Kid?!" Kearny laughed. "Maybe to you, old man!"

Their father laughed. "Old man? Then what am I?"

"Distinguished, Pop," Greer winked at him.

Thatcher laughed as his father sat up straighter on the sofa and preened. Everyone laughed harder when he broke into a yawn.

"I didn't realize it was getting so late," he said, patting their mom's knee. "You can stay and play, kids. I've got to get to bed if I'm going to open the grill tomorrow. You with me, Del?"

Their mother nodded and tossed her game tablet on the

coffee table. "I'm with you, Artie. Goodnight, kids! I love you all! Try to keep it down."

Thatcher was surprised to see it had gotten so late. He had to look twice at his phone to be sure he read it right. 11:15 p.m. Shit.

A chorus of goodnights and goodbyes began. Hugs and his mother's intentionally noisy cheek and forehead kisses went around the room. Thatcher half-rose from the couch to meet her when it was his turn.

"Night, Mom," he said, returning her kiss with a loud smack of his own. She giggled.

"You haven't done that in a long time," she smiled so genuinely that he couldn't help but smile back.

"No?" he asked. "Sorry about that. I love you."

Her smile widened. "I love you, too. Thanks for coming."

He nodded and plunked back down beside Sedona, who teasingly begged him not to go to bed. He helped her finish boxing up the game as the others gathered leftovers, purses, phones, and keys. As their folks started thumping up the stairs, Sedona bumped him with her shoulder.

"Wanna share a bowl of popcorn and watch something scary, like old times?"

He gave her a half-hearted grin. It was better than staring at the ceiling in the pool house, thinking of Kit all night. At least this way, he could break the monotony with a movie.

"I'm in," he said, rising to hug Payson and Page in turn.

As the ladies finished hugging and the guys finished tipping their chins at one another, his phone rattled on the table. Since Greer had so bluntly pointed out that everyone that called him was in the room, he scrambled to grab it, trying to tamp down the burst of hope that shot through his chest.

911 D gun drunk Lily 17N Anthem

He read the texted shorthand again, his heart crashing to

his knees.

911. D…David? Gun. Drunk. Lily. 17N Anthem.

Gun.

Lily.

The words went from his eyes to his brain and began sliding down into his core, turning to ice as they went. He tried to arrange them into anything else, anything other than what they were. Anything other than what they had to mean. A configuration that didn't mean that David had kidnapped Lily, possibly at gun point, and was driving—drunk, no less—on the I-17 freeway headed north toward Anthem. Or driving through it. Or passing it and heading further north.

Anthem.

He rushed to the door, calling over his shoulder, "Who's blocking my Jeep? I have to go!"

He ignored their bewilderment, their questions. He ignored Sedona's hands reaching for him. Glancing out the front door, he turned back in a rush, nearly slamming into Kearny.

"What's—"

Pushing past him, Thatcher thumped Greer's chest. "Keys!"

Greer barely had them out of his jeans pocket before Thatcher ripped them out of his hand. Ignoring Greer's "Dude, what?!", Thatcher hit the driveway at a fast limp, pressing the entry fob as he went. He was already climbing behind the wheel and reaching for the door when Greer's hand came down on his shoulder. "Christ, Thatcher, what's—"

With little time to feel guilt, he shoved Greer hard so that he cleared the door, fumbled with his still-fickle left hand, but managed to get the door closed while starting the ignition. As Greer continued to holler, even banging on the window, Thatcher hit the gas and lurched out of the driveway, peeling into the night with a single thought.

Kit.

~~~

Kit huddled in the dark, watching the SUV for signs of movement. It had been still since David spun out and hit the guardrail, but she didn't dare move.

She'd barely gotten out of the shower and dressed when someone started pounding on the front door like they were trying to break it down. Her heart leapt with hope.

Please be Thatcher. Please, please, be Thatcher.

But it wasn't.

"I want to see my daughter," David demanded.

She didn't see the gun at first. She was too busy being hit by the nauseating wave of his booze breath. She told him to fuck off as she was closing the door, but he stumble-rushed forward. A thunk too loud to be the thump of a foot or fist hitting the door drew her eyes downward.

"Look, David," she began.

No amount of begging, pleading, or, finally, belligerence would convince David to lower the gun. Still, Kit didn't move aside to let him in the front door. Unfortunately, Lily must've woken from their shouting. As Thatcher had predicted would happen one day soon, she managed to climb out of her crib and had toddled out without Kit noticing.

David noticed.

He didn't have to make good on his threats to shoot her if she didn't let him in to see Lily. All he had to do was swoop down and scoop her up.

None of her snarled threats stopped David once he had Lily. He rushed to the SUV, which he'd backed into the driveway for a quick escape, and plunked their screaming daughter down on the back seat. Kit lunged into the SUV
~~~

from the driver's side and grabbed Lily, but David slammed the door before she could lunge out again.

Fucking child safety locks!

He was in the driver's seat before she could attempt to climb over the console and escape through the front passenger side, so she buckled herself and Lily in, cursing the lack of a child seat. Trying to soothe her wailing child, she begged David to let them out.

"Okay," she cried over Lily's piercing wail. "You win. Let's go back inside and talk about some kind of visitation arrangement."

Over my dead body. But he didn't have to know she was bullshitting, buying time.

He saw through the empty promise and peeled out of the driveway.

She begged.

She bargained.

She cried.

She threatened.

Nothing convinced him to pull over and let them go.

Kit tearfully remembered her cell phone, tucked hastily into the pocket of her lounge pants as she'd rushed to the door. She'd never be able to make a call without him noticing. He was already weaving, wobbling all over the road like a stubborn old man in need of a walker.

"Shut her the fuck up!" he hollered over Lily's siren-like wails.

"Stop fucking screaming! You're scaring her to death, David!"

Under the guise of comforting Lily, Kit ducked her head, cooing comforting words to her terrified little girl while tapping out the quickest shorthand message possible, barely able to see the screen she'd hastily dimmed to the lowest setting. She only hoped Thatcher would get it, read it, understand it, and come.

Please, please. Please come. Please.

"Shut her up!" he hollered again, nearly colliding with a semi-truck in the middle lane.

Desperate, she held up her phone and bluffed.

"I just dialed 911, asshole! They're listening to this whole conversation and tracking the GPS on my phone! The cops will be looking for you. Pull over and let us out."

David swore viciously, calling her words she, with her not-so-clean mouth, wouldn't even utter. "Climb over and get yourself out!" He continued his stream of obscenities.

She didn't hesitate. She had the seatbelt off and was slipping over the console almost as soon as the words left his mouth. He jerked the car sharply to the right, launching the SUV onto the shoulder so quickly that the movement threw her into the front passenger door. Kit winced as her right shoulder took the impact.

He slowed the SUV but wouldn't stop it. "C'mon, bitch, get out before I shoot you!"

"Stop the car!" She cried terrified he'd decide he had nothing to lose by shooting her, anyway.

He didn't. He slowed further, held the gun up, and yelled, "Get out before I floor it!"

Kit leapt away from the door, clutching Lily in her left arm, stumbling as her feet hit the silty shoulder. She hit the ground on her right side, the force rolling her leftward. She locked her arms and tucked Lily against her like a football. She heard more than saw the SUV spin out as David hit the gas. But she sat up in time to see the SUV veer sideways, over-correct, and smack loudly into the guardrail.

She leapt to her feet and ran southward, half-blind in the overcast night. Remembering her phone, she faced it at her feet. The screen was too dim to help much. She stopped, too afraid to continue plunging blindly forward, and crouched down by the guardrail.

"Shhh, shhhh," she soothed, thumbing upward so the settings of her phone became visible. She increased the brightness as much as she dared, eyes glued on the SUV, watching for any sign of David. Lily's cries slowed. "Shhh, my precious. You're ok. We're ok." She tilted the phone to her disconsolate child, eyes roving over her little face and bare arms, searching for damage.

Once Lily slipped from wails to weary hiccups, she called 911 for real, stage whispering her best idea of where they were now, northbound on the I-17, somewhere past Anthem Way but still, she thought, south of New River. Then she left the line open but stayed quiet, still fixed on the SUV, poised to run at any sign of movement.

Lily grew heavy in her arms. Whether she was chilled by the cooler-than-usual spring evening or the circumstances, she didn't know. Each minute that passed felt like an hour. Every sporadic set of headlights lifted her hope and dropped it again, like a boat bouncing on water, when they passed without stopping.

Finally, an old white work truck with a tool box and a ladder rack on the bed burst onto the shoulder, skidding to a stop between Kit and the SUV. At her angle, she couldn't see the driver, but relief flooded through her at his call.

"Kit!"

The shadow of him passed in front of the headlights, something dangling from his hand.

"Thatcher!" she choked, staggering up from her crouch, legs like jelly as she stumbled toward him.

He crossed the distance in a few hitching strides, dropping the object as he folded her and Lily into his arms.

"Christ, Kit," he sighed into her ear, his voice ragged.

She trembled. Or he did. Or they both did. She wasn't sure.

He held so tightly, so deliciously tightly, that Lily let out a little grunt. She felt his reluctance as he released them, sliding his hands to her shoulders. Walking backwards, he tugged her into the outer glow of the headlights.

His eyes scanned over her and Lily slowly, head to toe and back again. He frowned and touched her forehead, gently stroking a place she hadn't noticed was sore.

"We're okay," Kit assured him. "I convinced him I'd called 911, and he pulled over and kicked us out. He slowed, but he didn't stop. Once I jumped out with Lily, he gunned it and skidded into the guardrail. I've been too scared to go see if he's okay."

"He's got a gun?"

She nodded. "Glock 19."

"Did you call 911?"

"A few minutes ago, yeah." She held up her phone, eyes widening as she remembered they were still on the line. "Hello?"

Or not.

"They were going to stay on the line with me until the police arrived, but I guess the call dropped."

Leaning forward, Thatcher kissed her forehead with such tenderness her eyes filled. Turning her toward the pickup, he said, "Sit in the truck and lock the doors. I'll be there in a minute."

He stood watching until she scrambled up with Lily, closing the door once she was safely inside. He didn't move until he heard the locks engage. When they did, he picked up the object he'd discarded earlier and edged toward the SUV.

As he left the circles of light shed by the headlights, Kit's arms tightened around Lily. She could barely see him now, and it made her nervous. She stroked Lily's hair, whispering comfort to her.

"Valiant saved the day again, Lily. You and me, we're okay. We're all better now, right?" Lily sucked her thumb and snuggled closer to Kit as if she understood the dire situation they'd escaped. "I would never have let him hurt you, precious. Never. But we're glad Thatcher is here, aren't we?"

Red and blue lights appeared, flashing, as first one and then a second police car nosed up at an angle behind the truck.

"We're safe, Lily Bug," she said, wiping at a fat tear. "We're safe."

CHAPTER TWENTY-SEVEN

Thatcher, standing beside the rear driver side door of the SUV, tapped gently on the window with an old pry bar he'd plucked from under the seat of Greer's truck.

He tapped again.

Nothing.

Warily, he pulled the door open. The acrid smell of alcohol and vomit wafted out.

David's head lolled back against the head-rest. His chest rose and fell. The bastard was either in a heavy drunk sleep or unconscious. Judging by the minimal damage to the front of the vehicle and the fact that the air bag hadn't deployed, Thatcher guessed it was the former.

Staring at the idiot that could have killed the woman and little girl who'd wormed their way into his heart over the past few months, he said,

"I went to bat for you, you stupid, drunk asshole. But Kit was right. You don't deserve Lily. And if Kit'll let me, I'll be the husband and father you weren't. And you, asshole, will never get near either of them again."

Flashing red and blue lights appeared, first one squad car, and then another. He stepped back from the SUV, squinting in the three sets of headlights pointed toward him. As an officer with a flashlight slowly approached, Thatcher realized he was still gripping the pry bar. He dropped it casually.

The door of Greer's pickup opened, and Kit slid out with Lily, watching as he slowly lifted his arms to show the officer he was no threat. Another officer appeared behind them.

After a very tense few minutes spent explaining the night's events to the two responding officers, he and Kit were cleared to leave.

He wrapped his left arm around Kit, kissing her temple. Lily was a soft, drowsy weight in the crook of his right arm. Looking down at her soft, tear-stained cheeks, the lump returned to his throat as he forced away dark thoughts about all the horrible ways the night might have ended.

Though she was overly fond of reminding him she didn't need him or anyone else, Kit offered no protest as he placed a watchful hand at her back as she climbed into the truck. Kissing her soft blonde hair, Thatcher carefully passed Lily to Kit, hovering at the door until they were safely buckled in.

Lily and Kit…his whole world. Or a good part of it, he was reminded as his phone vibrated itself off the driver's seat. No doubt his family was half insane by now.

Grabbing the phone, he slid behind the wheel, texting Greer a quick reply to one of his billion ***WTF?!*** messages.

All clear. Back soon.

"Are you really okay?" he asked huskily, reaching across the seat to cup her cheek.

She nodded. "Thank you for coming, Valiant," she replied in a wobbly voice that belied her insistence that she was alright.

"Always, Kit."

"I'm sorry, Thatcher," she said in a voice so small it twisted his guts.

"Why?" he breathed. "Jesus, Kit, that's my apology. That psychopath could have killed you both tonight, and I feel like I gave him the gun. You knew better than to let him near Lily, and I pushed you to hear him out, give him a chance."

"Maybe if I had, though, this wouldn't have happened.

And if I hadn't insisted on making all the decisions, you might have been at the house when he showed up." Sobbing now, she shattered him with her next words. "I opened the door without looking because I was hoping it was you."

Thatcher cursed the console between them and cursed his phone, which was blowing up anew. Reaching over the console, he knuckled the tears under her left eye.

"We'd better get back," he sighed. "I basically stole Greer's truck and ditched the end of game night to come find you. None of them have any idea what's happening."

In reality, what felt like an endless drive before took less than twenty minutes. While all he wanted was to get her alone, get his eyes and hands on her to verify she was truly unscathed, he knew he'd have some explaining to do first.

There was Greer's mix of indignance and worry, followed closely by outrage as Thatcher stood in the driveway and explained the last eighty minutes to an audience of twelve made up of his parents, brothers, sisters, Janine, Melody, and Shelby. There was his own tamped down impatience as his folks and siblings fawned all over Kit and Lily, ushering them indoors and offering food and drinks before finally, *finally* his parents retired to bed for the second time and everyone else trickled out to cars, trucks, and SUVs to head home.

"I'm sorry," he said, taking Kit's hand, guiding her down the hall to the nursery. "They can be a lot to take on a normal day. If you throw worry in, they're impossible."

Kit stroked Lily's round cheek one last time and whispered, "I like it. It was only Mom and me, and I always wished I had a brother or sister. Maybe I'm such a selfish control freak because I never had to share."

Cracking the nursery door closed, Lily safely tucked in the crib his folks kept for Hayden's visits, she pulled his head down, her lips fast and searching against his. Her tongue swept his mouth, taking the control she spoke of.

Thatcher offered no resistance. She needed that, he knew, after the vulnerability of her evening.

"I wasn't fair," she said, coming up for air.

"Shhh," he said, guiding her into the guest room across the hall from the nursery, knowing she needed to be close to Lily. The pool house was too far. Hell, it was too far for him, too.

He swept her against him, struggling to be gentle when all he wanted was to devour, drive into her, put his stamp on her. Erase any man that came before. Anything, everything to reclaim what he'd almost lost. When at last he lifted his head, she regarded him with eyes both sleepy and amused.

"I'm sorry, Kit. I should have let you decide what was right for Lily. If I'd backed you up, maybe he'd have stayed away. If he's going to drive drunk with you and Lily in the car, he's got no business being around her."

Before he could wonder why they were rehashing the same apologies, she said, "You were right, too, Valiant, as usual. If you're crazy enough to want to be with me, you've more than earned an equal partnership."

She flopped backward on the bed, taking him with her. She pressed her mouth to his again, tracing his lower lip with her tongue, nibbling gently, moving her mouth quickly to his throat to catch the vibration of the soft moan she knew would follow.

"I love that little girl in the other room, Kit, and I love you. I want you to be my wife," he said, stroking her face from temple to chin, pulling her mouth back to his for another taste. "And I want Lily to be my daughter."

She rolled on top of him, staring down with a love that lit him on fire from head to toe. "Yes," she said. "I'll marry you. I want you, too. For me. For Lily." She peppered his lips and then his neck with light kisses and nips that drove him half crazy.

"One condition," he whispered huskily, groaning as she

ground down against him.

She shook her head and did it again. "No conditions. Love is unconditional."

"You've got me there," he grinned, grabbing her ass and flexing his hips forcefully.

She closed her eyes and bit her lip.

"There's something I'd like, though. As a rule. Not as the exception."

She reached down for his fly. "What's that?"

As much as he tried to fight it, his mouth quirked. "I'd like my wife to call me by my given name."

"Okay, Valiant," she agreed with that rare, girlish giggle that socked him low in the belly, like an invisible hand closing over his arousal.

He growled, feigning irritation. "Tha-tcher," he coached teasingly, pulling down her lounge pants. He gave her ass a light slap. She yelped and giggled again.

"Groceries?"

He bit back a half-laugh, half-moan as she rocked downward again and kicked off the lowered pants, taking her panties with them. He tugged her shirt off, then shoved at his jeans and boxers. He caught her breasts in his hands, pinching her nipples playfully, a light punishment for her obstinance.

"Say it," he teased, pinching them gently again, giving each a light twist that elicited a throaty moan.

"Say it," he repeated, finding her wet heat and giving her one stingy stroke, wrestling free when she tried to guide his fingers back.

"No, ma'am," he admonished with a chuckle. "Not until you say it." He rolled her onto her back, pinning her under his weight, thrusting against her.

She started in with the happy noises, and he nearly gave in, his resolve weakening, especially when she reached down and gave him a squeeze, then stroked him firmly until his eyes nearly rolled back in his head.

Jesus, this woman.

He retaliated, slipping two fingers inside her, curling firmly upward, stroking that spot that reduced his strong, sassy Kit to whimpers, hips bucking, following his fingers in a not-so-silent plea for more. Suddenly, as he sensed she was about to shatter, he pulled them back, sampling a taste of her. Her eyes fixed on his fingers, mesmerized by his tongue licking the last of her from them. "Say it," he whispered huskily again.

With utter seriousness, she licked her lips and dug her heels into his ass so that he nearly whimpered, himself. "Warbucks?" she asked, giggling hard as he slid downward and opened her, fingers on either side of her inner thighs. She gasped loudly as he latched his mouth to that sweet, salty nectar, sweeping up, sweeping down, thrusting his tongue inside her so that her giggles melted into soft cries, those high-pitched little happy noises that pinged his cock. He let loose a moan against the sensitive flesh, then drew back, leaving her hips to rise toward nothing.

"Say it," he begged, no longer able to demand.

She met his eyes, her gaze full of heat and lust, tenderness and sassiness and, God help him, total trust. "Thatcher," she rasped, reaching for him. "Thatcher, Thatcher, Thatcher," she whispered over and over as he drove himself into her body. Into her life.

His love.

His heart.

His home.

END

THANKS, READERS!

Thank you for choosing *Through the Fire,* book four of the Phoenix Rise series. If you have read them all in order, you're now halfway through the series! Of course, they don't have to be read in order. They can be read as standalone novels, too!

As an independent author and publisher, I don't have the marketing power of the big publishing houses, so the best thing you can do if you enjoyed this book is leave a short review on Amazon or Goodreads. A few kind words go a long way to help independent authors get noticed! Reviews don't have to be fancy or long. A quick sentence will do just fine!

Other great things you can do if you enjoyed the book:
Sign up for my newsletter by visiting my website: www.lydiachelsea.com

Like and follow my Facebook page: Author Lydia Chelsea | Facebook

Like and follow me on Instagram: Author Lydia Chelsea

Follow me on Bookbub: Lydia Chelsea

What's next, you ask?

Book 5, *Fires of Eden*, is, of course, Eden's story!

Eden Myers is fed up with men.

It's been tough getting men to take her seriously since she started throwing sensual aid product parties in college to help with expenses. She's had it up to you-know-where with lecherous grins, raised eyebrows, crass assumptions and suggestive winks every time she tells a first date what she does for a living. And the ones who aren't making ridiculous assumptions are ashamed to introduce her to their family and friends. She's done being anyone's dirty secret!

Merritt Stafford is feeling trapped.

Being sole heir to a resort empire comes with his parents' hefty expectations: proper appearance, acceptable circle of friends, and marrying the "right" kind of woman. Delightful, sexy, sassy Eden Myers is…not that kind. But she is *his* kind…down-to-earth, genuine, and wealthy enough in her own right that he knows she's not a gold digger.

So, how does a man about to come into his
fortune avoid being disowned without losing the woman of his dreams?

Find out in winter of 2022/2023!

Made in the USA
Columbia, SC
17 September 2022

67441365R00178